'The unmatchable Joanna Trollope at her best'
Choice

'No one captures family dynamics like Joanna Trollope:
the shifts and rifts and nuances, the knock-on effects
of life decisions . . . A pitch-perfect novel'
Sunday Express

'An absorbing, slickly executed treat'
Daily Mail

'Joanna Trollope at her finest, writing about
the complexity of simple things'
Good Housekeeping

'Trollope is an extremely assured writer, with a brilliant eye
for detail and a finely tuned emotional intelligence'
Sunday Times

'With her compassion for her characters,
Trollope cuts to the quick of family life'
Fanny Blake, *Woman & Home*

AN UNSUITABLE MATCH

Joanna Trollope is the author of twenty highly acclaimed and bestselling novels, including *The Rector's Wife*, *Marrying the Mistress* and *Daughters-in-Law*. She has also written a study of women in the British Empire, *Britannia's Daughters*, and ten historical novels under the pseudonym of Caroline Harvey. She was appointed OBE in 1996, and a trustee of the National Literacy Trust in 2012 and the Royal Literary Fund in 2016. She has chaired the Whitbread and Orange Awards, as well as being a judge of many other literature prizes; she has been part of two DCMS panels on public libraries, and is patron of numerous charities, including Meningitis Now and Chawton House Library. In 2014, she updated Jane Austen's *Sense and Sensibility* as the opening novel in the Austen Project. *An Unsuitable Match* is her twenty-first novel.

JOANNA TROLLOPE

An Unsuitable Match

PAN BOOKS

First published 2018 by Mantle
First published in paperback 2018 by Mantle

This edition published 2018 by Pan Books
an imprint of Pan Macmillan
20 New Wharf Road, London N1 9RR
Associated companies throughout the world
www.panmacmillan.com

ISBN 978-1-5098-2350-5

3 5 7 9 8 6 4

A CIP catalogue record for this book is available from the British Library.

Typeset by Palimpsest Book Production Ltd, Falkirk, Stirlingshire
Printed and bound by CPI Group (UK) Ltd, Croydon, CR0 4YY

An Unsuitable Match

CHAPTER ONE

He had said it. He had actually said the words. All right, he'd been half laughing, shaking his head as if he couldn't quite believe what he was saying, and they'd been washing up at the time, so his hands had been in the sink, holding a saucepan to rinse it under the running tap, but all the same, he had said, 'D'you know, Rose, I have to tell you that I don't think – no, I *know* that I have never felt like this before.'

Then he'd put the saucepan down on the counter and turned the tap off. And said, 'I must have felt something like it, with Cindy, I suppose. I must have. Mustn't I?' He'd picked up a tea towel to dry his hands and he'd looked at her, straight at her, and he'd said again, 'But I've never felt like this. I've never felt about anyone as I do about you.'

She was standing by the central unit in her kitchen, the unit that housed the sink and the sleek glass hob, holding the salad bowl that they had just eaten from, and that he had washed up by hand because she'd bought it thirty years before, in Umbria, and didn't think that it would withstand the dishwasher.

She said only, 'Oh, Tyler.'

He said, 'I mean it.'

1

She nodded, without complete conviction. 'I – know you do.'

He moved towards her and took the salad bowl out of her hands, and set it down on the counter. Then he took her face in his hands.

'Rose Woodrowe,' he said, 'I'm in love with you.'

She nodded again. She felt something wild and wonderful surging up inside her, a mad kind of rapture. She said, idiotically, in a whisper, 'But I'm sixty-four.'

'So?'

'And a grandmother—'

'I'm sixty-three,' he said, interrupting. 'I could be thirty-three. Or ninety-three. It's irrelevant. Completely, utterly irrelevant. You are who you are. And I am completely in love with that. Get it?'

She blinked. She said faintly, 'It's – a kind of miracle . . .'

'No, it isn't. Well, I suppose it is, a bit, that we met again.'

She stepped back a pace, and dislodged his hands.

'I meant,' she said, 'that it's a miracle to me that you feel as you do.'

He took a step towards her and put his arms round her to prevent her retreating further.

'Typical of you,' he said, 'to put it that way. All *I* can think is that my younger self must have been off his stupid head not to grab you thirty years ago.'

'Forty-seven,' she said.

His eyes widened.

'*Forty-seven?*'

'Yes.'

'Are you sure?'

'Very. Tennis camp at some Dorset school, summer of

2

1969. I was seventeen and had just sat my A levels. You were sixteen and had precociously done the same.'

'I got four As,' he said proudly.

She pulled a face. 'Did you now.'

They both laughed. He held her hard against him and said, against her cheek, 'I was mad about you then. But I didn't dare –'

She closed her eyes. 'On the contrary, you were too busy daring with those flirty girls from Cranborne Chase.'

'Was I?'

She took her face away from his. 'I'm not going to humour you, Tyler. Or flatter you. You behaved like a classic teenage hormonal boy mess.'

He released his hold enough to look at her and said, soberly, 'Sorry.'

'No need to apologize.'

'I know I wanted you to notice me.'

She put her hands into his hair. Still thick, even if grey now, still with that kind of curve and bounce that gives even a plain face charm. And Tyler Masson's face was not at all plain.

She said, 'I think you were the kind of boy who wanted everyone to notice you. And we did. There was your name to begin with.' She seemed to focus suddenly. 'Yes, your name. Why on earth are you called that?'

'Tyler?'

'Yes, Tyler.'

'Well,' he said, smiling easily down at her, 'it was my mother's idea. She believed, being from Kent, that Wat Tyler of the Peasants' Revolt was some kind of ancestor. And my father drew the line at my being called Walter, which Wat is short for. So they compromised on Tyler.'

Rose made a face. 'With Masson, for heaven's sake.' She removed her hands from his hair.

'Ancient,' Tyler said breezily. 'The first Massons came over from France after the Norman Conquest. They were stone-masons. Any more useful etymology I can assist you with?'

She was giggling. 'No!'

'Go on about what made you notice me as a schoolboy.'

Rose made an effort at composure. 'Well,' she said, 'there was your height. And a kind of confidence—'

'Insecurity,' he said.

'Perhaps.'

'And what about you? What did you feel?'

She glanced at him. She said, 'I just wanted to be liked.'

'God,' he said, 'I like you. I like you so much. There isn't a way I know to express how much I like you.'

'I can't quite believe it.'

He bent to peer into her face. 'I don't get it. I absolutely, utterly don't get it. How can you doubt your total lovableness for a single second?'

'Upbringing, possibly. Character. Family position – the younger of two girls. I don't know. All I do know is that when you say what you've just said, I think I'm going to blow up like a firework.'

He linked his hands behind her waist. He said teasingly, 'What did I just say?'

'Don't . . .'

'Repeat to me what I just said.'

'I can't.'

'Rose.'

4

'Yes.'

'Rose. I, Tyler Masson, have never felt about a woman in all my sixty-three years the way I feel about you. OK?'

She nodded yet again. 'OK.'

'And in my blithe and arrogant male way, I am assuming that you feel something of the same about me. Do you?'

She looked up at him. His eyes, slightly magnified by the lenses of his spectacles were, she observed, not exactly matching in colour, one being a distinctly greener kind of hazel.

'Yes,' she said.

She was waiting for him to kiss her, but although he was looking down at her mouth, he made no attempt to touch it with his own. Instead he said, 'Just one more thing.'

'Oh?'

He released her waist and took her hands in his instead, bringing them up to hold against his chest. 'I've never done this before.'

'What?'

'Well, let's just say that if anyone proposed to anyone in the past, it was a mixture of Cindy doing the asking and me doing the assuming. But the thing is, Rose . . .'

He stopped. She waited. He lifted one of her hands up to his mouth and kissed the palm. Then he said, 'The thing is, Rose, that I desperately – really desperately – want to marry you.'

———

She had bought the little house seven years ago, after the divorce. It had been, in terms of the minimal employment of lawyers, a civilized divorce, largely because William Woodrowe wanted to marry someone else, and Rose was chiefly concerned about protecting the children from the spectacle of openly quarrelling parents. William, it transpired, had been having an affair with the senior nurse on his surgical cardiac team for well over a decade. It was an affair – if you could fairly describe such an established relationship as an affair – known, and after so long, largely accepted in both the London hospitals, public and private, where he operated, and Gillian Greenhalgh was treated with much of the deference that automatically accompanied the consort of a leading consultative surgeon. When Rose came to hospital functions as William's wife, Gillian stayed away. When Gillian was in charge of the nursing staff in an operating theatre, Rose was neither mentioned nor considered. And when new members of the surgical teams asked what on earth was going on with Mr and Mrs Woodrowe and Gillian Greenhalgh, there would be a lot of dismissive eye-rolling and shrugging and muttered mentions of a weird triangular way of doing things, search *me* how they all manage it.

They managed it, quite simply, because Rose did not know. Over the long years of their courtship and marriage, ever since she had encountered William Woodrowe at a cousin's wedding, she had been aware of his appeal as a doctor as well as his comfortably flirtatious manner. What else, for goodness' sake, had induced her to stand, precariously balanced on heels on the coconut-matting floor of a wedding marquee, and ply him for so long with eager questions about his research fellowship at Imperial College? He had sounded then as he sounded when he asked for a divorce thirty-two years later: confident, kindly and essentially reasonable. Then he had said, 'I think you are indulging me, encouraging me to go on about myself like this. But I would so much like to indulge *you*, if you would let me give you dinner in London.'

And later, just before her fifty-seventh birthday:

'I don't really think it's a question of you indulging me, exactly, in setting me free. I think it's more a matter of acknowledging that our marriage has been a great success, but that it has run its course. It really has, Rose. It's over.'

So although she had taught herself to expect and accept that William's personality and William's vocation would result in some inevitable straying now and then, she had equally instructed herself to regard them as the built-in hazards of a marriage such as theirs, a career such as his. There had unquestionably been episodes occasioning intense anxiety, but the long term, she had always told herself, would prevail over short-term threats. The idea that another, alternative relationship was quietly, steadily, secretly establishing itself did not occur to her, so when the solid fact of it was made plain to her, she was as psychologically winded as if the breath had literally been knocked out of her.

Once the first, violent shock was over, she had castigated herself, of course she had. How could she have been so blind, so *obtuse*, as to not see what was really going on behind the smokescreen of infatuated student nurses and susceptible junior doctors and patients longing to find a saviour in their cardiologist? How convenient it had been that her preoccupations as a mother and a part-time translator from French and Italian into English had involved visits out of London to schools and universities and European cities, and how stupid she was not to have suspected that William's encouragement of both roles in her life, maternal and professional, often gave him the liberty to be with Gillian in her useful absences.

She thought back, with a disgust initially directed purely at herself, at all the Christmas and holiday phone calls that she had never doubted to be from anxious patients, as William had calmly assured her they were – 'I'm just going to close my study door, darling, because I'm afraid this may take some time.' Nor had it ever occurred to her that the endless medical conferences in foreign hotels, which William had reassured her would be tedious for her in the extreme, might involve Gillian as his companion. Indeed he often mentioned that Gillian would be there, implying that her involvement was purely professional rather than revealing that she was really there to share his bed. The smooth and ingenious falseness was one thing; her own failure to perceive how thoroughly she had been deceived, and for how long, had been quite another.

Her older sister, Prue, a retired headmistress, had been characteristically firm.

'Now, Rosie, you can't make a career out of beating yourself up. Nor of being outraged at what a complete shit William has turned out to be. It's boring, frankly. Betrayed women who can't let go of their betrayal are beyond tedious. To be frank with you—'

'When are you ever anything else?'

Her sister had closed her eyes as if Rose had said something far best ignored.

'To be frank with you,' Prue repeated, resuming in exactly the same tone, 'you are not only better off without him psychologically, you are better off materially too. He has to give you somewhere big enough to house the children—'

'No he doesn't,' Rose said. 'The children are grown up.'

'When the children come to stay,' Prue said, in the voice

she had used with obstreperous fathers in the past, 'they need to be housed. So do their partners. And in Laura's case, their children. So you can choose where you want to live, and William has to fund it if he doesn't want to pay a great amount more in legal fees.'

'Um,' Rose said. She was trying to imagine wanting to live anywhere ever again. Prue took her shoulders in a purposeful grasp.

'I'll help you.'

'What?'

'I'll help you,' Prue said. 'To find a house.'

Rose gestured round Prue's retirement-cottage kitchen, as orderly and charmless to Rose's eye as Prue's kitchens had always been.

'But we have completely opposite tastes in houses.'

'Exactly,' Prue said. She smiled at Rose. 'What I like will help make up your mind to like the exact opposite. It will be an entirely constructive exercise.'

———

It was Laura, Rose and William's doctor daughter Laura, who had found the mews house. It had three bedrooms, a garage and even a garden, and it was at the end of a cobbled mews five minutes' walk from Oxford Street. Laura, a GP in west London, had heard about it on her professional grapevine. It was unmodernized and had been lived in by an old-school consultant in Harley Street, who wore a gold watch chain across his pinstriped waistcoat and kept a vintage Bentley in the garage.

The twins had been horrified at the idea of their mother ending up in the heart of London's medical district.

'Mum,' Nat said to her, his weekend T-shirt accessorized

with high-end earphones, 'are you off your head? The very bit of London you can't stand? Every quack in London as your neighbour? Seriously?'

Emmy, who had the most sentimental attachment of all of them to the house in Highgate where they had grown up, decided to be more personal.

'Why do you want to live anywhere, Mum, that has anything whatever to do with Dad? After what he's done. After how he's treated you. Why would you ever want to live somewhere that reminded you of him?'

But the mews house didn't. It was curiously detached, in character and atmosphere, from everything that surrounded it. Sure, as you emerged from the mews, you were confronted by a clinic for cosmetic surgery and a surgery specializing in dental implants, but beyond their front doors, you could turn into New Cavendish Street and in a few minutes be sitting in a coffee shop on Marylebone High Street with a little supermarket across the way that sold everything from milk to washing powder.

William said that the house was too expensive, and that quite apart from the asking price, modernizing it would be prohibitively costly. It was ten months on from his announcement that their marriage was over, and a satisfactory offer had been accepted on the Highgate house. William and Rose were in a cafe halfway up Highgate Hill, with a table firmly between them. Rose was drinking tea. She poured a second cup and said steadily, 'You can afford it. *We* can afford it.'

William looked at the ceiling. 'Out of the question,' he said shortly.

'I'm afraid,' Rose said, 'that you can't talk to me like that any more. I have created no real difficulties for you in all the years we've known each other. But now I want something and I intend to have it.'

'I thought your heart was in the Highgate house.'

'Once. Not now.'

'I thought,' William went on, clearly slightly aggrieved, as if Rose were the one who had created the situation, 'that you didn't care where you lived.'

'Nine months ago, I didn't. Till I saw this house, I didn't. Now I do. I can see myself living in this house.'

William put his elbows on the table, either side of his coffee cup.

He said, 'I suppose you should know that I have accepted a professorship in Melbourne.'

'Goodness.'

'The Cardiac Society of Australia and New Zealand have offered me the post. I'll be heading up a team at a major hospital and directing a research institute. And . . . ah . . . Gilly is to be head of nursing for cardiology and chest medicine at the same hospital.'

Rose looked out of the window. 'Hooray,' she said faintly.

'So we'll be out of your hair. You can live anywhere. We'll be in Australia.'

Slowly, her gaze swung back to him. 'But I don't want to live anywhere. I want to live in the mews house.'

'I can't afford it.'

Rose sat very still. She looked at him for a long time and wondered what had happened to the Rose that had once thought that life without him was too fantastical a notion even to be contemplated.

'It isn't you alone, William. It's us. It's the us who were married for over thirty years and had three children. It's the us who enabled you to have a fulfilling private *and* professional life. I'm not going to depend upon you for a single penny after we are divorced, but I am going to have this house, this particular house, which I shall make sure is my pension in the future, too.'

William looked down at his hands on the table and sighed. He is wondering, Rose thought, how he is going to tell Gillian – Gilly! – that he has agreed to buy a house for me that will cost much more than half the sale value of the Highgate house.

Rose said pleasantly, 'You both have pensions, after all. And you will both be earning, in Australia.'

Without looking up, William replied, 'You never used to be like this.'

She laughed. 'But I was never put in this position. Not that I knew about, anyway.' She added, 'You are wondering how to tell . . . Gilly, that you won't be able to afford a swimming pool *and* a tennis court in Melbourne, aren't you?'

'I think the children—'

'Leave them out of it, William.'

He straightened up abruptly and reached behind him for his coat. He said, in the professional voice she was used to hearing him use on the telephone, 'I'll think about it. I'll let you know.'

'Thank you,' she said. She was smiling. You didn't live with someone for over thirty years and fail to realize when you had won. 'Thank you, William.'

———

Her family were outraged at her choice. Her sister said that she couldn't understand how anyone in their right mind could possibly want to live in *London* if they had the chance not to. She made it sound as if it were some sort of punishment, rather than a choice. The twins said what they had said at the beginning, if with slightly less conviction once the value of a refurbished house in central London dawned upon them. Only Laura was affirmative; calm, steady Laura, with her architect husband and two small boys in the west London house that had been a neglected work in progress for the five years that she and Angus had lived in it together.

'Do you think,' Rose had said more than once, 'that Angus might get round to boxing in the bath? Or, perhaps, putting doors on the kitchen cupboards?'

'Sure,' Laura would say, a baby held absently on one hip while she emailed a patient on the phone in her free hand. 'One day. When he feels like it. When he finds the right panel. Or the right handles.' She would smile at her mother. 'Promise you, Mum. It doesn't fuss me.'

She was the only one to look round the mews house with approval.

'It's nice, Mum.'

'I know. And it's going to be nicer.'

Laura gestured towards the garden. 'The boys will be so safe there. And there are steps up to the lawn. They *love* steps.'

'I can have them to stay. There's a playground in Paddington Street Gardens.'

'Lovely,' Laura said. 'I can imagine you here, on your own.'

'So can I.'

Laura looked at her.

'Will you be OK, Mum, on your own? Really?'

'Darling. I think so. I am determined to be. The last year

has been so . . . . strange that it hasn't been a good indicator, and I can't quite picture how life will be, what it will be *like*, day to day, but I do know that I don't want you children fretting about me.'

'We want you to be happy,' Laura said, pushing up her sweater sleeves.

'Of course you do. Apart from anything else, a happy mother is less trouble. A happy mother in London and a father far away in Australia.'

'It's good for him.'

'I know.'

'And frankly,' Laura said, 'it's easier for us, not having to deal with him – and her – here. I mean, she's OK as a person, but none of it's actually very easy. I won't refuse to meet her, like Nat and Em, but I'd rather not, to be honest. I think I'll see them with the boys around. It's like having a dog there in a difficult situation. It gives everyone a kind of let-out.' She put her hands in her trouser pockets. 'But you are another matter. You liked being married, didn't you?'

'I did.'

'I like it,' Laura said. 'It's more interesting than people say. I can understand that you liked it.'

'But now,' Rose said steadily, 'I can't have it. I can't have what I had. It's over. Gone. So I have to make something else. And this' – she gestured at the dingy sitting-room walls with their faded oblongs on the dated grasscloth covering where pictures had once hung – 'is where it starts. This is the first practical project of my next chapter.'

Laura gave her the sweet, slightly absent smile she bestowed on everyone in her life who showed the smallest sign of independence.

'Good for you, Mum,' she said.

———

Rose enrolled for a twenty-six-day training course as a handyman in a north London college scheme for apprentices of all ages. She was the only woman in the scheme and, she reckoned, at least ten years older than any of the other trainees. In under a month, she learned the basics of plastering and tiling, how to lay bricks and how to hang both wallpaper and a door. At the end of the course, and still wearing her overalls, she was interviewed by a national tabloid under the headline 'Lady with a Spanner'. The organizers of the training course later told her that they'd had a fifteen per cent increase in female enrolment since the newspaper article. She waited for the children to say that they were proud of her. They said nothing. Angus, Laura reported in her neutral way, had boxed in their bath, which felt to Rose more like a mildly competitive reproof than any kind of compliment. It fell in the end to Nat, to the only son, emboldened by his new job with an asset-management company in the City, to corner her as she carefully spaced some tiles in one of her new bathrooms, and tell her that they were all worried.

Rose was holding a box of plastic tile spacers. She looked at them, rather than at Nat. 'Worried?' she said, with artificial vagueness.

'Yes, Mum.'

'Well,' Rose said, 'of course I'm getting professionals in to do the re-wiring and serious plumbing, and all that—'

'Mum,' Nat interrupted, 'don't play dumb. Don't do your

lady-with-a-spanner act on me. You can fanny about with wrenches and screwdrivers all you want, but you have to live in this house when you've finished it. You have to have an *income*, to live in an expensive house in one of the most expensive areas of one of the most expensive cities in the world, Mum. This house, whatever it's worth when you've done with it, isn't going to put bread on the table just by *being* here. We're worried, Mum, because we can't see what you're going to do for money.'

Rose stooped to put the box of tile spacers on the floor. She said quietly, 'I'm still translating.'

'That'll hardly pay your council tax!'

'I can do more. There's endless amounts of medical stuff to translate.'

'Not enough.'

Rose looked past her son. 'I couldn't ask Dad for more. I couldn't – bring myself to.'

Nat smiled at her.

'I get that. We all do. But the difference is that Dad can work for another eight years in Australia, and then he gets a pension. Never mind what – well, supplements there are to his income. But you've got this, only this. You chose to have this, rather than money. Fair enough. No criticism. But, Mum, you've got to *live* in this house, as well as own it. Do you see?'

Surrendering to deserved humiliation, Rose decided, could wait until Nat had gone. She took him down to her as yet untouched, old-fashioned kitchen and made him tea and gave him a chocolate-covered animal biscuit from the packet she had bought for Laura's little boys, and promised that she would most earnestly address his concerns. Then she escorted him out of the mews without allowing him to reiterate, as he was plainly longing to, everything he had already said, and stood waving until he disappeared around the corner towards Cavendish Square. Then she returned to the house, closed the front door and slid down against it until she was sitting on the bare boards of the hall, staring at her denim-covered knees. Here she was, fifty-seven years old, divorced and penniless, having lurched her way from one crisis to another and always, it seemed, with a blindfold on. 'Grow up, Rosie,' Prue would say, and she'd be right. Nat was right – and his sisters, on whose behalf he had spoken, were right too. She looked about her, at the scarred damask wallpaper that the old consultant had chosen for his hallway. Dark green. Dark green in an already dark passage. She wasn't actually penniless. She was certainly divorced, and unquestionably fifty-seven, but she wasn't penniless. She had the house. She struggled to her feet and put a hand protectively on the nearest dark-green wall. There was a reason the house had been so important and that same reason was going to enable her to live there. Somehow.

———

Now, seven years on, she was still there, and surviving. A series of lodgers – not hard to find, since she lived in the midst of an abundance of clinics and consulting rooms – plus a determined specialization in medical-translation work and a small legacy from her mother's estate ('You should invest it,' Prue said. 'It's so short-sighted just to *spend* it.') had enabled her to stay on in the mews house.

'There's no need, you know, to be defiant,' her daughter Emmy said once, propped in the kitchen doorway with a bag of crisps in her hand. 'I mean, we know you can do it, now. We know about how well you can cope.'

Rose was making tea. She paused, her back to Emmy, holding the jar in which she kept everyday teabags.

'It's not about coping, Em. It isn't even about defying anyone or anything. It's about having my eyes open.'

Emmy stopped crunching for a moment.

'Come again?'

Rose put the jar down and turned round.

'I just don't want not to see something crucial, ever again. I don't want to sleepwalk past something I need to see or into something I can't handle. I've *made* myself live here, not to show all of you that I could, but to show myself.'

'Oh,' Emmy said. She sounded genuinely astonished. 'Oh. OK.'

That conversation had been six months ago, two months before a friend – an ex-lodger who had subsequently become a friend – had taken her to a production of Ibsen's *The Master Builder* at a little theatre in north London, where the part of the bookkeeper, Kaia Fosli, was played by a young American actress called Mallory Masson, whose English accent, everyone around Rose was saying admiringly, was absolutely excellent. And in the interval, while she was talking peacefully to her friend over a glass of white wine, they had been interrupted by a man, a tall, personable, grey-haired man in spectacles, who said, 'Rose? Rose Guthrie? Is it really you?'

She'd stared at him; said, awkwardly, 'I haven't been Rose Guthrie for forty years.'

He laughed. He held out his hand.

'I'm Tyler. Remember? Tyler Masson. From forever ago.

That's my daughter on stage. Playing Kaia. That's my daughter, Mallory Masson.'

Four months ago. Four heady, extraordinary months, culminating in the scene in this very kitchen, next to the salad bowl. Rose put her hands over her face for a moment.

'I don't know,' she said to him, in answer to him, knowing that her face gave everything away. 'I can't think, I can't decide, I can't . . .'

He was still holding her hands captive.

'No hurry,' he said. 'Tell me when you're ready. You know, at least, what *I* want.'

She looked up at him, and she knew her expression told him everything he wanted to know. She was longing to tell him, to give him the ultimate satisfaction of knowing that she – joyfully, willingly – accepted his proposal.

'The thing is . . .' she began, and stopped.

'What?' he said. He was smiling.

'I just wonder how . . . I – we are going to tell the children?'

CHAPTER TWO

Tyler Masson had lost his American wife, Cindy, to cancer, three weeks after his sixtieth birthday. Cindy had first been diagnosed five years before, and had run the whole exhausting gamut of surgery and radiotherapy and chemotherapy at the celebrated cancer centre at Stanford near San Francisco, paid for – as so much in the Massons' lives seemed to be – by her father.

Cindy's father, who had died before his daughter, had not had any faith whatsoever that either of his sons-in-law could be trusted to look after their wives. That Tyler was English, in addition to his other disadvantages, only deepened the contempt. Cindy's father, still living in the substantial house in Pacific Heights where Cindy had grown up, had made sure that neither of his daughters would ever quite believe that they could manage without him, or his money. He had imprisoned his wife in the controllable social circuit of bridge afternoons, ladies' lunches and shopping that he deemed suitable. His younger daughter, Cindy's sister Diane, waited to divorce until her father was safely dead, and then set up house with another woman in a condo overlooking the Bay. Cindy, weighed down with the responsibilities of being the eldest and more vulnerably responsible child, developed terminal cancer.

Tyler had known all along, at some level, that he would never be a match for his father-in-law. His early academic promise petered out, almost without him noticing. He met Cindy in London at some kind of transatlantic university exchange in 1977, when he was twenty-two, and that initial meeting segued somehow into a summer some years later, in San Francisco, and the offer of a job in Cindy's father's commercial-property company, which included the promise of help in obtaining a coveted green card in order to live and work in America.

Tyler, coasting amiably through his post-student days, was a plum ripe for the picking. San Francisco, with its heady mix of new hippiedom and affluent tradition; sunny California; the easy sophistication of American life compared favourably with what he had left behind; Cindy herself with her lovely teeth and ability to both ski and play tennis, were all irresistibly seductive. After all, Tyler didn't know what he wanted to do with his life, beyond *not* wanting, fairly strenuously, to follow his schoolmaster father into teaching. The morning after his early spring engagement to Cindy – an arrangement that seemed to have come about with no actual decision made on his part – he stood in his bedroom in the Baker Street house of his future parents-in-law, and looked down into their immaculate garden, and saw, to his wonder, that the glossy-leaved trees trained as espaliers along one wall bore not only starry white flowers, but, unmistakably, actual *oranges*. He was entranced. He stood there, wrapped in a post-shower (a shower!) towel, drying his ears with a second towel, and gazed with rapture at the oranges. This spectacular place, with its exotically mixed culture and separate showers in the bathrooms, also grew orange trees in gardens, which they, the Americans, quaintly called yards.

'It's a Cara Cara,' Cindy's mother said later. 'Pink flesh. Very sweet. And beyond the oranges, you will have seen the Fuerte avocado trees.'

Tyler had never seen an avocado, let alone tasted one. He had never eaten an orange straight from its tree, either. He looked from the Cara Cara orange on his plate, across the table at a glowing Cindy, and felt that he had done very much the right thing in becoming her fiancé. This place, this city, had the feel of the future about it, an air of beckoning promise. When he had to face Cindy's father later in the day, for the inevitable interview, he felt he could do it buoyed up by being as much in love with what America held out to him as he surely was with Cindy.

He was given a job overseeing contractors on commercial sites, and a house at the unfashionable end of Pacific Heights where even a glimpse of the Bay was out of the question. He asked Cindy why they had to accept *this* house, and Cindy said simply, as if it was perfectly acceptable, that it was Daddy's decision. She had explained, very patiently, how much persuading she had had to do to bring her father round to the idea of her marrying Tyler Masson in the first place. Having won that enormous victory, she said, she wasn't going to confront her father with a further, if lesser, defiance.

Tyler said, trying to be rational, 'But if he doesn't pay for it—'

'Of course he's paying for it!'

'But why? Why don't we get a mortgage like everyone else, and be independent?'

Cindy had elements of her mother in her. She came up to Tyler and linked her arms behind his neck.

'Honey, it'd break his heart.'

'Would it?'

'Sure it would. Diane and me'll always be his little girls. I can't just – throw a gift like this house back at him.'

Tyler put his hands on her slim ribcage. Attempting a smile, he said, 'What about me?'

'What about you?'

'Well, suppose I would rather we looked after ourselves, even if we don't do it very well, at the beginning?'

She put her head on one side and her ponytail swung out smoothly. 'We're the kids, honey,' Cindy said, 'and Daddy knows best. When we're older, we can make changes. But not yet. You'll see.'

So Tyler waited. He waited through the birth of his son, Seth – named for his late maternal great-grandfather – and his daughter Mallory – named for her late maternal great-grandmother – and a change of job from overseeing contractors to liaising with architects. He waited through two changes of house, both dictated by his father-in-law. He waited for something to happen, that elusive something that had seemed to shimmer so tangibly close on the morning he had noticed oranges hanging on the trees outside his window. He waited for Cindy – blonde, trim, tennis-playing, conscientious – to promote him above her father in the pecking order of men in her life. It was only when she told him that her father was paying for her cancer treatment at the famous centre at Stanford that he realized he would never be first in her life, first in her consideration and estimation. In fact, since Seth was born, he, Tyler, hadn't even been second.

He'd looked at Cindy. She'd been crying at the confirmation of the cancer diagnosis, as neatly as she did most things.

'Couldn't we – go it alone? Together? Couldn't we try and fix this in our own way?' he said.

Cindy blew her nose. She shook her head.

'Why not?' Tyler asked.

She'd looked up at him. She was fifty-five years old, the children were in their late twenties and her father was reluctantly, angrily retired.

'I couldn't do it to him,' Cindy said. 'I couldn't refuse him.' And then she produced her usual trump card, the statement he had never had an answer to. 'I couldn't,' Cindy said, her eyes wide with intensity. 'It would break his heart.'

Tyler had gone out then into what he still determinedly called the garden. He had looked up at the American sky and then at the citrus trees and avocado trees that Cindy had planted trimly in pots against a white wall to reflect the sunlight. None of it, that day, looked exotic and full of promise. It looked, instead, alien and mildly threatening, as if this cruel and hideous illness of Cindy's was a manifestation of fundamental otherness in which he, Tyler Masson, with his American-accented children, would always be an outsider.

He looked back at the house. It had been given to Cindy by her father. Not to both of them: only to Cindy. And he, Tyler, had allowed that to happen, just as he had allowed the two previous houses to happen, and the jobs and the now perpetual state of being beholden to a man who was never, ever, going to surrender his elder daughter to any other man on earth. Tyler jammed his fists angrily into his trouser pockets.

'The trouble with you, my boy,' his father-in-law was fond

of saying, 'is that for all your fancy English education, you don't have the first idea about money. You think – no, don't interrupt me – that you are kinda *above* money. And I am here to tell you that' – pause for emphasis – 'it just ain't so. No, sir. Money is where it begins and money is where it ends. And I am the living proof.'

Tyler had never argued back. Arguing with his father-in-law would have been like hammering on a locked steel door with his bare fists. In their different ways, neither Tyler nor Cindy had ever done anything that had contravened her father's instructions, to the point where Tyler had begun to be overcome with shame at his own spinelessness. He had sat in the church at his father-in-law's funeral and felt, rather than relief at this longed-for release, only a bitter sense of self-censure. Goodness knows what Cindy, her sparse hair covered by an ingenious silk turban, was thinking, sitting quite still beside her weeping mother, dry-eyed and inscrutable. It would be only a year before another tumour, this time in her right lung, would make itself known and begin its final remorseless mission to carry her off.

Her father left his wife well provided for, for her lifetime, and a substantial sum to his daughters, in their unmarried names alone. To the sons-in-law he left cufflinks emblazoned with the crest of the California Institute of Technology, where he had studied engineering as a young man, and 'not one single dime', as Diane's abandoned husband said, throwing his cufflink box down in disgust. Tyler, nearing sixty and by then visiting Cindy daily in hospital, said nothing to her, telling himself that he was sparing her but knowing that he was, in truth, overwhelmed by self-disgust, and execrating himself for a whole lifetime of supine acquiescence. When she tried to talk to him about life after her own death, or her will and how she had disposed of her assets, he'd refused to listen.

'No, Cindy. *No*.'

'But don't you want to know?'

'No, I don't. I emphatically don't. I want you to be well again, that's all.'

'But honey, I won't be. You have to face the fact that I won't be. The children—'

Tyler said rapidly, 'The children will be fine.'

'I know. I know they will be. I'll make sure they are. That's one of the things I want to talk to you about.'

He picked up her hand. It was as thin as the rest of her, bleached to an unfleshlike pallor. He kissed it and said, 'I don't want to hear a word. I know you'll do the right thing. The kind thing. Like you always have.'

After she died, Seth and Mallory discovered that she had left the value of their house, when sold, to cancer research at Stanford, and enough money for Seth to leave the job he'd reluctantly taken in IT and enrol at the San Francisco Baking Institute on Grandview Drive, to study under a teacher who specialized in highly hydrated wholegrain sourdough breads. Mallory, who inherited a precisely similar amount, immediately headed east, to New York City, intent upon gaining a place at the American Academy of Dramatic Arts or the Juilliard School. When neither would accept her, she ended up at an acting academy on Pace Plaza, and became as immersed in the world of the theatre as if she had been on another planet. Within six months of becoming a widower, Tyler's working life came to a natural end, and he found himself having to leave his house because the sale was going through, as well as facing a weirdly blank and unanchored future. Cindy had left him enough to buy a modest apartment, and nothing more. The size of the legacy – only a fraction of what she had left her children – expressed her opinion of him very eloquently.

He bought an air ticket to New York and took Mallory out to dinner. She booked a table at a tiny Korean restaurant in SoHo, and arranged to meet him there. Tyler took one look through the steamed-up window at the crammed and clattering interior full of people eating kimchi out of pottery bowls, and rang his daughter.

'Sorry, sweetheart, but I can't eat there. It won't do. I want to *talk* to you.'

'Dad, we can talk there, it's cool—'

'It's deafening, Mallory. I'm going to see if Raoul's will give us a table.'

'Raoul's? Where you and Mom always went?'

'Yes.'

'But Dad—'

'I'm walking to Princes Street right now, Mallory. I'll see you there.'

Mallory had coloured the ends of her hair dark blue, and wore jeans and a black leather jacket. She looked, Tyler thought, like someone who had been right back to the drawing board and started again, transforming herself from a conventional West Coast beach babe to an edgy urban creative. She said she was really happy.

'You look it.'

'I mean really, *really* happy.'

'A man?' Tyler said, smiling.

Mallory rolled her eyes.

'Oh my God, Dad. *No*. So no. It's acting – I just love it. The theatre. I have never been as excited about anything as I am about the theatre.'

'So do you want to tell me? About the theatre?'

Mallory told him. She did not, he thought, stop talking for two hours. She talked right through a shared poulet de Bresse and a carafe of burgundy and a tarte tatin. At the end, rosy and replete with food and wine, she stood up to put her arms round him and tell him that although she hated that Mom wasn't there to know how happy she was, she was just blown away that he, Tyler, had come all this way to support her and see for himself. He had held her in his arms and felt, as he had always felt when Cindy insisted that refusing her father's loaded gifts would break his heart, that he couldn't say what he had flown from California to say. He couldn't dent her joyous mood by asking her what he was to do with the endless grey plateau of life that stretched ahead of him. So he held her and told her how happy he was for her and how she must tell him the minute she got a part in anything, however small, even if she was just a sundry spear-carrier like he had been, in school productions of the safely military Shakespeares.

'Of course,' she said. 'Of *course*. You'll be the first person I call.'

Only when she had gone, dancing down into the subway and leaving him standing staring after her, his hands in the pockets of his quintessentially American raincoat, did it occur to him that she had asked him nothing at all about himself. She hadn't asked him about being retired, or where he would live after the house was sold, or whether he had seen Seth recently, let alone how he was feeling. She had been warm and sweet and affectionate and completely self-absorbed. Standing there at the top of the subway steps in New York City with the world cheerfully jostling past him, Tyler wondered if he was now entirely alone, or whether, despite all the apparent human connections in San Francisco, he always had been.

He flew back to California because he had the ticket and had planned to. It had occurred to him to stay on in New York, or buy a ticket, on impulse, to Canada or Brazil, but in the end he docilely did what he had arranged with himself to do, and went home. Except, it wasn't home any more. It was the house he and Cindy had shared for over a decade, but it wasn't the house that Seth and Mallory had grown up in, and, in any case, it had been sold to a couple, the realtor said, who were just full of ideas as to what they could do with it.

Tyler didn't care. The house had become, for him, too much associated with Cindy's illness, Cindy's long, inexorable, stoical decline. He had no real desire to live there any more. On the other hand, he didn't want to live anywhere very much. He couldn't, in fact, visualize how life was to be lived, in the future, anywhere at all. In her quiet, considered way Cindy had left him enough money to buy his modest apartment, and his pension from his late father-in-law's business would enable him to live in it. If he could even start to imagine how that was to be done.

His ex-brother-in-law, Jack, had moved to a small apartment just off Mission Street after his divorce. Both Cindy and Diane had been disapproving. When they were growing up, Mission Street had been almost exclusively Latino, and now they heard that it had become a haven for hipsters. Jack bought an apartment above a Chinese–Peruvian restaurant, and said the nightlife was remarkable. There was a cinema restaurant there, he said, where you could eat while watching a movie projected onto a wall. He acquired a girlfriend not much older than Mallory and announced to Tyler that he and the girlfriend were taking off for Santa Fe for a while – the girlfriend was an abstract painter – and why didn't Tyler take over the apartment? So Tyler moved, almost sleep-walking, from a balconied house with a swimming pool on Pacific Heights to a two-bedroom apartment in the Mission, and sat on the edge of Jack's bed, which the girlfriend had draped in ethnic shawls, and had a long interior dialogue with himself about what he was to do.

The first person he tried to talk to about the future was Seth, who was now in his thirties, with long hair plaited down his back like a Sioux warrior. Having discovered bread, it was now his whole life, apart from the pretty Japanese woman who had been one of his first instructors at the Baking Institute and was now, he explained to his father, his partner in both life and love. He told his father that he was very happy to talk about the future. In fact, the future was exactly what he and Yuhui ('Pronounced Yoofy, Dad,' Seth told him. 'I don't want you embarrassing me by getting it wrong.') wanted to discuss with him.

They met, on Seth's instructions, at a bakery that was something close to what Seth and Yuhui aspired to. Tyler had imagined he might explain to them something of the alarm-ing lack of direction he was feeling himself, but it rapidly became plain that Seth and Yuhui had a definite plan for their own futures, which they were determined to explain, including what his own involvement in it was to be. They wanted, they said, to start their own coffee shop and bakery, and had found a site – 'Daringly, but bear with me, Dad, I have worked this out' – on the edge of the financial district.

'Lunchtime specialities,' Seth said. 'For the money crowd. Smoked trout on sourdough with chilli–lemon apple and mey choy greens. A house mayo. A four-dollar loaf of sourdough to take home—'

'Organic flour,' Yuhui said earnestly. 'Hand-kneaded.'

'—and drip coffee. We'll have wood countertops. The dough will be left to rise on wood countertops. We'll be experimenting all the time. Fresh apple, maybe. Maple oatmeal, wholewheat.'

It transpired that what they needed – wanted – was money. They had what Cindy had left Seth to buy a long lease on the building, but they needed more to convert it and equip it to the high-tech – but at the same time truly artisanal – standard that they aspired to. They were, Tyler thought, as he looked at their faces across the bakery table, evangelical. Bread to them was not just a passion, it was a mission. When Seth named the necessary sum for Tyler's contribution, revealing it to be almost exactly the amount Cindy had left him to buy an apartment, it had hardly caused a ripple in his thinking before he agreed. Of course Seth should have the investment. Why not? It would be purposeful, interesting, enterprising, to be involved in an exciting start-up like this. It even had a name. They were, they announced proudly, as if revealing the name of a first baby, going to call it Doughboy.

Only when he was home again, in Jack's apartment, hunting for a skillet in which to fry eggs, did it occur to Tyler that he could not in fact hand over all the capital he had to Seth, for Doughboy. He had two children, after all. If he was going to invest in Seth's future, then he would have to invest equally in Mallory's. He didn't in the least mind about being without capital – maybe, even, his father-in-law had been quite right about his lack of maturity over money – but he did mind very much about behaving equitably to both his children. He put the skillet down on the hob beside the eggs and called Seth immediately, to tell him that he was very welcome to half the amount they had discussed, but the other half was Mallory's.

Seth said cheerfully, 'That's fine, Dad. We haven't even started on asking Yuhui's family yet,' leaving Tyler yet again with the feeling he had had that night in New York – that he had somehow ceased to be of real significance, that he was, even to his own children, somebody important when they infrequently thought about him, but usually peripheral. Those two people, whose diapers – nappies, he had firmly called them – he had changed, whom he had taken to school, and heard learning to read, whom he had taught to swim, and ride a two-wheeler, and surf, and run with a ball, had now surged out into their own worlds and been gladly swallowed up by them.

It was a bad winter. For nine months, Tyler struggled, and he knew he was struggling. He could not bring himself to explain his overwhelming sense of lostness to his children, to his mother-in-law, to his sister-in-law, or to his few friends. He took care to have haircuts, to take his shirts to the Chinese laundry down the street, not to drink alcohol if he was alone, not to shuffle about in sneakers. The odd date was kindly arranged for him, but he hadn't the heart for them. He wondered, not infrequently, what he *did* have the heart for. It wasn't, if he was honest, that he was missing Cindy either, except as a habit whose very existence required some reciprocal effort. It was more – overwhelmingly more – that with Cindy gone, his identity in this wonderful city seemed to have vanished, like a cup of water thrown into an ocean. 'What,' he said to himself, over and over, 'am I *for*?'

At last, almost two years after Cindy's death, and with no sign of Jack and the girlfriend returning from Santa Fe, a call from Mallory offered a chink of light. She had been cast in a play, she said; it wasn't a major role but it was an Ibsen play, the director was a friend of hers, and the director was so excited because the play was going to have its run – 'four weeks, Dad' – in London.

'London?' Tyler said, '*London?*'

'Yes,' Mallory said happily. 'Can you believe it? London. London, England. Can you come?'

'To London? Sure, I can come to London. I haven't been to London for ten years.'

'You still sound so English.'

'Not to the English, I don't.'

'Dad . . .'

'Yes?'

'Will you – well, I want to sound more English. For this part. For my part. She's the bookkeeper. Will you coach me? To sound like you do?'

He had his telephone pressed to his ear. He closed his eyes. He could feel an extraordinary warmth beginning to spread down his limbs. He nodded vigorously, holding his phone.

'Of course.'

'Come soon,' Mallory said. 'Come now. You can sleep on my couch, the one in the living room. My roommates won't mind, they are so cool. Come to New York and be my voice coach.'

He flew at once, to New York. Mallory's roommates seemed to take to him immediately. He went from a feeling of utter futility about everything in general, to its polar opposite of feeling of value and purpose, in a matter of days. And when Mallory said, 'Come to London with me. For the rehearsals, as well as the run. *Please*,' he didn't even, in his English way, prevaricate.

'Of course,' he said. 'Of course I'll come.'

He emailed ahead to old school friends and university friends. He sat at the sharp-edged glass dining table in Mallory's rented Brooklyn apartment and typed cheerful email after cheerful email. The thought of going back to London, of finding a flat there instead of staying in the kind of stately central hotel that Cindy had been brought up to regard as the only residential destination possible in that city, was almost heady. He felt both excited and strangely liberated, and when he looked at himself in the bathroom shaving mirror, he saw someone, at last, that he was quite pleased to see.

The theatre where Mallory was acting in *The Master Builder* was in Kilburn, and she planned to share a flat with other members of the cast, suggested by the theatre, nearby, on the High Road. Tyler, anxious not to crowd her after the weeks on her couch, and equally anxious to exploit his own green shoots of revived independence, took a flat – a room, really, with a bathroom the size of a cupboard – on the edge of Little Venice, where his grandmother had once had a house and a conservatory full of tangled vines and orchids. On his first night, staring out of his huge studio window at the moving lights of cars speeding along the Westway, he told himself sternly that he must not, *not*, surrender to any romantic rapture at being home.

His days were busy, busier than they had been in over a year. The emails had borne fruit here and there, lunches and dinners, weekends in houses in the country, even a modestly paid offer of a consultancy with an old college friend who was handing his construction business over to his son. He went to the occasional rehearsal – by now something of a pet voice coach to the cast – and to other plays in other theatres; he made friends with the Bangladeshi from whom he bought milk and newspapers, the Latvian girl who took his shirts in to launder, the Cypriot Greek who gave him a haircut. In emails to Seth, he outlined his vigorous life back in London and reported that the opening night of Mallory's play had been a solid success, so critically acclaimed that he, Seth, would have been proud of his sister. It was so good a produc- tion, in fact, that he was going to go back on other nights and see it again, during its month-long run. And, he con- fided to his son, he was thinking that maybe, just maybe, he might stay in London. Just for a year perhaps, just long enough to see if what he was feeling was transitory or indica- tive of something he could build on.

'I want something of what you've got,' he wrote to Seth, dangerously late at night from his London room. 'And what Mallory has, with the theatre. I want to belong. I want to feel that I'm in the right place, for Christ's sake.'

Seth didn't reply in kind. Seth never replied in kind. He replied with his own, and Yuhui's news, with the progress they were making on the Doughboy project, how Yuhui's father had lent them fifty thousand dollars for bread-making equipment and ovens. It didn't matter, Tyler told himself, it didn't matter that his children were so fired up by their own lives that they had no bandwidth left, in modern terms, to absorb anything of his. Especially when he was bursting – the feeling barely, explosively contained – to tell someone close to him that Rose Guthrie, or Woodrowe as she now was, had, by some miracle, walked back into his life.

CHAPTER THREE

Nat was insisting on a family conference. Rose had demurred – 'Try not to be so pompous, darling' – but Nat ignored her. He said that there was nothing she needed to do beyond being at home, and that he and Emmy and Laura would come and see her at a given time to, he said, 'discuss this situation'.

Rose had, of course, told Tyler. They were in bed, on a wonderfully quiet Sunday morning, with pale sunlight falling onto the disordered folds of Rose's grey embroidered bedspread. It was, Rose thought, both an image and a moment of complete contentment: her head on his shoulder (his still-tanned shoulder), his arm supporting her while he read aloud from the Sunday newspaper, an article about pedestrians in the streets being too absorbed in the screens in their hands to notice either traffic or anyone else. He was reading beautifully, she thought, with just an edge of irony, and she could feel the faint vibrations of his voice resounding in the ear she had pressed against his skin. His skin. His smooth, astonishingly youthful, perfectly toasted skin, which she could now feel all down the length of her body. She closed her eyes. It had never been like this with William.

Sex with William was efficient but brisk, with little talking. With Tyler, it could, in the best sense, take all day – leisurely, exploratory, full of conversation.

She had even been able to say, quite frankly, the first time, 'I am very nervous about this, you know. I'm so out of practice.'

He said, smiling, 'You don't have to do anything.'

'But I do, I can't just lie there.'

'Why not? Don't you trust me?'

'It isn't that. It's nothing to do with trusting you. It's me, it's this – this *body*, it's being sixty-four, it's—'

'Shush,' he said. He was smiling. He came close to her but didn't touch her. He said, 'Just leave it to me.'

'Oh, Tyler . . .'

He put his hands on her shoulders and pressed her gently down onto her bed. 'Lie back.'

'I – don't want to disappoint you.'

'You couldn't.'

'But . . .'

'Even if you tried, you couldn't. Just remember, Rose, that I am getting what I never imagined I could have. Close your eyes.'

'I can't.'

'Close them.'

She had. She had closed them as instructed and only opened them again what felt like a long time later, when he said softly, 'Look at me.' And now, lying against his shoulder, she remembered not caring how surrendered she had looked, how dizzy, and suffused with a new and exhilarating liberty.

'Tyler,' Rose said now, opening her eyes.

He stopped reading. 'Is this actually very boring?'

'It isn't that.'

'Ah?'

'It's the children.'

'Ah,' he said, in a different tone, 'the children.'

Rose sat up in bed and tucked the duvet under her arm-pits, like a bodice. Tyler lay where he was, his spectacles on, lazily smoothing a lock of her hair – streaked with toffee-coloured highlights now, since his arrival – behind her ear.

'Yes.'

'Tell me,' he said.

'They – my children, that is – have asked for a meeting. Here. Nat suggested it, Emmy wants it too and Laura is, as usual, going along with it. There's – there's a purpose to this meeting.'

Tyler's hand was now gently massaging her shoulder. He said, as if he were thinking only about her shoulder, 'A purpose?'

She turned slightly to look at him.

'I think,' she said, 'it will be about money. About money if – if we get married.'

Tyler smiled at her. 'Of course.'

'But—'

'I'd expect your kids to be concerned about the money.'

'Would you? Don't you mind?'

'Why should I mind?' Tyler said.

'But if we marry – and I have this house?'

'Sweetheart,' Tyler said, 'I don't care about the money. I never have. It drove Cindy and her father round the bend that I didn't care, couldn't care. Your money, your house. Fine by me.'

'Really?'

He shrugged. He said easily, 'Really really.'

'I – was dreading telling you. I thought it would put you off my children. And I so want you to like each other. I can't tell you how much it matters to me that you like each other.'

Tyler moved his hand to stroke it up and down her back.

'I'm sure we will,' he said. He gestured with the free hand that wasn't touching her back. 'You'll see.' He was smiling again. 'I'm completely indifferent to money.' He rolled sideways so that he could kiss her nearest arm. 'It'll probably infuriate you, my attitude to money. But it won't scare the children.'

———

There was a mild argument about where the meeting should happen. Rose wanted them all to be in comfortable chairs, and on the sofa, in her sitting room, but Nat wanted them round her dining table, with something to write on, and iPads to look things up.

'No,' Rose said. 'It's a family discussion, not a board meeting.' She had thought of adding, 'Try not to be so like your father,' but had restrained herself. Instead she said, 'We can't have a meeting as if we hardly know each other. In any case, I am not going to be *lectured* by you, so I will be in my own chair, thank you very much.'

Nat made a face.

'As you wish, Mum.'

'I *do* wish.'

'Whatever makes you happy,' he said irritatingly.

'I *am* happy.'

'You look it,' Nat said. 'You look amazing. Wonderful.

You look – well, you haven't looked like this for as long as I can remember. Well done, Mr Masson.'

'Please don't talk about him like that.'

'Like what?'

'With just an edge of sarcasm,' Rose said.

Nat moved to put an arm round her shoulders.

'Sorry, Mum. Perhaps when I meet him . . .'

'Of course you'll meet him. It's just been so fast.'

'Telling me.'

'But don't patronize me, darling. Don't talk down to me, as if I need saving from myself somehow. This meeting, for example, isn't just unnecessary, it's far too soon.'

Nat took his arm away. 'Not if you intend to *marry* this man, Mum.'

'I only told you he had asked me.'

'But you'll say yes.'

'Probably.'

Nat said warningly, 'Mum . . .'

Rose looked towards the door. 'Is that someone at the front door? Emmy?'

'Useful timing.'

'I managed not to say it earlier,' Rose said, 'but sometimes you sound exactly like your father.'

Nat looked at her. She had always been attractive, he thought, but there was a glow to her now, an extra energy that he couldn't help admiring while at the same time feeling almost unable to bear knowing why it had come about. For a split second, he wanted to hurl himself into her arms and beg her to return to being just his mother. A second later, the impulse was gone. He walked towards the door.

'I'll go and let Emmy in, shall I?' he said.

Rose went to find Laura, in the kitchen. Laura was on her phone, as usual, but she had assembled a tray of glasses and bottles of wine and water, and filled Rose's salad bowl with the crisps that she had brought, ignoring Rose's suggestion of providing smoked salmon perhaps, or slices of salami.

'No,' Laura was saying, 'no. Tell her I'll see him tomorrow if his temperature isn't down. One more spoonful of Calpol only. *One*. Keep him drinking. Yes. Yes, thank you.' She took the phone away from her ear and peered at it. 'Honestly. Poor woman, she gets in such a state.'

'Is the child a baby?'

'Heavens, no,' Laura said. 'He's seven. And far too fat. I want to see their *ribs*, at seven. Hungry and skinny.' She glanced at her mother. 'You look terrific, Mum.'

'Thank you, darling. Even Nat said so.'

Laura smiled at her. 'Your mummy's boy.'

'No, he isn't.'

Laura leaned forward and said, almost conspiratorially, 'Well, he won't like this new development in your life. Will he?'

Rose picked up the tray. 'Perhaps turn your phone off?'

'I was going to, Mum,' Laura said, unperturbed. 'I'm not on call tonight anyway.'

Rose glanced at her. 'I'm not looking forward to this.'

Laura put her phone in her jacket pocket. 'Why not?' she said. 'It's your life, isn't it?'

———

Emmy said that they had all been brought up by Rose not to be in any hurry about relationships, always to wait until the first giddy madness had subsided a bit before deciding anything about anyone. She was sitting on Rose's sofa with a glass of wine in her hand and the bowl of crisps on the sofa beside her, and because her office in public relations prided itself on its informality, she was in jeans and boots worn with a sleeveless T-shirt and an immense muffler swaddling her neck.

Rose said nothing. Nat was checking something on his iPad. Laura said, 'Angus and I knew each other for three years before we lived together. And then another two before we got married.'

'There you are,' Emmy said to Rose, 'five years. And you've known this Tyler man for four months.'

'I knew him long ago.'

'But not properly. Not really. It wasn't like I *knew* all the boys at school. They were just kind of there.'

'I wasn't making a point *against* Mum,' Laura said. 'I was just saying. I think I take ages to fall in love anyway – I mean, Angus knew long before I did – so I'm not really much of a guide.'

Nat put his iPad down. He said to Rose, 'Don't you think Em has a point, though? Don't you think this is all far too fast? Far too fast, at least, to think of marrying.'

Rose looked down at her wine. She hadn't touched it. It occurred to her that she didn't want to touch it, that she felt, for the first time ever, not much warm pleasure in having all her three children in her sitting room together. In fact, she thought, she was so far from feeling pleased and proud to have the children there that she really, if she was alarmingly candid with herself, wanted them gone. Nat was sitting in the chair Tyler usually sat in. Rose would have preferred, at that moment, to raise her eyes from her wine glass and look across the room and find Tyler there, and not Nat. It was, she told herself, an immensely improper thought: unnatural, unmaternal, unacceptable. But she could not deny that it had happened, that the thought was there.

'Perhaps,' she said, not looking up, 'you would allow me to know my own mind.'

Laura, absorbed in her phone again, said almost absently, 'Of course.'

'Not actually of course at all,' Emmy said. She had made a neat pile of crisps of approximately the same size and was eating the resulting sandwich in small bites. 'Laura, don't be exasperating. You don't mean it. You are just as concerned about this – this *infatuation*, as we are.'

'I really can't listen to this,' Rose said.

'We mustn't fall out,' Nat said to Emmy, ignoring his mother. 'Don't pick on Laura.'

'Maybe don't pick on me either,' Rose said.

Emmy finished her crisps and took a swallow of wine.

'We're not picking on you, Mum. We're just worried. It's worrying when your mother suddenly completely falls for someone like you seem to have done.'

Rose looked up at her. She said levelly, 'Why?'

Emmy made a face. '*Why?*'

'Yes. Why? Why can't I have a life in just the way you expect, even demand, to do? Of course, you're none of you *used* to there being a man in my life, are you, because there really hasn't been one since your father, so I suppose I ought to expect a bit of over-reaction—'

'We are *not* over-reacting,' Nat said.

'Aren't you? Wanting a meeting, coming round here in a gang to tick me off . . .'

'Not tick you off,' Laura said.

'What then?'

'Just,' Emmy said, picking up more crisps, 'to try and help you to see that it would be a good idea – or the best idea – to slow down a bit.'

'Yes,' Nat said, emphatically.

Rose looked at her eldest daughter.

'Laura?'

Laura looked up from her phone. She said almost vaguely, 'Well, I certainly don't want you hurt to any degree, but I also think you should be allowed to make your own choices.'

'Thank you,' Rose said, at the same moment that the twins shouted '*Laura!*' in exasperation.

'You aren't helping,' Nat said to Laura, and then to his twin sister, 'Put those crisps down.'

Emmy immediately put the handful of crisps back in the salad bowl. 'Sorry.'

'It's odd, isn't it,' Laura said, her eyes on her phone screen, 'how she's always done exactly what Nat says?'

'I don't.'

'Oh you do,' Laura said, raising her eyes. 'You always have. I mean, if Nat was all for this man in Mum's life—'

'Stop it,' Rose shouted. '*Stop* it!'

They gazed at her, three pairs of eyes fixed upon her in astonishment.

'Goodness,' Emmy said faintly. 'You never shout.'

'Perhaps,' Rose said more quietly, 'I don't usually have cause. But I do now. I *do*. I will *not* have you dictating who I see and who I – I *love*, and I will not have you telling me how I should conduct my relationships. I have stood by you all, supportively, through all your emotional ups and downs, and, I'll have you know, I've been no trouble to you as a mother. I've never asked for anything, I've refused you nothing, I never interfere or criticize, and now, when I have a chance of happiness – no, not just happiness, but immense, *profound* happiness – all you can do is carp and judge and behave as if all I deserve is to be sent to some naughty step of your disapproving devising. Don't you think I deserve some support? Don't you think, after all these years of what you've had from me – which I've gladly given, I have to say – you might consider seeing things from my point of view, rejoicing that I have found someone who loves me, someone, I might add, that you haven't even *met*? Don't you think that after all I've been through, never mind all I've protected you from, that you might manage to feel just a fraction of the *joy* that this relationship brings me?'

There was a stunned silence. Then Nat, under his breath, said, 'Wow.'

Laura leaned forward in her chair and stretched her arms out towards her mother, her phone sliding unheeded to the floor. 'You're a fantastic mother,' she said.

Emmy was crying softly into her muffler. She said incoherently, 'That's why, Mum. That's why we're just worried that it's all going too fast, that you'll be taken advantage of.'

Nat got out of his chair and came to kneel beside Rose. 'Sorry, Mum.'

Rose put a hand out to ruffle his hair. She didn't speak.

Nat went on, 'Emmy's right. We're just worried. It's made us all jumpy.'

Rose flung an arm sideways to squeeze one of Laura's hands. In a calmer voice, she said, 'What exactly are you worried about? Why can't you trust me to pick a trustworthy man?'

Emmy sniffed. 'Because you're out of practice.'

'So I don't know what I'm doing?'

'None of us does.'

'I meet a man again,' Rose said, 'a man I first met when we were teenagers. And he's a widower. And retired. And his children have inherited money from their mother and are launched on their careers. And I am alone, and solvent, and making do with a life I have learned to quite like, but didn't sign up for when I married. And we fall in love and he asks me to marry him, and you react as if I was a teenage heiress being seduced by a scheming adventurer. Just stop. Just – just *stop*. Try to see it all from my point of view and *rejoice* with me.'

Laura nodded. She bent to pick up her phone.

Nat got off his knees, sighing, and stood looking down at his mother. 'We should meet him.'

Rose gestured, as if to indicate that that was what she had been aiming for all along.

'Here,' she said.

'No.'

'Why not?'

'Somewhere impersonal,' Emmy said, putting her hand into the salad bowl.

Nat swooped across the room and snatched the bowl off the sofa.

'Emmy's right. And would you *stop* eating crisps, Em.'

'I like them.'

'But you hate yourself for eating them all the time. Look how you are in the pub. Why don't we meet in a hotel?'

'A *hotel*?'

'Angus could come,' Laura said. 'He ought to be there, really.'

'Why?' Emmy demanded.

'He's known Mum since before – well, he's known Mum for over ten years.'

'That's no reason. He isn't her child, after all.'

'I'd like Angus to be there,' Rose said. 'I'm very fond of Angus.'

'Right,' said Nat. He was standing in the middle of the room, holding the salad bowl. 'Right. We'll meet in a hotel.' He glanced at his mother. 'OK?'

Rose looked back up at him. Her expression was impersonal.

'If it makes you happy,' she said. 'Certainly OK.'

———

Nat and Emmy lived in adjacent, hilly streets in Clerkenwell, Nat in a penthouse with a lodger, high above Crawford Passage, and Emmy in a studio flat round the corner. Both were heavily mortgaged, and in both cases the flats were jointly owned by themselves and their father in Australia, who had paid the deposits. Between the two flats, at the bottom of Eyre Street Hill was a pub, banded in white stone and red brick like a giant humbug, where the twins often met after work, and to which they now repaired after the meeting at Rose's house.

Nat set a glass of ginger beer down in front of his sister.

'Are you sure that's what you want?'

Emmy nodded. 'It's fine. I don't really know what I want. Except for Mum not to be like this.'

Nat put his bottle of Belgian beer down beside Emmy's glass and straddled a stool opposite her.

'I know.'

Emmy said gloomily, 'She looks fantastic.'

'Years younger. And her hair. What's she done with her hair?'

'Highlighted it.'

'It's always been just – hair. Brown hair.'

'Well, now it's got highlights.'

Nat said crossly, 'Floodlights, more like.'

'Don't be a meanie.'

Nat picked up his beer and put it down again untasted. 'Did you feel like this about Dad and Gillian?'

Emmy was chipping varnish off one thumbnail with concentration.

'Nope.'

'Why not?'

Emmy didn't look up. She said, 'It was old news by the time it got to us.'

'It was more than that.'

Emmy said nothing. Nat picked up his beer bottle again, took a pull and held it loosely between his knees.

'I think,' he said, 'that Dad doesn't mean as much to us as Mum does.'

Emmy stopped chipping and glared at her brother.

'He does. He's our father just as much as she's our mother.'

'No, Em. I mean, yes of course he is, biologically, but Mum is the one we know really well, Mum is the one who always did stuff for us and came to see us. And we saw Mum in pieces, didn't we? We caught her crying when she didn't think we were looking. We have *intimacy* with Mum.'

'You mean you do.'

'Em,' Nat said patiently, 'being childish like this just proves my point. You're close to her, you *know* her. You're probably going home to sleep on pillowcases she bought for you. You don't want her belonging to anyone else any more than I do.'

Emmy stopped fiddling with her thumbnail. Without looking at her brother, she said, 'I just find her, really, really embarrassing like this.'

Nat put his beer bottle down on the table. 'I know.'

'I mean, she's sort of all girlish and giddy. It's awful.'

'What d'you think he's like?'

Emmy gave a little shudder. 'To be honest, Nat, I don't really want to think about him.'

'But we've got to meet him.'

'I know.'

'I'm quite angry about that. I'm angry with her for putting us in this position.'

Emmy nodded. 'Yes. But it's happening. And we have to protect her from it being worse than it has to be.'

'When we meet?'

'No,' Emmy said, 'after. We have to make sure she sees a lawyer and that we're there when she does.'

'Em, that's my line.'

'Well, I've said it for you. She isn't thinking straight. She's kind of high on all this. I mean, she shouted. She actually *shouted*. I don't think I've ever heard her shout in my life. It's like someone has cast a spell on her, transformed her.' She stopped and looked at her ginger beer. 'Did I order that?'

'Yes,' Nat said. 'It's what you asked for.'

'I must be mad,' Emmy said. 'It must be catching.' She stood up and dusted flakes of nail varnish off her T-shirt.

'I'm going to get a proper drink,' she said, 'and then we can make a plan of action.'

———

When Laura got home, Angus had bathed the boys and read them bedtime stories, and was sitting at the kitchen table slicing peppers with the Japanese chef's knife he had bought because, he said, it combined beauty with complete functionality.

Laura dropped her bag on the floor, her phone on the table and came over to give him a kiss.

'Boys OK?'

'Clean. One asleep, one allowed to shine a torch on the ceiling as an incentive to stay in bed.'

Laura said, 'I'll go and kiss them. What are you cooking?'

'A stir fry. How was the family meeting?'

Laura sighed. She pushed her hair behind her ears. 'Oh, you know. What you'd expect.'

'Your mum standing her ground and the twins up in arms?'

'Pretty much,' Laura said.

Angus stood up and carried the board of sliced peppers over to the modern industrial cooker that stood against one raw and unplastered wall.

'And you?'

'What about me?'

'What do you feel about your mother falling for someone after all this time?'

'I feel . . .' Laura said slowly, and stopped.

Angus poured oil into a wok. He waited.

'I feel,' Laura said, 'quite a lot of things. I'm thrilled to see her so elated but I am a bit concerned she's too elated. I think she has every right to any kind of happiness she wants, but I'd ideally have liked her to take it a bit more steadily and slowly. She looks about forty.'

Angus tipped the vegetables into the wok and said loudly, above the sound of the hissing oil, 'What about him?'

Laura shrugged. 'She wants us to meet him. She wants you to come too, to meet him.'

Angus turned round. '*Me?*'

'Yes. She said she wanted you to be there too. I think she just wants a bit of a buffer against the twins.'

'Are they very anti?'

'Of course,' Laura said. 'You know them.'

Angus turned back to his wok and began to turn the vegetables rapidly. 'Perhaps they're right.'

'Of course they are,' Laura said. 'A little bit. Just as I am.'

'What a mess.'

'Yes.'

'And it'll get worse.'

'Don't say that.'

'I speak as the son of a man on his fourth marriage. Dealing with one's own emotions is one thing. Facing a parent's roller coaster of a love life is quite another. I haven't felt like my father's child forever. *He's* the child, if anyone is.'

The kitchen door opened six inches and a powerful torch beam was directed through the gap.

'Jack?' Laura said.

The torch beam wavered.

'It isn't Jack.'

Laura went over to the door and opened it wider. Jack, in his Kylo Ren pyjamas, was standing barefoot on the uncarpeted boards of the hall outside.

'Where were you?' he said.

'I was with Grandma Rose.'

'Why didn't you come and kiss me?'

'I was going to. But I think you were only allowed the torch if you stayed in bed. And you aren't in bed.'

Jack switched the torch off.

'There,' he said triumphantly.

Laura propped herself against the doorframe and looked down at him.

'I can't kiss you unless you're back in bed.'

Jack thought for a moment. 'Am I your first and best person?'

'What are you talking about?'

'Grandma Rose says to me, "You are my first and best". Then she says to Adam, "You are my second and best".'

'Ah,' Laura said. She stood upright. 'Grandma Rose.'

Jack tucked the torch under his arm as if it were a truncheon.

'Did you know that Grandma Rose is your mummy?'

'I did, actually.'

'Like you are my mummy.'

'Yes.'

Jack turned and began to march back towards the stairs. 'You'll always be my mummy, won't you?' he asked.

'Of course I will.'

'Because,' he said, his back to her and his arms stiffly at his sides, like a guardsman, 'That's what mummies do, isn't it? They are just there, forever and ever.' He paused at the bottom step and looked back at her. Then he said warningly, 'OK?'

CHAPTER FOUR

It was difficult, Tyler found, to catch Mallory these days. Either she was on stage, or winding down from being on stage, or asleep after winding down, or rehearsing for the next – very different, very contemporary – show she was going to be in in New York, so that both her days and her nights seemed to be completely spoken for. Add to that the fact that she was never alone, that she and her theatre friends seemed to hunt in convivial, chattering packs, and it was, Tyler thought, almost impossible to engineer the opportunity to tell her about Rose.

He had, at least, made a beginning. He had arrived at her flat at ten o'clock one weekday morning, armed with a tray of coffees and a paper carrier bag of croissants, and had scored rather a success with her half-asleep flatmates, stumbling round him in the rags and tatters of their rehearsal clothes and smudges of the previous night's eye makeup. They seized upon the coffee with theatrical relief, and scattered flakes of croissant around them like confetti. Under cover of the distraction they caused, Tyler said quietly to his daughter, 'I've met someone.'

Mallory was crouched on the sofa next to him, squinting

into a hand-held mirror while she drew a careful black line behind her eyelashes. She finished the line and then she said, not looking at him, 'Someone? A woman?'

'Of course a woman,' Tyler said. 'Someone I knew years ago, when I was at school. I have re-met someone from my past.'

Mallory turned to regard him over her shoulder. 'Someone you like.' It was a statement rather than a question.

'I'm crazy about her,' Tyler said. 'She's called Rose Wood-rowe.'

'Uh-huh.' Mallory began to draw across the other eyelid.

'I wanted you to know.'

Mallory waited until her eyeliner was applied. Then she said, 'Thanks, Dad.'

She began to get up off the sofa. Tyler put a hand on her arm, to detain her. 'Can I . . .'

She was standing by now. She looked down at him. She was smiling but she took her arm away, all the same.

'Gotta run, Dad.' She glanced up and called, '*Avanti*, peaches!' to her flatmates, then she looked back at her father. 'Happy for you, Daddykins,' she said, and she was gone.

Since then, despite many attempts, Tyler had not been able to pin her down for long enough to tell her that his feelings for Rose were serious, serious enough for him to have proposed and to have been, in so many words, accepted, and, in consequence, to be considering taking up permanent residence in England. These were all matters that he wanted Mallory to pay attention to, because although he told himself that nothing Mallory could say or do would change what was rapidly becoming a settled intention, he wanted her to know, and to have the chance to express an opinion. He also wanted to be able to say, truthfully, to Rose, 'My kids are fine with the whole idea. Completely fine. In fact, they see you as nothing but a blessing, taking me off their hands.'

He even had additional sentences lined up for the right moment.

'They're longing to meet you. Of course, you can meet Mallory here, before she goes back to New York, and then we can go to California together, and you can meet Seth. And Yuhui, of course. You'll like Yuhui.'

She would, of course, like Seth. You couldn't not like Seth. Not only was Seth easy-going and good-natured and comfortable to be with, but his reaction on the phone to his father's news about Rose had been both welcome and welcoming.

'She sounds a doll, Dad.'

'She is. You'll see.'

'You sure sound happy.'

'I am.'

'You're allowed,' Seth said, 'to say you don't think you've ever been happier, you know.'

'Am I? I thought maybe—'

'Mom was different. Mom'll always be special to all of us. But we don't want you moping alone forever. Did I tell you that Doughboy has been named in the top ten of San Francisco's hottest foodie start-ups?'

'No.'

'Social media has gone wild, Dad. We can't bake fast enough. At lunchtime we got lines out the door and round the block.'

'I was thinking,' Tyler said, 'of bringing Rose out to meet

you. I'd love you to meet her. I'd love her to meet you. And Yuhui of course.'

There was a fractional pause and then Seth said, too heartily, 'Sure thing!' And then, 'Sorry, Dad. Gotta go.'

'Of course.'

'Sourdough bread,' Seth said, 'is a way of *life*.'

There had not been an opportunity, Tyler reflected rue-fully, to expand upon Rose as he would have liked; nor to ask Seth if he and his sister had communicated on the topic of their father's love life. On the evidence of their strange life-long detachment, Tyler could only assume that whatever discussion they might have had on the subject would have been minimal at best. Even as little children, they had not really been close enough to fight, but had pursued their parallel existences as they grew up almost irrespective of one another. Now, as adults, they displayed a remarkable indifference to each other's lives. Neither, Tyler imagined, had interrogated the other about their father's news. In fact, neither had seemed in the least inclined to interrogate *him*. Tyler thought he should feel relieved but found that he only felt neglected, even a little isolated and exposed. Walking to the hotel in Holborn which had been selected as the venue for his first meeting with Rose's three children, plus son-in-law, Tyler felt only the intense anxiety of being scrutinized while undefended and alone.

Mallory had said that she might come. If she could. If the rehearsal didn't run over, but they nearly always ran over. It was that kind of show. She sounded as if she was mildly irri-tated to be asked to fulfil a family obligation that was, in fact, no concern of hers in the first place, but yes, she would try to come as a favour to her father. Seth had said that he'd talk to Rose via FaceTime if he could, during the length of the meeting, but it was, after all, morning in San Francisco, and the mornings were, like, *crazy*, round Doughboy. All in all, Tyler thought, crossing Holborn in a jostle of other pedestrians, and wondering if his Brooks Brothers blazer was too stuffy and conservative a sartorial choice, nothing about this encounter or its attendant circumstances was in the least confidence-making. Except Rose herself. Without Rose, Tyler decided, pulling his shirt cuffs clear of his blazer sleeves, the prospect of meeting her children was a matter of mild, but distinct, dread. If Mallory had been with him, trotting by his side with her newly red-rinsed hair glowing like a beacon, he would have felt so much better . . . . *furnished*. He paused at the vast archway that led to the hotel's courtyard and squared his shoulders. He was, he told himself, over six foot after all, well dressed and personable. It was ridiculous to be nervous of a bunch of kids the age of his own children. Ridiculous. What did it matter if they didn't like him? Not a jot. Rose loved him. That was all that mattered. Rose loved him and he loved her. God, he did!

—

'Are you all right?' Laura said to Rose.

They were in the open-air courtyard bar, sitting in wicker armchairs around a table under an electric brazier suspended beneath a huge green canvas parasol. The twins had taken chairs either side of their mother in a way she was trying to see as protective rather than aggressive, and Laura and Angus were sitting opposite, leaving an empty chair next to Emmy, who had already pulled her own chair away from it, as if to emphasize that Rose was part of an impregnable family unit.

Angus had secured a bottle of white wine, which now sat in front of them in an ice bucket, and half a dozen wine glasses plus two dishes of salted almonds, which Emmy had already inspected with disappointment.

'I'm fine,' Rose said firmly. 'But I would like a drink.'

Angus and Nat both stood up.

'Silly boys,' Laura said fondly.

'Angus pour,' Rose said. 'Nat sit down again.'

Nat said, 'I don't want to sit down.'

'Why can't Nat do the pouring?' Emmy said.

Angus looked at his wife. 'Shall I?'

'Yes,' Rose said. 'Do it. Just *do* it. Don't be childish, Nat.'

Nat sat down again. 'I really don't like the way you're speaking to me these days.'

Rose, who was concentrating on not looking towards the entrance arch, said with elaborate calm, 'I'm talking to you exactly as I've always talked to you, darling.'

'No, you aren't. You're talking to me as if I was six. Why can't I pour the wine?'

Angus swung round and accosted a passing waiter.

'Would you pour for us, I wonder?'

'There,' Laura said. She had her phone in her hand. 'Simple.'

'This poor guy,' Angus said, settling himself again with a tiny air of triumph. 'If we're all this jumpy, how must he be feeling?'

'I'm not jumpy,' Rose said.

Emmy looked at her.

'Yes, you are. We all are.'

'He said he might be able to bring his daughter.'

'The *actress*,' Emmy said, with emphasis.

The waiter placed modest glasses of white wine in front of everyone, and laid a folded napkin across the mouth of the ice bucket.

'Will that be all?'

'For now,' Nat said, 'yes. Thank you.'

Emmy picked up her glass. 'Cheers,' she said meaningfully.

Rose raised her own glass. 'Happy days, darling.' She gestured round the circle. 'Happy days, *all* darlings.'

'D'you know,' Nat said, pushing back his chair and getting up, 'I think I'm going to get a beer.'

Rose began, 'Can't you—'

'No, Mum,' Nat said, 'I can't.' He picked up his wine glass and set it down in front of the empty chair. 'Tyler can drink it.'

'What,' Tyler said, emerging from the courtyard, 'can Tyler do?'

There was a small and sudden silence. They stared at him. Tyler tried very hard to think that the twins' stares, in particular, weren't unmistakably hostile. He smiled across the table at Rose. 'Hey, Rose,' he said.

She didn't move. She sat where she was, wine glass in hand, and gazed at him. She said softly, almost dreamily, 'Hi there.'

He blew her a leisurely kiss. Then he looked at the rest of them. He held a hand out to Laura.

'You must be Laura.'

She nodded. Next to her, Angus stood up. He held out his own hand.

'I'm Angus. I'm married to Laura.'

'Good to meet you. Which means that you are Emmy and you are Nat.'

Rose seemed to swim to consciousness. She said faintly, 'My twins.'

Emmy said nothing. She glanced at her brother who was still staring at Tyler as if he were some sort of phenomenon. It was hard to imagine that whatever phenomenon Nat was visualizing was not something distinctly unpleasant. With determined cheerfulness, Tyler motioned towards the wine glass in front of the empty chair.

'Is that for me?'

'Yes,' Rose said. She looked at him as if no one else were there.

'I was going to get a beer,' Nat said again. He sounded as if he were issuing a challenge.

Rose tilted her head back so that she could see him. 'No one's stopping you, darling.'

Nat reddened slightly. Emmy said plaintively, 'Mum . . .'

Tyler sat down. He turned to Laura. 'So you're the doctor.'

She smiled at him and put her phone on the table. 'I am.'

Tyler pointed round everyone in turn. 'Doctor, architect, IT, PR. Is that right?' He glanced up at Nat. 'If you're going to get a beer, make it two, would you?'

Wordlessly, but still managing to convey immense resentment at Tyler's request, Nat turned from the table and vanished in the direction of the bar. Emmy said clearly to her mother, 'I think he's upset.'

Rose regarded her. She smiled. She said, as easily as she could, 'I can't think why.'

'Oh, *Mum*.'

'Is your daughter coming?' Laura asked Tyler.

'I hope so.'

'Me too,' said Rose.

Emmy leaned closer to her mother. In a low and deliberately private voice, she murmured, 'You know why Nat's upset.'

Rose put a hand out and squeezed her daughter's arm. Then she said across the table to Laura, 'Tyler's daughter was so good in the Ibsen. Her English accent was perfect.'

'She had an excellent coach,' Tyler said.

'Ibsen was Norwegian,' Angus said. 'So why does anyone playing him need to sound English?'

Tyler smiled at him. 'Tradition, maybe?'

Nat came back to the table and dropped into his chair.

'Where's your beer?' Emmy said.

Nat shrugged slightly. 'The waiter's bringing them,' he muttered, staring at his lap.

Angus said to Tyler, 'You must get almost sick of wine, in California.'

'Well,' he said, pushing his glass away, 'I grew up here, so I grew up drinking beer. It's a kind of habit, I guess.'

Rose said teasingly, 'I hadn't noticed.'

He turned to smile at her, his face softening. 'There's a lot for you to learn yet.'

'Clearly.'

'Please!' Nat said suddenly.

Laura shook her head at him. 'Honestly, Nat. So – *squeamish.*' She glanced at Tyler. 'Apologies for my brother.'

'None needed or expected. But thank you.'

Rose said to Nat, 'Explain your job to Tyler. Just describing it as IT doesn't begin to do it justice.'

'Yes, please do,' Tyler said encouragingly. He leaned forward.

Nat didn't look at him. He said, with elaborate reluctance,

'It's – um – part of a financial institution. Like – a hedge fund.' He stopped.

Tyler said helpfully, 'I know what a hedge fund is.'

'Go on, darling.'

Nat looked at the table top. In a slow and surly tone of extreme indifference, he continued, 'I kind of devised a system for them. Special algorithms for their needs. I wrote the programmes.'

'Impressive,' Tyler said politely.

Emmy was looking at her brother. 'They promoted him.' She sounded defiant.

'I'm sure they did.'

'It'll be a seat on the board next,' said Rose.

Nat gave a sigh of exasperation. He rolled his eyes at Emmy as if to say, 'What did we do to deserve a mother like this?' Then he said, in a voice of barely concealed vexation, 'Mum. You don't *know* that.'

'But I'm expecting. And hoping. I'm very proud of you, darling.'

'Don't embarrass him, Mum, Emmy said.

'I'm proud of all of you,' Rose said, determinedly. 'I'm proud of Angus, if it comes to that, and he isn't even mine. You are all doing interesting worthwhile things and you are all in paid employment. I think both those things are worthy of huge pride.' She looked at Tyler. 'Don't you?'

He smiled at her. 'Indeed.'

Laura said, 'I'd have expected you to say "sure", after all those years in America.'

'I took a perverse pleasure in staying as English as I could.'

Emmy was staring at a point above Angus's head. The waiter stood there with two bottles of beer on a tray, and beside him was a small girl with ruby-red hair and a huge slouch bag on her shoulder. Tyler sprang up.

'Mallory!'

She allowed herself to be embraced.

'Hi, Daddy.'

Tyler turned round, his arm encircling Mallory's shoulders.

'Everyone, this is my daughter, Mallory. Mallory, this is Rose. Rose. Who I have talked to you about. And this is Rose's elder daughter, Laura, and her husband, Angus. And these are Rose's twins, Emmy and Nat. If – if we had Seth here, we'd have everyone. Everyone who matters.'

Mallory looked at them all slowly, her gaze flicking from face to face. She adjusted a piece of chewing gum from one cheek to the other. Then she smiled at Rose.

'Hi,' she said.

She motioned to the waiter to bring an extra chair and place it next to Nat, and dropped her slouch bag off her shoulder. A tiny jewel inserted into the side of her nose flashed sudden fire as she bent to release her bag. Then she straightened up again.

'Wow,' she said. 'Look at you. You all look like you need some lines to say.'

—

'Thank goodness for Mallory,' Rose said.

They were sitting side by side at the back of a crowded pizzeria, sharing a wheel-sized Napoletana that Tyler had cut into manageable strips. He had taken his blazer off, and rolled up his shirtsleeves, and Rose had been unable to help noticing that his forearms contrasted impressively with the

T-shirt-exposed arms of men around him who were less than half his age.

Tyler tipped his head back to receive the end of a pizza slice. He said, round the pizza, 'It wasn't so bad.'

'It *was*,' Rose said. 'It was awful. The twins . . .' She stopped and then said, 'I'm used to being so proud of the twins.'

Tyler put the remaining half of his pizza slice down. 'You could be tonight.'

'Not really. Not seeing them being so babyishly possessive. I didn't like it.'

Tyler wiped his mouth with a paper napkin. 'Can't be easy, can it? They have you all to themselves for seven years . . .'

'But they're not fourteen,' Rose said, 'they're *adults*. Technically, anyway. Adult enough to hold down jobs and live independently. It was like wading through treacle till Mallory came.'

Tyler gave a tiny smirk. 'She was pretty great.'

Rose looked at him. She said sharply, 'I can say that. *You* can't.'

He raised an eyebrow. 'Oh?'

'As the father of the best-behaved child, you are obliged to say nothing at all in her favour.'

He turned to face her. 'You're not serious.'

'I am,' Rose said. 'I am deadly serious. I am the tiger mother whose cubs have let her down and it makes me very dangerous.'

'Goodness,' Tyler said. 'You mean it.'

'I do.'

'Are – are we having a row? Our first row?'

Rose said nothing.

'Rosie?'

'I don't know,' Rose said. 'I just want to cry. And hit something.' She clenched her fists. 'I just wanted tonight to go well. I *so* wanted it to go well.'

'It did.'

She turned to face him. 'It did *not*,' she said furiously. 'You did your best, and Laura and Angus were fine, but the twins were *awful*. Rude and childish and awful. I was . . . I was ashamed of them.'

Tyler pushed away the remains of the pizza and rolled his shirtsleeves down. Buttoning the cuffs, he asked, 'Were you ashamed of me?'

'No.'

'You don't sound very certain.'

Rose picked up her water glass and took a swallow. 'It wasn't you.'

'Wasn't it?'

She said, with difficulty, 'I felt so sure, when we got there. I was longing for you to come. And then you did come, and I was so thrilled, and then somehow, sitting there between the twins, I began to feel that – oh, I don't know, I just didn't feel so . . .' She stopped.

'Convinced?'

She looked down and said, almost in a whisper, 'It suddenly didn't seem so glorious.'

'What didn't? Please look at me.'

Rose sighed. 'Not here.'

'Rose. *Tell* me. What didn't seem so glorious?'

'Being in love with you,' she replied sadly, not looking at him.

He let a beat fall, and then he said, 'Do you really think

it's fair to take your disappointment over that one little meeting out on me?'

She looked away from him. 'Probably not.'

He waited.

'I'm not used to not being in my children's good books,' she said. 'Well, their *best* books if I'm honest. And I'm not used to them being less than wonderful.'

'Laura was lovely.'

'Please don't,' Rose said. 'Please don't make comparisons.'

'I wasn't.'

'I *know* I'm not being reasonable. I *know* it isn't fair to you. But I feel so jangled up and jagged.'

Tyler reached behind him for his blazer, dropped on the back of his chair.

'Let's go.'

Rose picked up her bag. 'OK.' Then to the bag, rather than to Tyler, she said, 'I don't think I want you to come home with me tonight.'

———

Sleep proved impossible. The tensions of the evening, only exacerbated by the courteous walk to her front door – he delivered her home, she reflected, with all the formality of an old-fashioned chauffeur – were only lying in wait until they could get her to themselves. She had thought, in a wild, unmanaged way, that all she needed was to be alone and no longer in Tyler's tolerant if faintly reproachful company, but the moment the front door was closed behind her she was consumed by a longing to have him there with her once more.

He had kissed her cheek. Firmly. One side and then the

other, holding her shoulders as he did so. He'd said, 'Good night, Rosie. Sleep well.'

But he hadn't said he'd call in the morning, or made a plan to meet her the next day, or made a single reference to the future. He had kissed her cheeks, and let her go, and she had heard his footsteps going resolutely down the mews until they faded around the corner. She went into the kitchen and made chamomile tea, organizing her vitamin supplements for the next day and checking her phone and emails for messages. Then she inspected the locks for the night, climbed the stairs and ran herself a bath. Once in the bath, she began to cry. She was not, by nature, a weeper, but this was hardly weeping. It was, she thought, giving way completely, with her mouth open, more like bawling.

It was very tiring, to cry and sob and howl like that. She dragged herself out of the bath exhaustedly and climbed into her pyjamas, then leaned against the basin to brush her teeth and cream her face. Over the edge of the washcloth, she looked at herself with loathing. Red-eyed, blotchy, with weird striped hair standing up in tufts and hanks. Hideous. *Hideous*.

She went slowly out of the bathroom towards her bedroom, feeling along the walls as if she were very old and frail. Once in bed, she lay in the darkness and stared into it, worn out and defiantly, suddenly, sleepless. She put out an arm and switched on her bedside radio and there was the Speaker of the House of Commons intoning, 'Order, order,' over a rabble of men shouting about transport systems in the north of England. She switched the radio off again, and lay there, just staring, her mind darting hither and yon, hurling itself against one unacceptable memory after another.

She heard midnight strike, and then one in the morning.

She told herself, variously and unstoppably, that she was a bad mother, that Tyler was in essence a bad idea, that the twins were not to be blamed, that Tyler was entirely right, that the twins had behaved disgracefully, that she had defended the wrong people, that she had destroyed her last chance of romantic happiness, that she had got all her priorities wrong – or right – that Tyler would want to have nothing further to do with her and that that was probably the best solution, while being simultaneously the one idea she could not bear. At two o'clock, she disentangled herself from her bedclothes and went down to the kitchen to make more tea, which she carried back upstairs, intending to re-make her bed and try to start the night again.

Her mobile phone lay charging on the carpet inside her bedroom door. She bent to see if there were any messages. There were none. Nothing. She stood there, a mug of chamomile tea in one hand and her phone in the other. And then, before she could change her mind, she put the tea down beside her bed and impulsively dialled Tyler's number.

CHAPTER FIVE

William Woodrowe telephoned one of his children, in strict rotation, every Sunday morning. It was, of course, Sunday night in Melbourne, convenient for someone who prided himself, as William did, on his alertness in the evenings, and he always made whichever child he was speaking to carry their phone to the nearest window and describe the inevitably dismal English weather outside to contrast with whatever was magnificently happening in southern Australia. It had become something of a standing joke for his children. They learned to paint a perpetually sodden picture of low grey skies and relentless drizzle, whatever the actual weather, in order to allow their father his regular triumph of having had yet another day of cloudless skies and record temperatures. It was a kind of ritual. He needed to be able to congratulate himself on a weekly basis, as if Australia itself was confirming the rightness of the decisions he had made that had so rocked his children's world.

Laura was still in bed when her father rang. Angus had got up soon after seven, taking the two little boys downstairs for bowls of cereal in front of their permitted Sunday morning treat of television cartoons. He had returned with tea for

Laura and then disappeared to his own office on the top floor where he was working, he told Laura, on the specific uses architects might find in a 3-D printer. Laura, who was much more interested in the workings of physiology than of 3-D printers, smiled at him in her famously absent way, and thanked him for the tea. She squinted at the clock. It was almost nine. As it was her turn for a call from Australia, nine o'clock was when it would come. William was a punctual man; as punctual, Laura reflected, sipping her tea, as his younger daughter was not.

'I *mean* to be,' Emmy said, perpetually arriving late in a flurry of bags and breathlessness. 'I *start* punctually and then something always, always happens.'

One minute after nine, Laura's phone rang. She held it to her ear.

'Morning, Dad.'

'Darling,' William said. 'Not on call then?'

'Not this weekend.'

'It's still light here. Spectacular sunset. How are the boys?'

'Watching *SpongeBob SquarePants*.'

'What?'

'Doesn't matter,' Laura said. 'It's their Sunday morning treat – an hour of telly rubbish.'

'What's the weather up to?'

Laura looked towards the window. '*You* know, Dad,' she said, humouring him.

'Sunday,' he said with satisfaction. 'Grey and damp. Such an enervating climate.'

'I think it's quite peaceful,' Laura said. 'It kind of allows one to flop about.'

'How's things?'

Laura flapped a hand in the air. 'Fine,' she said. 'You know. Rather too much work for both of us, but that's our choice. Jack says he has a wobbly tooth but I don't believe him. He's at an age where he thinks it gives him status to have a wobbly tooth.'

William said, in a slightly different tone, 'Emmy rang me.'

Laura sat up a little. 'Did she?'

'Yes. About your mother.'

Laura pulled herself up against the pillows. 'Go on,' she said neutrally.

'It appears that your mother has met someone.'

Laura closed her eyes briefly. 'So?' she replied, in a friendly voice.

'Well,' William said, 'it sounds serious. It sounds as if this is rather more than a . . . than a romantic friendship. Emmy said that it had only been going on for ten minutes but that your mother is already talking of – of *marriage*.'

'She's allowed to, you know,' said Laura reasonably. 'She's been alone for over seven years. She's allowed to have a relationship.'

'A relationship,' William said heavily, 'is very different from a marriage.'

Laura looked towards the door. It would be wonderful if the little boys decided to burst in at that moment, or Angus appeared to see if she would like a refill for her tea. She badly wanted to say to her father that she didn't think her mother's love life was any of her ex-husband's business, but at the same time, she was very conscious of how easy it was, on long-distance phone calls, to create the perfect opportunity for misinterpretation. So she said, lamely, 'Oh, it's early days.'

'Not from what Emmy said. Emmy told me you had all been summoned to meet him. At a hotel.'

Laura said nothing.

'Laura?'

'Yes?'

'Did you hear me?'

'Dad,' Laura said. 'Just let Mum do her own thing, would you?'

'Of course,' William replied. 'I wouldn't be telling you any of this if Em hadn't sounded so concerned.'

'Well, you know Em . . .'

'She and Nat have found a solicitor to advise on the situation, and I just wanted to say that I know someone—'

'No, Dad.'

'Laura—'

'Listen,' Laura said again, stretching out for her glasses, which were on the low cupboard beside her bed. 'You know how Emmy is. You know how Nat is too, about Mum. They just want to make sure—'

'Suppose they're right?' William demanded. 'Suppose this man of your mother's sees a vulnerable woman with a very nice central London property and—'

'He's a nice man,' Laura said.

'How can you tell, on the strength of one meeting?'

Laura put her glasses on. She took a deep breath.

'Don't you think,' she said to her father, half a world away, 'that whatever Mum does or doesn't do is really no concern of yours?'

There was a silence and then William said, in a hurt tone, 'Laura.'

'Em shouldn't have rung you. She's got me and Nat to talk to, if she's worried.'

There were sudden rapid small footsteps on the stairs, coming up, accompanied by babble – Jack and Adam, with blessed timing. Laura smiled into the phone. 'Dad, I can hear the boys. They'll be two seconds. Wouldn't you like to talk to them?'

———

Sundays, Emmy thought to herself, were supposed to be for relaxing. *Constructive* relaxing. Ideally, according to the conformity laid down by social media, Sundays started with a lie-in, followed by a leisurely brunch somewhere with friends, and perhaps a cycle ride along the Regent's Canal, followed by an evening on the sofa with a box set of a Nordic noir drama, all bridges across the Baltic and snowflake sweaters. That is, if you were in the mood. And you had a boyfriend, someone – she couldn't picture more than his outline – called Matt or Andy, who had a good job somewhere and was very attentive and supportive – but not clingy – and could cook, and perhaps played rugby, but who never left wet towels on the bed or cut his toenails in front of the television. Someone that Nat liked. Someone to whom she could say, 'Am I making too big a deal out of this whole Mum thing?' and who would say seriously, in return, 'It *is* a big deal, Em, and you are quite right to be worried, but I have a brilliant idea about how to distract you.'

Which might mean taking her out to do something unexpected, or making love to her, or spoiling her in some imaginative domestic way – whatever it was, Emmy thought, would be not just fantastic in itself, but would also deflect her from her intense, almost obsessive preoccupation with her family.

It wasn't, she thought, either right or fair to be so influenced by what was going on with her mother. She had never really – apart for the odd and largely manufactured teenage tantrum – had any problem with her mother. Rose had always been a reasonable mother, a mother who might sometimes be firm, but who was invariably fair. And who was always, *always* on her side. Emmy remembered being sent to detention once, at school, for something she hadn't done, and Rose just . . . sorted it. She had come to the school and been very charming to the teacher who had given Emmy the undeserved detention, and very charming to the real culprit, and the upshot was there was a private moment in which the teacher said sorry to Emmy in front of Rose, and all three of them were smiling. Rose wouldn't let Emmy talk about it later. She wouldn't even talk about it herself. She simply said, 'It's over, darling, *over*,' and Emmy, who was thirteen at the time and poised to see injustice erupting everywhere, had felt nothing but admiration. Which was what she felt when her father told them that he was leaving both the family and the country to live and work in Australia with Gillian Greenhalgh, and Rose had not uttered a syllable of condemnation or vengefulness in her children's hearing. She had been, all Emmy's life, someone she could *trust*.

Until now. Seven years on from William's announcement and all its complicated fall-out, managed by Rose with familiar fortitude and application, and . . . *this* happens. The person of the greatest stability and reliable sustenance in Emmy's life had abruptly morphed into someone she hardly recognized, a capricious, erratic person whose emotional priorities seemed to have been scattered to the four winds, as if – as if, Emmy thought, she was like some teenage kid whose head had been completely turned by flattery.

'She's too *old* for this!' Emmy had cried to Laura.

Laura was sending an email with one hand and feeding banana slices to Adam with the other. 'No one ever is,' she replied annoyingly.

'That's why,' Nat said later in the pub, looking at his iPad, 'I want to get a solicitor in place. If she's gone a bit bonkers, I want to make sure at least her assets are safe. I can't control her heart, much though I'd like to, but I can at least look after the nuts and bolts.'

He'd tried to make an appointment with a solicitor in a firm in Lincoln's Inn Fields. He'd told Emmy that the firm specialized in wills and the protection of assets, and that he would accompany Rose.

'Can I come too?' Emmy said.

Nat looked at her appraisingly. 'Of course,' he replied.

It had crossed Emmy's mind to say, 'You don't think Mum will mind, do you? If we both come?' but she had quelled the thought. Even if Rose minded, she reflected now, fidgeting round her studio flat with irritable Sunday apathy, she would have to put up with it. Being accompanied to see a solicitor by two of her three children, who were only concerned for her and her future, was not oppressive, Emmy told herself, but supportive. She paused in front of a mirror and inspected her teeth. Maybe what was wrong with her wasn't Sunday, or the lack of a mythically satisfactory boyfriend, but the abrupt reversal of roles; the very fact that her mother had become, apparently, the feckless child and she, Emmy, the responsible adult. Perhaps that accounted for her malaise. It was, now it had occurred to her, an illuminating thought. Surely that reversal of roles, happening almost overnight, was enough to send the most balanced person into a tailspin. Wasn't it?

—

'No,' Rose said.

She wasn't smiling. Nat waited for her to add 'I'm sorry' to the 'no', but she didn't. She picked up the cappuccino she had ordered in the City coffee shop and took a neatly managed mouthful of foam, then she put the cup down again and regarded it. Not Nat, but her coffee cup.

He glanced at his watch. He had ten minutes left before his official lunch hour was up. Rose had not wanted lunch, so Nat had eaten a crayfish and rocket wrap with his Americano on his own and explained, through mouthfuls, that he had found a solicitor who specialized in exactly Rose's situation, and he would like to make an appointment to see her whenever her and Rose's and his and Emmy's diaries could be co-ordinated. Rose did not demur about the principle of seeing a solicitor. She didn't say anything helpful and accommodating like 'Of course, darling, how very thoughtful and caring of you to think of it,' but she didn't object, either. She said instead, 'If you children really, really think that it's necessary.'

And Nat had nodded vigorously around his mouthful of crayfish. As soon as he could speak clearly, he said, 'Mum, I do. We all do. I've talked to the girls, and we are unanimous.'

Rose gave a little sigh. 'I've no wish at all to be difficult. Or . . . or silly.'

'Good,' Nat said firmly. He took a pull at his bottle of water. 'That's great. So I'll make an appointment some time next week for you and me and Emmy to go and see this Grace Ashton woman—'

'No,' Rose said with emphasis.

'But you just said—'

'I said I agreed to see a solicitor. But I'm not going to be frogmarched in by you and Emmy as if I were a – a *prisoner*. Like someone who has done something wrong that needs to be punished.'

'Mum, we need to be there, we need to know what the legal position is, over protection of your assets, we need—'

'*You* need,' Rose said, raising her eyes to look at him. 'I don't need. I might permit, but I don't need you to be there as if I were too old and gaga to be able to understand how not to be exploited.'

'Mum, *please*,' Nat said wearily.

Rose said nothing. She wasn't looking mulish, he admitted, but unquestionably removed, as if the urgency of his position was a matter of indifference to her. After what felt to him an unnatural length of time, she said, 'I've got several things to say. Could you please not interrupt me until I've said them?'

He nodded. Time was ticking on, but the delicacy of the negotiation was going to have to take priority. Rose picked up the teaspoon in her saucer and scooped up a small cushion of milk foam.

'I expect it was very naive of me to think you would all see something of what I see in Tyler straight away, but I really did not consider how antagonistic you and Emmy would be. No, don't interrupt. You agreed to hear me out, and I have hardly started. So – it was an unsuccessful first meeting and I imagine I am partly to blame in being so idiotically hopeful that you would understand both what I see and appreciate in him. But – there we are. Monday night happened and it was as it was. I was very upset by Monday night, *very*, and I owe it almost entirely to Tyler's generosity and good nature that I'm not upset still. I rang him at two in the morning and he came at once and – this is important, Nat – he understood far better than I did how you and Emmy, especially, felt about meeting him. He was completely generous, Nat. Completely. In fact, he said that if you hadn't been protective of me, he would have been surprised and distressed himself.'

She paused, lifted the spoonful of foam to her mouth. Then she put the spoon back on the saucer precisely. Nat opened his mouth, and Rose raised a hand to silence him.

'In a minute, darling. In a minute. So, because of Tyler's understanding and general forgiving nature, I am prepared to see a solicitor. I don't want to, I don't like having you dictate to me this way, but I will. But I'm not going with both of you as if I'm not of sound enough mind to go on my own. Laura isn't insisting on coming too, is she? If you and Emmy want to come, why shouldn't Laura come too, so that all three of you can sit round me like guard dogs?'

Nat looked at his watch again. 'Laura doesn't want to come. But I do and Em does. We want to come – oh God, Mum, I'm so sick of saying this – not because of us and some agenda you insist we have, but because of *you*. We want to be there because we care about you, we want to look after you. Mum, I've got to go.'

'Of course,' Rose said politely. She didn't move.

Nat slid off his stool and stood up. He looked down at her and said, in the tone of one addressing a tiresome and recalcitrant child, 'I'll make an appointment, then. For you and me and Emmy.'

Rose stood too, and gathered up her bag and umbrella. 'Just you and me, darling. Just the two of us. Or Emmy and me. I don't mind which of you it is, but I'm only going with one of you.' She straightened up and smiled at him. 'I think that's called a compromise, isn't it?'

———

Prue came to London in order to see her sister. As was her wont, she did not telephone ahead to make arrangements that suited them both, rather she announced her own plans and was, as she had managed to be all Rose's life, curiously difficult not to obey. William had always found Rose's compliance with her sister's instructions completely incomprehensible. Rose herself said that she could see how it looked, but that try as she might, she was weirdly unable to do other than submit. So, although she had made her usual token resistance to Prue's imposition of herself for a night at the mews – 'Don't go to any trouble for me, Rosie, an omelette is all I'll want for supper' – she had given in.

Tyler said, 'Of course you should see your sister. I look forward to meeting her.' He had then waited for Rose to say how eager she was herself for such a meeting, how keen her sister would be to meet the first man of real significance in Rose's life since William, but she didn't. Instead, she gave him a swift kiss, an almost placatory kiss, and said, 'All in good time. Or, at least, in Prue's good time,' and then added, to head him off before he even uttered the question, 'Not this time. I need to talk to her alone. Next time perhaps.' He glanced at the photograph of Prue that Rose kept in what she called the Family Gallery, in her sitting room. Prue was on the Isle of Skye in the photograph, on a walking holiday, pausing with both hands clasped on top of a thumb stick, stoutly booted with wind-ruffled hair. She looked formidable.

She arrived within five minutes of the time she had informed Rose to expect her, wearing a new nylon backpack which she said was an innovation in her life, and very successful so far. From it, she extracted a jar of her homemade chutney – 'Such a glut of green tomatoes last year' – and a cult Italian novel – 'I know how narrowly you read, Rosie, unless pushed' – and then looked round Rose's sitting room in search of criticizable changes.

'Actually,' she said in mildly surprised tones, 'it looks charming.'

'Why wouldn't it?'

'Well,' Prue said, 'I did wonder if the advent of Mr Masson in your life might have had a palpable influence.'

'He isn't that kind of man,' Rose said firmly. 'He doesn't want me to be different. That's what's such a relief, Prue. He just wants me to be as I am. That's what he likes.'

'Ah,' Prue said. She lowered herself into an armchair and crossed her legs, thrusting one foot in the air for Rose's inspection. It was clad in a large grey trainer with a blindingly white sole and fluorescent orange laces. 'My newest find. Indecently comfortable. Nine ninety-nine in the market. What do you think?'

'Honestly?'

'Honestly.'

'I think they're practical but hideous.'

Prue lowered her foot. 'Me too,' she said cheerfully. 'But

practical is what I'm after. Now then, Rosie. How are the children?'

Rose sat down on the sofa opposite her sister. 'In what way?' she asked warily.

Prue put her fingertips together. 'About Mr Masson, Rosie.'

'I was afraid you'd ask that. I was afraid, Prue, because as usual, I'll probably tell you.'

'Not good then.'

'Laura's fine. Or at least, behaving in a manner that makes it easy for me, or as easy as it could be.'

Prue studied Rose over her steepled fingertips. 'So the twins are being tiresome.'

'Not exactly tiresome . . .'

'Rosie.'

'What?'

'The twins do not want you to have another serious relationship in your life after their father.'

Rose noticed that her sister had declared this a fact, rather than a possibility. She plucked at the piping on the nearest sofa arm.

'It's protective. I know it is. They just don't want me to be taken advantage of, even though Tyler is the last man to want to exploit me.'

'Or . . .' Prue said, and then stopped.

Rose stopped plucking and looked up. 'Or what?'

Prue lowered her hands so that they were lying on the arms of her chair. 'Or Nat doesn't want any other man to supplant him as number one in your affections. And Emmy – well Rosie, in my opinion, Emmy is jealous.'

Rose stared at her sister. *Jealous?*'

'Yes,' Prue said calmly, 'jealous. Even her mother, her elderly mother in her sixties, has a boyfriend before she does.' She re-crossed her legs and the orange laces flashed. 'Never underestimate the power of the primitive in any emotional situation. Our veneer of civilized conduct is paper thin. Don't look so shocked, Rosie. It isn't blasphemous, what I've just said. It's common sense.'

———

Tyler found, as he had intermittently found all his life, that he needed to *do* something. These impulses for action were, he knew, both random and unreliable, but they were also urgent and seductive. They had accounted for, in the past, his decision to go to California in the first place and, more recently, his decision to marry Cindy, and even more recently, his decision to fly to New York to find Mallory, and then London to support Mallory, which had resulted, so spectacularly, in the life-changing relationship with Rose.

When Rose had rung at two o'clock that morning, so distressed and confused, he hadn't even hesitated. Of course he'd been awake himself, miserable and troubled, and had felt nothing but a surge of sheer relief at hearing her ask him, with a diffidence he found irresistible, if he would come round. Of *course* he would come round! He would gladly have crossed hot coals, nay continents, to come round. He was engulfed by sheer thankfulness at being able to act, being able, by going to the mews within half an hour of her call, to sort things, soothe them, disentangle them. He stood in Rose's narrow hallway, holding her and stroking her hair, while she said all kinds of apologetic and complicated things that he wasn't really listening to. It didn't matter to Tyler, what had happened, what she'd said, what she'd been thinking, how deranged she had been by her twins' conduct; it only mattered that he could hold her and stroke her and make her better.

'There, there,' he'd said, his eyes closed in order to focus on the rapture of relief. 'Don't worry, sweetheart, it's over. It's over.'

That moment and what followed had been, Tyler thought, heaven sent. He thought that such opportunities – rare and precious – were what he had been designed for. He didn't congratulate himself on being good at forgiveness, he just recognized it as something that came naturally to him and gave him a satisfaction like no other. Cindy had sometimes pointed out that this capacity was the good side of his inability to take a stand, or make a forceful decision, or exhibit a mildly ruthless but attractive male desire to dominate, all of which drove her mad. Tyler would say, trying to deflect her exasperation, 'You've got your father for all that,' and Cindy would slam out of the house to try and take her frustration out on the tennis court. Her reaction to him made Tyler sad, but not powerfully so. Not sad enough, in any case, to consider in any depth how he might change his ways.

And he certainly didn't want to change his impulses to action and reaction. He loved the surges of energy they brought, the rushes of adrenalin, the sudden blinding clarity of focused vision. Responding to Rose's pre-dawn distress had been, in truth, a luxury to Tyler, and his newest idea, a determination to see her son alone was almost as compelling. Nat had been virtually unable to look at him the other night, so consumed was he by various emotions which Tyler had no doubt were both enormous and unmanageable. Poor boy,

Tyler thought. Poor boy, with a father in Australia and a raw sense of obligation and filial duty to his mother that had never been exercised, let alone tested before. The thing to do, Tyler decided, brushing his hair back with two brushes as his father had taught him, was to see Nat on his own, and possibly without telling Rose, and persuade him that he really had nothing to fear by Tyler's presence in his mother's life. Nothing at all.

———

Nat had made an appointment to see Grace Ashton for himself and for Rose. He had finally acquiesced, over the course of three phone calls, to Rose being accompanied by just him, but had insisted – since it was, he pointed out repeatedly until she told him to stop, Rose's decision, not his – that she had to tell Emmy herself that she couldn't come. Emmy had, of course, raged about this. They had met as usual in the pub between their flats, and Emmy had seemed unnecessarily furious about Rose's decision, almost as if she were badly stung by something quite other, although she insisted she wasn't. She had been drinking tonic water, on its own, which Nat always took as a sign of some turbulence or other going on that she wasn't ready to talk about yet. He'd have to wait. He knew of old that waiting till Em was ready to talk about something on her mind always resulted, in the end, in being told what he needed to know. Some twins, Nat knew, could read each other's minds. Some were more like two halves of a whole. That was how he and Em were. It made them, he thought, infinitely patient with each other. Em might be, justifiably in his view, furious with their mother over seeing the solicitor, but she wouldn't, for a moment, countenance feeling that her brother had in any way let her down. Sometimes it occurred to him that that other people, other women and men, found it tricky to persist in any romantic relationship with either he or Em, because that relationship always had to accommodate the given of twinship as well. It wasn't exactly an obstacle or a disadvantage: it was just *there*. He had promised Em he would ring her the moment he could after the meeting with the solicitor, and she had been, as he knew she would be, quite content with that. With Dad overseas and absorbed in his own life, Nat said to Emmy, it was up to the three children – when Laura could be made to focus – to ensure that their mother didn't fall prey to any person or set of circumstances that might not be to her advantage. Emmy had wholeheartedly agreed. Her agreement added to Nat's sense of having both undertaken and fulfilled a responsible filial duty. It buoyed him up to feel so confident and in charge, and to have a solicitor's meeting firmly in place. He felt so surely that he had done the right thing in the right way by Rose, that he was able to be quite breezy about Tyler's unexpected phone call and his request.

'Of course,' Nat said to Tyler, as if he were a completely different person to the one who had been so visibly disconcerted at the meeting on Monday night. 'Of course I'll meet you. I can usually get away from work about six.' He squinted up at the ceiling and took imaginary aim at the ergonomically designed light fitting in his office. 'Tell me where you'd like to meet, and I'll see you there.'

CHAPTER SIX

The solicitor, Rose couldn't help observing, wore a wedding ring and a half-hoop of sizable diamonds. She was possibly in her mid-forties, buxom and self-possessed, and on her desk were photographs of teenage children and an appropriately aged man, all with wide smiles and excellent teeth. In one photograph, Rose noticed, there was also an enthusiastic-looking dog, with the man's hand resting on its head. They looked very much like the kind of family Rose had, at the same age as the solicitor, comfortably assumed her own to be: healthy, happy enough and not too visibly successful to create insecurity and resentment in anyone else. She had not then, of course, known definitively about Gillian Green-halgh, even if a mild but persistent anxiety about William's susceptibility to colleagues clouded her peace of mind like a perpetual shadow. Grace Ashton did not look like someone who permitted perpetual shadows: she gave off, instead, an air of intimidating decisiveness. The man in the photograph would not, Rose suspected, be given a second chance, of any kind.

Grace Ashton shook Rose's hand with a firm grip. Then she shook Nat's hand. Then she motioned them both, with a gesture that expected immediate compliance, to two up-right armchairs in front of her desk. Her rimless spectacles were blindingly clean, as were her well-kept unvarnished nails. When she sat down behind her desk and regarded them both, it was hard not to feel dishevelled by contrast. Rose found herself regretting the navy-blue jacket she had rejected in her bedroom that morning as too formal.

'Please,' Grace said, smiling at Rose, 'don't feel at all self-conscious. We are seeing more and more people seeking advice about late relationships. In fact, my firm has seen a twenty per cent increase in situations like yours in the last three years.'

Nat opened his mouth – to agree, Rose suspected, so to forestall him she said quickly, smilingly, 'I'm sure that's the case, Mrs Ashton, but I would much prefer it if you didn't regard me as just another example of a category.'

Nat swung round to admonish her, eyes wide. Grace Ashton, however, didn't blink.

'Of course not, Mrs Woodrowe. I was merely trying to reassure you that our practice has considerable experience of situations like yours,' she said smoothly.

'*Mother*,' Nat said, under his breath.

'Perhaps you should know,' Rose went on pleasantly, 'that I'm here not under duress, exactly, but certainly reluctantly.'

'Of course.'

'Why of course?'

'Because,' Grace said, 'people in your position don't usu-ally feel they need any advice. And,' she smiled at Nat, 'it is always difficult to accept pressure from one's children.'

Nat said, as if stung, 'I'm not pressuring. I'm protecting.'

'Which is where I come in,' Grace replied. She clasped her

hands together lightly on the desk in front of her. Then she smiled again, this time at Rose. 'May I explain?'

Rose gave the most imperceptible of nods. She was here, she must remember, not just because the children wanted it, but because Tyler had said it was the right thing to do. Tyler had told her that Nat and Emmy were quite justified, and when she had cried to him, 'But I *trust* you!' he had simply said, 'All the same, sweetheart. All the same.' She badly wanted to tell Grace Ashton that they were dealing with, in Tyler, one of the least avaricious men in the world, but Mrs Ashton's manner did not encourage spontaneous confidences of that kind. She was regarding Rose through her shining spectacles as if emotional displays of any sort were completely out of place in her office, and would be firmly, if courteously, discouraged.

'Mrs Woodrowe?'

'Of course,' Rose said. She did not look at Nat. He would, no doubt, be looking exasperated and she had no wish to see his expression.

'Perhaps I could just start,' said Grace, 'by explaining the legal position? With no specific reference to your personal intentions.'

'Please,' Nat said tightly.

Out of the corner of her eye, Rose could see his crossed knees, in charcoal-grey suiting, and his ankles in fine black socks and the shine of his polished black brogues. It occurred to her to marvel, despite everything, at how grown up he looked, how professional, what an impression he must make at meetings where his advice was sought, and how miraculous it was to have been the witness of his transformation from a little boy clinging to her at the nursery school gates to this self-possessed adult. One foot jerked, slightly and involuntarily. Rose might have said, but didn't, to Grace, 'He wants you to get on with it. I might not, but he does. He's always been impatient, with everyone but his twin sister.'

Mrs Ashton said evenly, 'The position, in my firm's experience, is to answer this question: on re-marriage, later in life, how do you make the assets that both participants have accrued in their lifetimes both fair and safe? And how do you ensure that what satisfies the wishes of both parties also satisfies the wishes of their children? In our experience it is, of course, absolutely *key* to protect the assets of both children and grandchildren. Do you have grandchildren, Mrs Woodrowe?'

'Two.'

'And Mr, er, Masson?'

'None,' Rose said. 'As yet.'

Mrs Ashton looked at Nat. 'You are unmarried, I believe? As is one of your sisters?'

He nodded, swallowing. Rose had an impulse to put a hand out and touch his arm, or squeeze it, for comfort. She wanted to say, 'I'm sure you *will* marry, darling. So will Emmy. There's so much less hurry these days than there used to be,' and was struck, simultaneously, by how idiotic and inappropriate such an impulse was.

'We have five categories to consider,' said Grace. She unclasped her hands, and held up one in order to tick items off on her fingers. 'One, property. Two, businesses. Three, pensions. Four, joint assets. Five, wills. All these elements have to be considered, which is why we often recommend pre-nuptial agreements.'

'*Pre-nups?*' Rose was truly startled.

'Yes,' Grace said. 'A good idea, Mrs Woodrowe, in cases like yours where both parties have been married before and there is an inequality of wealth or debt between the couple.'

Rose half got to her feet. She looked from Nat to Grace. 'What do you mean? What are you *talking* about?'

Nat cleared his throat. 'I told her. I told Mrs Ashton about your house. I told her Tyler doesn't seem to have any money. I just said. Sit *down*, Mother.'

Rose subsided, her face flushed. She wanted to say, stupidly, 'He never calls me "Mother",' but instead managed to confine herself to stammering, 'I never thought – I never imagined . . .'

'It is always better, Mrs Woodrowe, to look at every possibility. Just as it is best to make full disclosure of both facts and assets. The law may seem a cold fish but it isn't there for the best of all worlds but to save and protect in the worst.'

Rose stared at the carpet. She heard Nat say, sounding disconcertingly like his father, 'As I said on the telephone, Mrs Ashton, we need to know as precisely as we can what to prepare for,' and Mrs Ashton replying, almost as if Rose wasn't in the room.

Rose raised her head and said clearly, to Nat, 'Perhaps it would help if I knew exactly what you have already disclosed?'

'Only that you have a valuable house and that Tyler doesn't appear to have anything.'

'He has a pension in America.'

'We might suggest a discretionary trust,' Mrs Ashton said. 'Which would constitute a pre-marital agreement. *If* you intend to marry.'

'I do.' Rose sounded very certain.

'In that case, the house would remain yours, and Mr

Masson would have no interest in the value of it, but he would have the right to live in it for his lifetime. In other words, if you were to die before your husband, he, as your husband, would have the use of your assets until his own death. You need a trust to protect your assets for your children, but if you have a trust, your ability to choose and the exercise of your own discretion becomes limited. If you were to divorce—'

Rose looked horrified. 'Divorce!'

'We have to consider everything,' Grace Ashton said, unperturbed. 'A divorce court will only take notice of the terms of the trust if you and your husband have made full disclosure of all your assets when you marry.'

Rose glanced at Nat. 'Did you know all this?'

He sighed. 'Mum, it's why we're here,' he said wearily. 'Because it's complicated.'

'It is,' Grace agreed. 'And there might be tax issues to add to it – capital gains tax, possibly. A trust—'

'I don't want a trust!' Rose almost shouted.

There was a brief and startled pause and then Mrs Ashton went on as if the interruption had hardly happened. 'A trust would need trustees, Mrs Woodrowe. Yourself, of course, and also perhaps your children. It would be quite a drastic and unusual thing to do but in the circumstances—'

Rose stood up abruptly. 'I think I've heard enough.'

Slowly, Mrs Ashton and Nat rose to their feet. Mrs Ashton said, more to Nat than to Rose, 'I think we have covered all the ground necessary for a first meeting.' She held a hand out across her desk. 'Goodbye, Mrs Woodrowe. I hope that this has been helpful at least.'

Rose looked at the proffered hand as if the last thing she

had any desire to do was to shake it. Then she looked straight at Grace Ashton.

'I wouldn't call it that,' she said.

———

In a cafe downstairs from Emmy's offices, Nat was staring into a takeaway cup of peppermint tea. 'She wouldn't really speak to me afterwards,' he said. 'I mean, she did all the mum stuff and asked if I was doing anything nice this evening and was my eczema better, but she wouldn't talk about the meeting.'

'Did you try?'

'I didn't get the chance. She said, the minute we were outside the door, "We've learned what we've learned and I am not discussing *any* of it until I've had time to digest it, so please don't go for me," and then she started down the stairs, ignoring the lift, at breakneck speed and I could see it was hopeless.'

Emmy made a face. 'D'you think any of it went in?'

'Oh yes. That was the trouble. She saw what her position would be if she persists in this marrying thing and she didn't like it, Em, she didn't like it one bit. I guess that she's got used to the freedom she's had since Dad, whatever the pressures and anxieties, and it didn't occur to her that she might be compromising them if she gets married again.'

Emmy said sympathetically, 'Oh, Nat.'

'I felt so sorry for her, Em. I really did. I'd got used to just feeling exasperated and fed up with her and suddenly I just thought – oh God, Em, it made me think of when Dad said he was leaving and she wanted to spare us and not blame him or have us think badly of him, and –' He stopped and gave himself a little shake and then said miserably, 'It was a whole lot easier when I just felt irritated with her, I can tell you.'

'But it's what we wanted really, isn't it? I mean, we wanted her to come down off cloud nine.'

Nat looked at his tea without enthusiasm. 'Not really. It's not falling for someone.'

'Isn't it?'

'It's wanting to *marry* them. It's this marriage thing. You could see Mrs Ashton was trying to tell her not to get married.' He raised his eyes and looked at his sister. 'Em. Why is she so fixated on getting *married*?'

Emmy shrugged. 'Dunno. Generational?'

'What? Being married because people her age always did?'

'Maybe.'

'But she isn't like that,' Nat said. 'She doesn't usually care about convention. She's learned to manage alone brilliantly.'

'Until him,' Emmy said.

Nat sighed. 'I've got to see him for a drink. He asked me. Got my office number. God knows why.'

'Yes,' said Emmy absent-mindedly.

'I'm wondering whether to head him off.'

Emmy wasn't listening. She said, almost bitterly, 'I think she just wants to show the world she's *got* someone. That's what this marriage thing is all about.'

Nat looked at her. He said, after a pause, 'Em?'

Emmy picked up the scarf she had put on the banquette beside her and began to wind it around her neck.

'Maybe,' she said, 'Mum just wants to show us all she can still pull and then get proposed to.' She stood up. 'Good luck with that drink.'

'Where are you going?'

'Back to work. Back to wooing a dry-cleaning company to let us re-brand them, if you must know.'

'What are you so cross about all of a sudden?'

She stepped away from the table and slung her bag on her shoulder.

'I'm not cross,' she said. 'I just sometimes get bored with the whole Mum thing. Like Laura does.'

'But you aren't a bit like Laura. Laura's only ever focused on her own life, her own family.'

Emmy bent and gave his cheek a quick kiss.

'Bye Nat,' she said. 'Thanks for telling me.'

———

Tyler was early, on purpose. He had suggested that he and Nat meet in the bar of a hotel off Piccadilly, which was furnished in a clubby and masculine manner with leather chairs and panelling. He had told Mallory on the phone that he had asked Nat Woodrowe to have a drink with him, in the interests of being above board about all his plans, and Mallory had said, as if she were half attending to something else, 'Oh, OK, Daddy. But why?'

'Why what?'

'Why d'you want to meet the guy all buddy-buddy just the two of you?'

'Because, sweetheart, I want to reassure him that I don't have designs on anything of his mother's but only on his mother herself.'

'Doesn't he know that already? I mean,' Mallory said, her voice just edging into the contemptuous, 'it's not as if she's a Hilton heiress exactly, is it?'

Tyler said, 'Would you like to come too?'

'No. Why would I?'

'I thought maybe you could get to know each other a little better.'

'Daddy,' Mallory said, 'I don't need to know these people. I came the other night because you asked me, but I don't need to make a habit of it. I have my life and you have yours. I'm happy for you, Daddy.'

'Are you?'

'Yes,' Mallory said. Her voice changed suddenly and she sounded close to tears. 'Of course I am. Enjoy your drink. I gotta run.'

Well, Tyler thought, surveying the hotel bar and mentally selecting a pair of bucket chairs against the back wall, Mallory's attitude, whatever it meant, wasn't going to throw him off his stride. Probably it had only just dawned on Mallory that his feelings for Rose meant that he had, in her view, got over grieving for her mother, and this was taking some adjusting to. She had given no sign of distress in front of Rose's family; had, in fact, conducted herself with more poise and social confidence than the rest of them put together. But maybe that was a front, a by-product of being an actress. Maybe, underneath, Tyler's falling for Rose had awakened all kinds of feelings of grief and loss. Odd, that, if so. Cindy had been a conscientious mother but a faintly distant one, as if the lifelong allegiance to her father could not be compromised by any competitive devotions. Tyler indicated to the barman that he was heading towards his chosen chairs. Why did things – people, his children, Rose's children – have to be so complicated? Why couldn't they just look at him and Rose together, neither of them breaking up a marriage for God's sake, and just *be happy*? He slid his raincoat off and draped it over the back of one of the bucket chairs. At least he was going to have a chance to reassure this boy of Rose's that as far as any assets were concerned, he had less than nothing to fear.

Nat was late. By the time he reached the bar, it was nearly forty minutes after the agreed time. Tyler stood up to greet him, holding out his hand and smiling. 'I thought you might stand me up.'

'It was the traffic, you know.'

'Plus,' Tyler said in a friendly voice, 'you regretted agreeing to see me?'

Nat lowered himself into a chair. 'Sorry. Bit of a day.'

'I know. You went with your mother to see a solicitor.'

'You know!'

'Of course I know. She rang me.' He sat down again and said affably, 'We speak several times a day. What are you drinking?'

Nat looked at Tyler's glass.

'It's a vodka and tonic,' Tyler said helpfully. 'Want one?'

Nat shook his head. 'Could I have a beer?'

Tyler gestured for a waiter. He said solemnly to Nat, 'I want you to know that I think you were quite right to get your mother to see a lawyer. Nat, which beer do you want?'

Nat looked up at the waiter. 'Could I get a Punk?'

'Sorry, sir. We only have Budweiser here. Or Stella Artois.'

'Mallory would tease me,' Tyler said, 'for choosing to meet you somewhere so staid.'

'A Bud, please,' Nat said to the waiter, and then, looking down again, 'I don't know what Mum told you. And a Bud's fine.'

'But it's not craft beer.'

'It's fine.'

'Nat,' Tyler said, 'could you just look at me?'

Nat raised his eyes reluctantly. 'OK.'

'I'll say it again. I'm only interested in your mother herself. That's all. I have no designs on anything she has, anything that might be deemed as belonging to the family. I'm not materialistic. In fact, it used to drive Mallory's mother round the bend, that I wasn't.'

Nat sat up a little straighter. He said, 'Can I ask you something?'

'Sure.'

Nat cleared his throat. 'Why do you want to marry my mother?'

Tyler smiled broadly. 'Isn't it obvious? I adore her. I want to be with her all the time. I think the absolute world of her, Nat; in fact, I didn't know that there could *be* anyone like your mother.'

Nat's beer arrived in a tall-waisted glass with a crest emblazoned on the side. He glanced at it, and then he looked back at Tyler.

'OK. OK. But marriage. Why *marriage*? Why can't you just – be together, if that's what you want? I mean, you aren't exactly going to have a family, after all, are you? I can't see why you can't just be a couple and not do the marriage thing.'

Tyler said solemnly, 'I've never actually proposed to anyone before your mother. I can't remember exactly what happened with Mallory's mother, but I think it was a kind of understanding that never quite got articulated; we just assumed, and her family did too, and then her mother produced an heirloom ring and gave it to me to give to Cindy.

But when it came to your mother, I just *knew*. I knew I wanted to marry her, I wanted the world to know she had agreed to be my wife just as it will know and acknowledge when she *is* my wife. Nat, it is incredibly important to us that we are husband and wife for everyone to see. I can't tell you how proud I am that she's agreed. I can't tell you how proud, even ecstatic I'll be when she *is* Mrs Masson.'

Nat sat quite still and looked at him. Then he said hoarsely, 'Please . . .'

'Please what?'

'*Please* don't marry her,' Nat said. 'Please don't put her in that position.'

'What position?'

'The complicated legal position that will happen if you marry her.'

Tyler took a swallow of his drink. 'No, it won't,' he said, smiling at Nat.

'It will. It will! Didn't she tell you what the solicitor said?'

'Something about a pre-nup? A trust?'

'Yes. If you get married.'

Tyler waved a hand. 'I don't mind, Nat. I don't care what I sign. Anything any of you want that reassures you. Makes you happy. I'll do whatever needs doing legally, no problem. But I'm set on marrying Rose. It's what I want. I haven't wanted much in my life that I've been willing to go to the wire for, but I do want this. I want to marry your mother, Nat. I want it more than anything. And what is more, she, bless all the angels in heaven, wants to marry me.'

'Suppose,' Nat said, almost wildly, 'she has agreed because, being the person she is, she sees how much you want it and doesn't want you to be disappointed?'

Tyler looked at him benignly. 'Sorry, Nat.'

'Sorry?'

'Your mother and I are absolutely at one about this. Whatever the legal hurdles, whatever documents you want drawn up, all fine by us. We'll do whatever you want, whatever it takes. But' – he picked up his glass again and tipped it towards Nat in a kind of jaunty salute – 'we are going to get married, and that, my boy, is final.'

———

'Laura's out,' Angus said. 'She's at the hospital. Some patient she's fond of mightn't last the night. You can come in and wait for her if you want.'

Nat stepped inside, past his brother-in-law, who was holding open the door from which he had scraped all the old varnish, but had not yet got round to re-painting.

'Please,' Nat said tiredly. 'I left a message on her phone.'

'She won't pick it up if she's working. I gave her a second phone for Christmas so I know I can always get through if I need to. You hungry?'

Nat looked vaguely round the kitchen. Angus had papers spread across the huge kitchen table under the precisely aimed pools of light cast by three industrial metal lamps hanging on stout rubber flexes from the ceiling.

'I'm doing our VAT return,' Angus said. 'I can make you an omelette. Or there's cheese. Want a beer?'

Nat slumped into the nearest chair. 'I'm full of beer.'

Angus crossed to the fridge, extracted a block of cheese loosely wrapped in greaseproof paper from a shelf in the door and put it in front of Nat, on the table. Then he added a knife and a plate, and the heel of an artisan-looking loaf on a breadboard.

'Better eat, Nat. Have you had dinner?'

Nat shook his head. 'Peanuts. Literally. A handful of peanuts.'

Angus filled a tumbler with water from a filter jug and put it beside the plate.

'Where've you been?'

Nat sighed. He began to saw a hunk off the loaf. 'Is there any chutney?'

Angus got up again, and went back to the fridge.

Nat said, 'I had a drink with Mum's man in some hotel bar. And . . .' He paused, the bread knife in mid-air. 'And, Angus, he says nothing, absolutely nothing, will stop them marrying. He's as fixed on it – more, really – as she is.'

Angus put a jar of chutney and a plastic box of olive-oil spread in front of Nat. Then he sat down opposite him. 'Did you think you could talk him out of it?' he said.

Nat opened the greaseproof packet and cut an uneven wedge of cheese. 'Yes. I thought I could tell him how complicated and unwise the lawyer told us marriage would be, but there wasn't a chance. I mean, Mum was clearly shaken by this morning. She wouldn't talk about it afterwards at all, which meant she was in shock, really, and I thought I could build on all that later, with him; I could say that it wouldn't be fair on her, to drag her through the legal mangle, just to put a ring on her finger. But there wasn't a chance.' He bent forward and took a large and messy mouthful of bread and cheese. Round it, he said indistinctly, 'God, I was hungry.'

Angus said, 'Have you talked to Emmy?'

Nat shook his head, chewing. 'I told her what happened

this morning. But I haven't told her about meeting – Tyler. It's really hard to say his name, you know? Em knew I was meeting him, about his request, but she doesn't yet know what happened. It was crazy, Angus. Crazy.' He bent forward again and took another bite. 'We were at complete cross-purposes. He wanted to tell me he isn't remotely interested in whatever she's worth and I wanted to persuade him not to marry her.'

Angus put his elbows on the table. 'Does Rose really want to get married?'

Nat nodded, his mouth full again.

Angus pushed up his sweater sleeves. 'Woodrowe women are pretty hard to persuade not to do something they've set their hearts on. I didn't want Laura going to the hospital to-night. I said, "Look, you're Mr Nagdi's GP, not a hospital doctor," but she was determined to go because she likes him, she likes his wife and his whole family. She'd made up her mind. It sounds as if Rose has made up hers.'

Nat drank half a tumbler of water with the same appetite he had applied to the bread and cheese. Then he put the glass down and wiped the back of his hand across his mouth. He said, 'She was really upset to hear what the lawyer had to say this morning. You could see she was. But I think they talked today, I think he won her over. *I* think she couldn't resist him wanting to marry her so much. And' – Nat pulled a face – 'he was kind of OK tonight. Not smarmy. Not scheming. He just sat there smiling and saying how he adored her and wanted to marry her and I just wanted to *hit* him.'

Angus grinned. ''Course you did. She's your mum.'

'You know how it is.'

'Well, actually, I don't. You know my story. But Rose is as

good a mother-in-law as it gets, I suspect, so I get how you're feeling.'

Nat picked up the bread knife to cut another slice. 'Can I?'

'Go ahead.'

'To be honest,' Nat said, 'I didn't want to tell Em all this. She seems really upset by it, really angry as well as sad, and I don't want to dump on her till I've sorted it all a bit in my head myself. That's why I wanted to talk to Laura.'

Angus pushed the cheese packet towards his brother-in-law. 'That Mallory girl . . .'

'She was cool.'

'Mightn't she be able to give you a bit of a steer on her father?'

Nat paused with his knife in the olive-oil-spread tub. 'What do you mean?'

'Well, won't she have a view? I mean her mother died of cancer, and here's her father proposing to marry someone else, from another country to boot. She won't exactly be unaffected, will she? Maybe he's done it lots of times before, maybe he's always proposing to people, maybe he was a bad husband and made her mother miserable. Won't Mallory be able to help? In fact, now I come to think of it, shouldn't Mallory be as involved in all this as you three are?'

Nat was laying thinner slices of cheese carefully across the bread on his plate. 'Good thinking,' he said soberly.

'It's only just occurred to me.'

'She seemed the only person who could even begin to cope, on Monday.'

'Call her,' Angus said.

At the far end of the table, a mobile phone began to

vibrate. Angus sprang up to answer it. He peered at the screen.

'She's on her way back. Twenty minutes, she says.'

Nat put the heels of his hands into his eyes. 'Brilliant,' he said. 'Thanks, bro.'

Angus crossed the kitchen and picked up the kettle. 'Coffee?'

CHAPTER SEVEN

'I have no idea,' Rose said, 'what I want to do.'

They were in her garden, and Rose was showing Tyler how to prune rose bushes. Tyler had never pruned anything in his life; had never, he said to Rose, been allowed to, because a gardener called Moses who travelled across the city from Mission Bay had looked after Cindy's father's garden, as well as Cindy and Tyler's. Moses, Tyler told Rose, had very fixed ideas of how a garden should be, which was formal and precise and above all, controlled.

'He'd have despaired of English gardens,' Tyler said. 'I think a herbaceous border would have been his idea of a horticultural nightmare.' He looked down at his feet, where spring growth was beginning to push up between the paving stones. 'He would hate this. What's it going to be?'

'Alchemilla mollis,' Rose said. 'Lime green and vigorous.'

Tyler gazed at her. 'I love you. I love you when you know things like that.'

Rose blew him a kiss from her gardening glove. 'Every woman my age in England knows about alchemilla mollis.'

'Bet they don't.'

'Tyler,' Rose said, clipping out long rogue fronds from a

rose bush, 'I've thought about it a lot, and I don't want to do any of the things the lawyer suggested to me.'

He took a breath. 'OK,' he said. He sounded deliberately measured.

She said, snipping and not looking at him, 'I can't bear all this talk of agreements and pre-nups and discretionary trusts. I really hate it. I hate the bloodlessness of it, the underlying assumption that we need, somehow, *guarding* from each other, like dogs who can't be left in the same room together in case they fight.'

Tyler put the secateurs Rose had given him in his trouser pocket. He came to stand close to her. 'I don't think that's the intention.'

'It is,' Rose said indignantly, snipping on. 'It *is*. You should have heard this Ashton woman. I mean, she acknowledged that the law sounded cold, but her whole subtext, in everything she said, was to undermine all emotion, all human connection, only to do what was to my – but mostly the children's – material advantage, as if money was all that mattered. As if this house' – she gestured in its direction – 'was a sort of gold mine.'

Tyler said carefully, 'Well, looked at in terms of assets, I suppose it is.'

She glanced at him. 'Whose side are you on?'

'Yours. And only yours. I'm just trying to see the situation from Nat and Emmy's point of view.'

Rose said, 'What do Seth and Mallory think?'

'I have no idea.'

She stopped snipping and looked at him. 'What d'you mean, you have no idea about your own children's opinion of you re-marrying?'

Tyler shrugged. 'Seth can only think about bread and Mallory gives me the brush-off every time I broach the subject. In any case, Cindy left them money, and before you say don't I resent the fact that she left money to them, and not anything much of her estate to me, the answer is absolutely no, I don't at all. It was her family money and she left it to her family. Fine by me. You know how I am about money.'

She put her head slightly on one side. Then she said fondly, 'I do.'

He grinned. 'You may not feel so affectionate about my attitude to money in time. It drove Cindy insane. It drove my poor parents insane. I cannot mind about it, Rosie. I really try, but I can't make it matter like it does to most people. Like it does, understandably, to Nat.' He glanced towards the open doors to the sitting room. 'Nat is plainly really worried about this house.'

Rose followed his gaze. 'I love it.'

'Yes. But not, perhaps, like you love your children. Or even me.'

'Why do you say that? This house has rescued me. Living here was where I didn't just heal, I came alive again; I found liberty and independence.'

'Rose . . .'

'Yes?'

'Those feelings, what you've felt about this house, well, they were before me. Weren't they?'

She was standing looking at him, her hands in their suede gardening gloves hanging by her side. She said, a little uncertainly, 'Yes.'

'I mean,' Tyler continued, stepping forward and putting his own hands either side of her waist, 'I can quite see how this house saved you, gave you a purpose and a goal as well as liberty and independence. And I know how hard and ingeniously you've worked to live here, all the lodgers and the translations and probably the deprivations. All of which is magnificent. It really is. Magnificent. But now it's going to be different. Very different. Because there's me.'

She didn't speak. She stood in front of him, his hands warm through her shirt and her sweater.

'I've had an idea,' he went on.

'Oh?'

'It's an idea that maybe means we don't even have to think about those bleak legal suggestions of pre-nups and asset-protection trusts. It's an idea I think your twins will like.'

'We can't do something just to please the twins.'

'No,' Tyler said, 'but if they're mollified because of what we decide to do, that's surely a plus?'

Rose raised one hand to rub an itch on her nose with the back of one wrist. Then she said, 'You've been thinking.'

'I have.'

'Since your drink with Nat.'

'Yes,' Tyler said. 'I've been thinking of a way to stop him and Emmy fretting about us getting married. Because we *are* getting married.'

Rose nodded. Tyler leaned forward and kissed her mouth. Then he said, 'So this is my idea. I suggest that you sell this house, give a wallop of money to your three children, and with the rest, we'll go to the country and find a cottage for you and me.'

Rose said, almost in a whisper, 'A cottage.'

He beamed at her. Then he slid his arms around her waist and pulled her to him.

'Yes,' he said, 'a cottage. For you and me. Don't you think?'

———

Mallory and her friends were sharing a flat above a couple of shops – a pizza place and a hardware shop – on Kilburn High Road. There were four of them in the flat, sharing two bedrooms and a single cupboard-sized bathroom, but the rent was a manageable £350 a month each, and as all of them were on an Equity minimum wage on account of the theatre being deemed Category C for Small Theatres, a reasonable rent was significant. Mallory, who earned just over £600 a week for playing Kaia Fosli, also had a £25 supplement as the understudy for the part of Hilde Wangel, which she was careful to spend for the benefit of the whole flat, on extra wine, or a takeaway Chinese from the restaurant down the street. That she had money from her late mother in America was never mentioned: she would have regarded any display of prosperity as tactless to the point of crudity. She was, to her infinite gratification, a working actress sharing a flat with another actress, an assistant stage manager and a girl whose job it was to oversee both costumes and props. Money, Mallory knew from her time in New York, was a useful commodity, but in artistic, creative, self-expressive terms, beside the point.

She was completely relaxed about having Nat in their chaotic sitting room. The stage manager and the props girl had both departed for the theatre and an audition for the next job, and only she and her friend Jess were lounging around the cheap dining table with its peeling veneer, drinking coffee among the detritus of last night's wine bottles and last week's unironed laundry. Jess Ballantyne, who played

Hilde, and whom Mallory understudied for her princely £25, had long, thick auburn hair bundled up into a casual knot on the back of her head and wide grey eyes still smudged with the previous night's makeup. Both girls wore leggings and oversized hooded tops. Their toenails, Nat observed, were carefully painted, and they had obviously slept in both earrings and rings. When Jess Ballantyne stretched her arm out to break off a piece of the brioche he had brought – 'Take something,' Emmy had urged him. 'Breakfast or flowers or something' – he noticed that although her fingernails were unpainted, there was a snake tattooed on her inner wrist, its head almost reaching the ball of her thumb. It gave him a small thrill to imagine where the snake ended, where its tail finally stopped. It was a thrill akin to the one he experienced when he realized that Jess, languid and supple in all her movements, wasn't even bothering to look his way.

'It's good of you to see me,' he said to Mallory.

Mallory shrugged. Her red hair, concealed under a mouse-brown wig for the stage, was roughly tied back in a ponytail, with long fronds left to wave round her face. The nose stud, which he had noticed and been slightly disconcerted by at the hotel, was missing, and Mallory's early-morning face, clean of makeup, had the innocent pallor of a child's.

'It's not good, it's just OK. Believe me. We may never see each other again.'

Jess licked her fingers. She said, 'Won't you? I thought you guys' parents were hooking up.'

Mallory sighed. She rubbed her eyes. 'Nothing to do with me.'

Jess broke off another piece of brioche. She said, not looking at Nat, 'Mal, he's your *dad*.'

'He is,' Mallory said. 'But it's still nothing to do with me.'

Jess turned suddenly and gave Nat the full force of her huge questioning grey gaze.

'*What?*'

Nat swallowed. What a girl. What an amazing girl. A little unsteadily, he said, 'That's . . . really what I came to ask you about. Your father, I mean. Which means – or, it kind of follows, I suppose – what do *you* feel about our parents?'

Mallory raised her eyes. She looked straight at Nat. 'Nothing,' she said.

Jess gave Nat a quick glance, which he hardly dared to interpret as conspiratorial. She turned to Mallory. 'Babe, you can't mean that. You can't mean nothing. Nobody loses their mother and sees their father fall for someone else and feels nothing. No one does.'

Mallory said steadfastly, 'I don't feel anything.'

'I do,' Nat said with emphasis.

Jess flashed him another intense look. 'There you go.'

Mallory picked at something encrusted on the table. 'Dad can fall for whoever he wants to.'

'Mal,' Jess said. 'That's not very nice for Nat to hear.'

Nat's heart swelled within his chest. He said, striving to sound gallant, 'That's OK.'

'No, it isn't,' Jess replied. She bent towards Mallory. 'If you really felt nothing, you wouldn't sulk.'

'I'm not sulking!'

'Oh?' Jess said. 'So this display of teenage indifference is for real, then?'

Nat felt dizzy with gratitude. Mallory said, looking at her nails, 'Your mother's a doll.'

Jess took her nearest wrist. 'Mal, this guy's come for *help*. Can't you see? He wants to know about your father.'

Mallory extricated her wrist and held it with her other hand as if it had been damaged.

'I can't tell you anything.'

'Why not?'

'Because,' Mallory said, suddenly flaring up, 'I don't *know* him. I didn't know Mother either. She was always playing tennis, and if she wasn't doing that she was doing something for, or with, *her* father. 'If you want to know,' she said, abruptly glaring at Nat, 'I don't know why they had kids except I don't suppose they knew how not to; I don't suppose contraception was very efficient back in the day. We were just four people living in the same house genetically connected but completely separate. I had my friends from school; Seth had his. Mother was out all the time, Daddy was at work.'

She stopped as abruptly as she had begun. Nat said diffidently, 'How – how would you describe your father?'

Mallory looked at her nails again. 'He's OK.'

'More than that?'

'He's a nice guy,' Mallory said. 'He never fitted in to Grandpa's family; he was always kinda . . . *English*. To tell the truth, I have no idea why they thought it would be a good idea to get married. They didn't fight, they just didn't – have a connection.'

'But,' Nat persisted, taking courage from Jess's evident sympathy, 'you don't like to see him having a connection with someone else?'

Mallory pulled a face. 'It means nothing to me.'

'I think it does,' Nat said bravely.

'I said, she's a nice lady.'

'But you don't want to see him blown away by her.'

Mallory sat back in her chair. She looked at Nat. 'Why d'you think I'm an actress? Why do you think I love belonging to a company? Why d'you think I talk like this about my father? Or my baking-obsessed brother? Why do you think I've trained myself not to care?'

'But you *do* care,' Jess said.

Mallory stood up. 'If my father decides to stay in London because of your mother, then I'll know, won't I? I'll know where his priorities lie. Where they've probably always lain. I'm going to take a shower.'

Nat stood up too. 'Mallory—'

'When the play closes Saturday,' Mallory said, 'I'm going back to New York. And nobody will care, one way or the other, will they?'

'Your dad will miss you,' Jess said. She was twisted round in her chair, and the snake on her arm was visible almost to her elbow. 'Don't you want him to be happy?'

'Oh, sure.' Mallory said, moving towards the door. Then she added, 'It's his life, poor guy. Maybe he thinks it's just starting. Maybe he's really excited to be a Brit back in Britain. Whatever, I wish him well.' She paused in the doorway and looked at Nat. 'Let them get on with it. You can't ever stop people doing what they're determined to do, anyway. So let them do what they want to do, why don't you?'

When she'd gone, Nat sat down again and Jess twisted back round in her chair. There was a small silence, then Jess said, 'I don't think that's what you came for, was it?'

He let out a long breath. 'What was all that about?'

'Old history,' Jess said. 'Old resentments. Did you have a happy childhood?'

Nat picked up a nearby pen that was lying on the table and rolled it in his fingers like a cigar. 'Hard to say. Yes, at the time, but clouded later by knowing what my father had been up to for so long. Maybe happiness when you're little isn't very formative.'

'Mal's a good actress.'

'I'm sure.'

She looked at him. 'Seen the play?'

'No. Only my mother has. She thought it was wonderful.'

Jess scratched her arm thoughtfully. 'Want to see it?'

He grinned. 'Now I do. Yes, please.'

'I'll get you a house seat. Friday? Saturday?'

The sound of the shower splashing onto a plastic curtain was audible. Nat felt strangely buoyant, even though he had hardly obtained a fraction of what he had come for.

'Both, please,' he said.

———

Seth Masson's bakery was easy to find online. There it was, Doughboy, listed as one of the top new bakeries in San Francisco, famous for its artisan breads, for its farmer's cheese and green-onion turnovers at lunchtime, for sourdough loaves which were, said the reviews, sensational even in a sourdough-rich city. There were photographs of the exterior of the bakery, and close-ups of the best-selling tartines with burrata, and loaves piled in a wicker basket. There were also, Emmy discovered, photographs of Seth in a long ticking apron with 'Doughboy' printed across the bib, and a pretty, solemn-looking Japanese girl holding an open miniature hamper of muffins. She looked long and hard at photographs of Seth. He looked slighter than his father, with hair pulled back into what was presumably a single pigtail like an eighteenth-century mariner's, and round John Lennon glasses, but his smile was like Tyler's, wide and welcoming but not, somehow – unlike Tyler's – to be resented. He wrote a weekly baker's blog, full of words like 'passion' and 'commitment'. There were Biblical references to bread being both the stuff and staff of life. He looked, as did the Japanese girl who was plainly his partner both personally and professionally, as if he really meant all the high-flown things he said. Perhaps you could only do that, without being laughed at, if you were American. Earnestness, Emmy thought, reflecting on the slogans she devised for work, was only valued in England as a target for mockery.

She messaged Seth on his Facebook page, in response to his advertising Doughboy's new range of jams – conserves, Seth called them – developed to be spread on their thick slices of sourdough toast.

'Hi,' Emmy wrote, 'you don't know me, but our parents know each other. Does the name Rose Woodrowe mean anything to you? I'm her daughter and – watch out – I'm going to act the pedant . . . doesn't the word "conserve" only apply to jams made of small fruit? Isn't the word you're looking for "preserve"? Sorry! Love the photos of Doughboy – the bread looks amazing! Emmy W.'

She added a couple of kisses, then took them off again. This was so weird, messaging the bread-mad son of a man your mother was insisting she was going to marry. Who wasn't your father. When your mother was sixty-four. Sixty-four! Ye gods, as her Aunt Prue was wont to say in extremis, you couldn't make this up: not the situation, not Emmy's screen being filled up with the picture of some random sandwich shop in California which had suddenly become of intense significance. I mean, Emmy thought, bringing up the picture of Seth in his apron again, what are we all *doing*? What has she made us do, acting as she is? Here am I, online with someone I've never heard of to whom I am suddenly intimately connected, and there is Nat going off to pick the brains of an American actress with cranberry-coloured hair, all because our mother has gone ever so slightly off her head? Is she taking us all round the bend with her?

On the table top next to her laptop, her mobile began to play its programmed carillon and spin round. She peered at the screen. It would be Nat. It wasn't Nat.

'Aunt Prue!' Emmy said, holding her phone, slightly angled, under her hair.

'Hello, dear.'

'I haven't talked to you for ages.'

'I rang,' Prue said, 'to see if you are all right.'

'All right?'

'Yes, Emmy. If you and Nat and Laura are, let's say *comfortable*, with what is going on with your mother.'

Emmy closed her eyes briefly. 'Oh. That.'

'Yes, dear. That.'

Emmy said in a rush, 'To be honest, I don't know what to think.'

'Nor me, dear. I have yet to meet him.'

'We only just have.'

'And?'

'And,' Emmy said, 'he's fine. I mean, he's – well, I suppose he's OK.'

'Two arms, two legs, two eyes, nose et cetera?'

'Yes.'

'Hair?'

'Yes. Lots, actually.'

'Glasses?'

'Yes. Oh, Aunt Prue . . .'

'What, dear?'

'I've just got a knot in my stomach about it all.'

'Well,' Prue said briskly, 'I have my own ideas about that knot.'

'Please don't tell me.'

'It isn't easy, being obliged to witness the spectacle of a parent in love. Quite apart from the insanity that being in love induces in everyone, there is the added awkwardness of seeing a parent in the grip, as it were. How is Laura?'

Emmy leaned against the table. 'She's managing better than me. Than us. You know Laura. A bit distanced, a bit live and let live, a bit . . .'

'Annoying?'

'Only because I can't be like her. I mean, she's got her work and her boys and Angus and all that. This whole thing isn't making her so – lonely.'

'Lonely?'

'I miss Mum,' Emmy said simply, suddenly and profoundly feeling it to be true. 'She's sort of gone away, because of him. We argue about stuff. We never used to argue.'

'If it's any consolation,' Prue said, 'I haven't heard from her in a month. I've left her the odd message but she hasn't rung me. I expect she thinks I'll tick her off.'

'Would you?'

'Hard to tell till I've met him,' Prue said. 'I have to admit that the *idea* doesn't exactly appeal.'

'She would say that's because you've never married.'

'I didn't,' Prue said resolutely, 'because the right person never asked me. And all the drips and weeds who did were out of the question.'

'Nobody,' Emmy said, 'has ever asked me.'

'Have you ever hoped that anyone would?'

Emmy closed her eyes again. 'Not yet. Not – in real life.'

'No. But your mother—'

'I don't get it,' Emmy interrupted with a burst of energy. 'I don't see what she sees in him. I can't see *any* of it.'

'Is he an adventurer?'

'A what?'

'Is he after her,' Prue said in her explanatory, headmistressy voice, 'for her money?'

'I don't know. I don't think so but that's why Nat took her to see a solicitor.'

'A solicitor!'

'Yes,' Emmy said. 'Didn't you know?'

'I think,' Prue said solemnly, 'that I had better come to London again.'

'I don't want her cornered, Aunt Prue. She's already told us that we make her feel threatened and bullied. I don't want her to feel worse, I just want her back. I just want my mum back the way she's always been.' She glanced at her laptop. It was sleeping, but if she touched the mousepad, Seth Masson would be there again in his ticking apron, reminding her that there was now, because of Rose's feelings about Tyler, a whole new and unwanted yet intriguing cast of characters in her life.

Prue said, with as much gentleness as she was capable of, 'She's my sister, Em. My only sister. I've always looked out for her.'

'I know. I know. The painful thing just now is that she only wants to look out for herself,' Em said.

———

Laura lay in the dark across the end of Jack's bed. He had taken, since he graduated to a proper bed, to getting out of it half a dozen times after his supposedly good-night story, and padding down in spurious search of drinks of water and trips to the toilet. Neither Laura nor Angus had wanted to close his bedroom door or threaten him with a return to the baby status of a cot, like Adam's, so an uneasy compromise had grown up involving a parent lying down in the dark at the end of his bed after his story and staying there until he was asleep.

Jack liked this new arrangement. It was a pity that neither parent was at all inclined to use it as an opportunity for interesting conversation – how did aeroplanes stay up, were there angels, what happened if you never cut your nails? – but it was oddly empowering to feel an adult gradually becoming heavier and heavier somewhere near one's feet as they sank into the slumber that somehow always eluded you. Jack lay in the dark, flicking his fingers against his teeth, or twisting his hair into instantly unravelling ropes, and listened to his mother's breathing as it gently deepened into unconsciousness. She talked, sometimes, about feeling tired. Jack didn't really know what she meant. He knew what it was like to feel anxious or busy or fractious or – occasionally – hungry, but this tired thing was a mystery. He never felt tired. When people said, 'Go to sleep,' he looked at them as if they were bonkers. You couldn't *go* to sleep; it was impossible. It was just something that seemed, most nights, to happen.

Laura held her breath in order to hear Jack's own breathing lengthen and regularize. If she rose, however stealthily, before he was in a deep sleep, he would spring up and remind her sternly of her promise to stay.

'That's the *arrangement*,' he would say, wagging a finger.

Laura was never in a hurry to leave his bed, in any case. There was something eternally comforting and secure about lying there, idly watching the revolution of star shapes from his nightlight wheel across the ceiling and allowing her mind to float in neutral, bobbing about gently like a cork on water. Daydreaming, she supposed it was; or duskdreaming, more accurately: a peacefully unfocused contrast to the rest of life, which was so full of urgent need and demand. Those times on Jack's bed, while he fought not to sleep, were some of the most luxurious of her days.

His breathing was now definitely the breathing of someone properly asleep. She peeled herself slowly off his bed until she was upright and bent to look at him, his thumb half out of his slack mouth. She wouldn't kiss him. Experience had taught them both that kissing him sometimes meant an instant, confused and miserable re-awakening which meant he could then take a whole evening to settle again. Instead, she blew a kiss into the air and barely touched his shoulder with a forefinger. Then she went in to check on Adam, asleep on his knees as usual, his cheek pressed to the sheet, his nappy-padded bottom in the air, and crept downstairs into the lamplit kitchen.

Angus was standing by the table, his reading glasses pushed up onto his forehead, staring at his phone. 'Asleep?' he asked.

'Yes, at last. Is that my phone?'

Angus held it out. 'Sorry. All yours. It's a message from your brother.'

Laura took the phone. 'Nat? He never texts.'

'He has now.'

'Goodness,' Laura said. 'Did you read this? He's – wow, I've never known him like this. I think he's met someone. I think Nat has really *met* someone!' She looked up. Her expression was sober.

'What?' Angus said.

'Well,' Laura said, 'lovely and all that. For Nat, anyway. But if he's met someone, what about Emmy?'

CHAPTER EIGHT

Prue had always made a point of being straightforward. She did in fact, Rose often remarked, pride herself on it. So she didn't just turn up unannounced at the mews house, to catch her sister in an unguarded moment, but rang ahead to say that she was coming up to London for the day and intended to see Rose and – if possible, although she made it plain that it was her settled wish – to meet Tyler.

'Of course I'll meet her,' Tyler said. 'I'd like to. In fact, as she's your only sister, I'd love to. Shall we give her lunch here?'

Rose was brushing her hair. Prue would notice her new highlights. She would also notice that Rose had a leather skirt and suede ankle boots and that her face had, these days, what could only be described as a glow. It had an inner light that cosmetic companies were always promising could be achieved with the application of a new and miraculously engineered foundation, but that in truth only ever came from a state of mind and heart. She couldn't, she thought, leaning forward towards the mirror, manufacture that shine in her eyes. They'd been, all her life, perfectly acceptable unre-markable brown eyes, but these days they had a luminousness, a depth and texture that someone who had known them all their life couldn't fail to observe. And, being Prue, also comment on.

From where he was sitting on the edge of Rose's bed, putting his socks on, Tyler said,

'Selfishly, I rather hope she'll be struck by how gorgeous you look.'

Rose turned from the mirror. 'D'you know, I wasn't thinking exactly that because I've never thought of myself as anything more than perfectly OK to look at, but I was sort of realizing . . .' She stopped.

He said tenderly, 'Of course you were.'

She ducked her head. 'Oh, Tyler . . .'

'You're a beautiful woman.'

'No, I'm not.'

He got up and crossed the room to stand behind her so that he could regard her over her shoulder, in the mirror. 'Look at you.'

'Oh.'

'You look all of forty-two.'

'Stop it!'

He put his arms round her from behind and rested his chin on her shoulder. He said,

'Do you like our faces together like this?'

She nodded. He turned slightly to kiss her cheek.

'Together,' he said.

She waited, still holding her hairbrush.

'I think . . .' Tyler said. 'Well, I think two things. I think we should invite your sister for lunch here. And I think we should go shopping for an engagement ring.'

Rose's mouth fell open a little. 'Goodness.'

He released her slightly and stepped back. 'It's not a major decision for you, like selling this house now, is it? It's something we are completely agreed on. And, my darling, it will be something we can show Prue together, won't it? In fact, why can't Prue be the first person to see us officially engaged?' He smiled at her in the mirror. 'Shall we look for something old? What do you say, future Mrs Masson, to an aquamarine?'

———

Prue arrived with a bunch of supermarket tulips for Rose – an uncompromising yellow – and the air of one who is resolutely opposed to being charmed. She kissed Rose briskly and glanced at Tyler as if she were assessing him as a possible new accountant.

'Hello, dear. These are for you and the label on them promises that they will last for five days, which is the very least I would expect. I don't know what you have done to your hair, but it's very pretty. Dyed it, have you?'

'It's highlights, Prue.'

'Ah. Yes. Well, you look very bonny altogether. I imagine leather is very practical, isn't it?'

'Prue,' Rose said, moving the tulips to the crook of her arm, 'this is Tyler.'

Prue regarded him. 'I guessed as much.'

He held his hand out and after a moment's apparent consideration, Prue shook it.

Tyler said, smiling, 'I suppose I'd better not kiss you.'

'You suppose quite right, Mr Masson.'

'Tyler. Please.'

Prue transferred her gaze back to her sister. 'To be perfectly frank, Rosie, I really need to see you alone.'

Rose tried to laugh it off. 'I don't want to be ticked off by you as well, Prue. The children have been bad enough as it is.'

'They have reason.'

'Tell you what,' Tyler said, as if an illuminating thought had just struck him, 'I'll go out. Why don't I go out and leave you two alone together, and then I'll come back at lunchtime.'

'Suppose,' Rose said, 'I don't want to be left alone with Prue?'

'It's quite safe,' Prue said. 'I only have things to ask, not things to say. That seems to me, Mr – Tyler, a very sensible suggestion.'

His arm twitched, as if he had been about to put it round Rose's shoulders, and thought better of it. He said, still smiling, to Prue, 'Thank you.'

She lifted her capacious cross-body bag over her head and shoulders, and handed it grandly to him. 'I like a practical suggestion.'

Tyler, stowing Prue's bag on a hall chair and then coming quickly to help her out of her padded coat, said to Rose, 'I can continue our jewellery trawl.'

'Jewellery?' Prue demanded.

He removed the padded coat and hung it on the newel post of the staircase.

'Tyler,' Rose said, almost pleadingly.

'Yes,' he said to Prue. 'Jewellery. We've been looking for an engagement ring. We really hoped – or, at least, *I* did – that we could find one to show you today, but so far nothing has been quite right. Has it, Rosie?'

Rose shook her head.

'What happened to the one William gave you?' Prue asked, almost accusingly.

'I sold it,' Rose said. 'It paid for the twins to go skiing and Laura and Angus to buy a new hot-water tank.'

'And now you want another.'

'No,' Rose said, 'I don't. I mean, I don't not, but I don't need another ring.'

'I do, though,' Tyler said. 'I want her to have a ring given to her by me. I want people to look at her left hand and know why she is wearing an engagement ring.'

Prue looked at him thoughtfully. 'Do you now?'

He returned the look. 'Yes, I do.'

'Look what I've got?'

'No,' Tyler said. 'No. It's not about possession. It's about my amazement, my . . . my *rapture* that she has agreed to marry me.'

Prue moved back towards the front door and unlatched it. She opened it wide and made a sweeping, ushering gesture. 'Then I think, Mr Masson, that that is your cue to leave us alone together for an hour. Don't you?'

———

'He's very personable,' Prue said, settling herself into an armchair with her chosen glass of bitter lemon. 'I'll give him that. And nice manners. Tactful.' She surveyed her sister. 'You look extremely well, Rosie. Quite apart from your hair, that is. I'm intrigued by your hair. I don't remember it ever being so thick before. In fact, I don't remember it being the kind of *asset* it plainly is now.'

Rose put her own glass of water on a side table and settled

herself, with as much nonchalance as she could manage, on the sofa. She said firmly, 'I'm happy, Prue.'

'Mm.'

'I don't just mean I'm excited to have someone in love with me. I mean that I feel safe. I feel safe in the way he loves me. Of course it's lovely being in love, but it's even lovelier not being anxious, not feeling that he's being comparative, not worrying that he'd love me more if I were just a bit different.'

'Ah,' Prue said. She took a thoughtful sip of her drink. 'And might the unspoken corollary of that be that I wouldn't know what you were talking about?'

Rose sat very still, her suede-booted feet together almost primly. 'That hasn't crossed my mind. What I am trying to convey to you is that I haven't lost my head.'

'Why do you think I might suspect you had?'

Rose shrugged. She looked out of the French doors to the garden where there was a green glaze on the shrubs as the new young leaves began to emerge.

'Is that,' Prue persisted, 'what you think your children think?'

Rose went on gazing at the garden.

'Is it?'

'I hate being out of step with them,' she said eventually.

'And they are used to being your priority. They have come first with you all their lives.'

Rose switched her gaze to her lap. 'Laura has told me that it is my life. That I must live my life the way I want to live it.'

'And the twins?'

'I think,' Rose said unhappily, 'that the twins and I have got thoroughly at odds with each other. Somehow.'

Prue crossed one trainered ankle over another. She said, 'Wasn't Nat right about making you see a solicitor?'

'I suppose so.'

'Rosie,' Prue said sternly, 'don't be childish. Although I always think that using that adjective is very unfair to children. What I mean is, that refusing to understand your legal position would be a deliberate act of immaturity. Nat was quite right to insist on it. Just as he is quite within his rights to ask you to think, very seriously, about why you insist on getting married. I'll ask you the same, Rosie. Why on earth, after all you've been through, all you've survived, all you've achieved, why do you want to get *married*?'

Very slowly, Rose lifted her gaze from her lap and looked at her sister.

'I love him.'

Prue waved the hand not holding her glass of bitter lemon. 'Not a reason.'

'He loves me. He has never proposed to anyone before. He wants the world to know I am his wife.'

'He,' Prue said with emphasis. 'He. He. He. What about *you*?'

'I love him,' Rose repeated, unblinking. 'I'm in love with him. Nobody has ever made me feel as remarkable and as complete and as safe as Tyler makes me feel.'

'All descriptions,' Prue said steadily, 'of being in love. None of them, as far as I can see, good, sound reasons to be married.'

Rose looked back down at her hands, at her left hand where one day this as yet unbought aquamarine would sit.

She said simply, 'I just want to.'

There was a silence. Then Prue replied gravely, 'Do you?'

Rose nodded. She said, almost in a whisper, 'I really do. I can't explain it to the twins, because it seems almost improper somehow, but I just want to. Long to. Perhaps a part of me wants to get marriage right, for once?'

Prue took another swallow from her glass. 'How long have you known him?'

'Four months. Well, fifteen weeks, to be precise.'

'Exactly.'

'What d'you mean, exactly?'

'I mean that it's very fast. If Emmy said she wanted to marry someone she'd known since Christmas, say, you'd tell her to wait a bit, wouldn't you?'

'I'm not Emmy,' Rose said, 'I'm a grandmother. I've been around all kinds of houses she hasn't even encountered yet.'

'Rosie,' Prue said. 'Just wait.'

'What?'

'I said, just wait. Be engaged if you must, but don't do anything else that might limit your options.'

Rose said nothing.

'For example,' Prue went on, 'this house.'

Rose's head jerked up. 'What about this house?'

Prue swivelled her head to survey the room. 'A house like this, Rose, has to come into the equation.'

Rose took a deep breath. She said, 'Tyler isn't interested in this house.'

'Oh?'

'In fact,' Rose said in a rush, 'he is so not interested in this house that he'd like me to sell it and give the proceeds to my children and then he and I could go and find a cottage in the country together.'

Prue put her glass down and clasped her hands in her lap. She regarded her sister solemnly.

'Oh, Rosie.'

'Yes?'

'What do you feel about that?'

Rose looked at the celling. Then she looked out at the garden again. Then she suddenly flung her arms wide in a clumsy gesture and said, with a kind of anguish, 'Awful. If you want to know.'

———

It was really difficult, Emmy thought, to talk to Laura. Laura always said that she was – soap-opera phrase – *there* for her, but then she said the same to Angus, and the children, and their mother, and Nat, and her patients. It was fine in theory, as an attitude, but in practice it meant something quite different. It meant that Laura was almost always giving her attention to some person or cause that was absolutely unimpeachable, which in turn meant that you were earning yourself moral black marks by trying to claim even fifteen minutes of her focus. Emmy had sometimes wondered if this elusiveness had been one of the most powerfully attractive elements of Laura for Angus, and whether, one day, he might suddenly find it as pointless and exasperating as it had once been a turn-on. In Emmy's view, it wasn't worth risking relationships by taking such chances. But then, she wasn't Laura, and Laura had inherited from their father just the same quietly determined confidence as he had, even if, since she was female, it had a subtler manifestation. Laura loved Angus, but she didn't need him as he manifestly needed her. As Emmy had always known she needed Nat, and had, until this week, assumed that dependency was returned in full: was in fact – Emmy liked this word – symbiotic.

When Nat asked her to come and meet an actress he'd met called Jess Ballantyne, and had sounded elated and – and, *estranged*, in a way he never had in all his life before, Emmy's first appalled impulse had been to call a girlfriend. Her second impulse, hot on the heels of her first, was not to expose herself, not to divulge how violently, primitively, she felt abandoned and overlooked, to anyone outside this family. In the old days, she told herself, she would have gone to talk to Rose, but that was out of the question at the moment. The only thing to do, she decided, was to send uncompromising WhatsApp messages to Laura, entreating a conversation. She didn't actually type the words, 'as my big sister, you owe me', but she implied them in a way even Laura couldn't mistake. But even if she couldn't mistake them, Laura could just sidestep them in that blithe but intractable fashion that seemed to come so naturally to her. And made other people, Emmy thought crossly, making the compli- cated tube journey to waylay Laura at her west London surgery, go far more than the extra mile for her in conse- quence.

Laura's surgery was a member of the West London Group Practices and her colleagues teased her about being their token white Englishwoman. With the exception of their senior partner, who had done his initial medical training in Dhaka, they had all been students, and junior doctors, in the National Health Service, and Laura, except for her skin colour, was no exception. Nor was she an exception in having a doctor father. Five of her eight general-practitioner col- leagues were the daughters and sons of doctors, even if none of their parents had worked in the kind of shiny new premises that now housed Laura's practice, complete with a primary-coloured play area floored in plastic-covered foam rubber. Stepping among the babies – Emmy was, being unfamiliar with them, nervous around babies – she arrived at the reception desk and announced to a girl in telephonist's headphones behind it that she was Doctor Mayhew's sister.

The girl didn't smile. She had an immaculate head of complicated cornrow plaits and painted nails decorated with Union Jacks. She said only, 'I'll tell her.'

'Could you say it's Emmy?'

The girl indicated the line of chairs set out for patients, with a flash of flags. 'Wait there.'

'Well, I will, but I'd be really grateful if you'd tell Laura it's me.'

The girl said, into her microphone, 'Your sister's here, Doctor Mayhew,' and then, not looking at Emmy, 'I'll tell her to wait.'

Emmy marched over to the line of chairs and sat down with emphasis. She had never been in Laura's new surgery before, with its Scandinavian skylights and general air of trying to look anything but medical. There was even, she noticed, a coffee machine, and a room designated for baby changing, and round the walls hung cheerful exhortations not to smoke or take drugs, to eat fruit and vegetables – to be part, in fact, Emmy thought sourly, of a jaunty modern population who had no trouble in being responsible for their own health. She looked at her phone and checked her messages. She looked at the spring sky fading through the skylights. She remembered how she had told her boss that there was a family crisis and she had to go and talk to her famously busy sister who was a doctor and so, you know? Her boss had looked very sympathetic and respectful. Of course Emmy should go: Emmy should go *now*, in fact. So she had, and here she was, sitting on a moulded plywood chair in the reception area of Laura's surgery, waiting for Laura to finish having all the time in the world for everyone who wasn't her sister.

Of the eight doctors holding surgeries, Laura was the last but one to finish. She came out of the glazed door that led to the corridor of designated doctors' rooms and made for Emmy with a wide smile that completely quelled Emmy's mounting temper.

'Em. *So* sorry. One thing after another today. Have you been here ages?'

'Rather.'

Laura sat on the chair next to Emmy's.

'Why didn't you phone me?'

'I did. I WhatsApped you. Twice.'

Laura made a clucking noise of despair.

'Oh Lord. I didn't look at my family phone. It drives Angus mad that I only look at my work phone. He gave me this one especially.'

'I know.'

'Em,' Laura said, 'I'm really sorry. I am. But that's that. I'm not saying it any more. Come home with me and tell me why you're here. It isn't an accident or anything, is it? It isn't Mum?'

She stood up. Slowly, Emmy stood too. She said, 'No, it isn't Mum. Mum's fine. It's – oh, Laura. It's Nat.'

'What's happened? Is he OK?'

'Oh yes,' Emmy said. She attempted a laugh. 'He's fine. He's – *really* fine.'

Laura got her car keys out of her bag. 'What then?'

'I'll tell you in the car.'

Laura put a hand out and held her sister's arm. 'Tell me now. What's the matter? Or can I guess?'

Emmy looked round her. The waiting room was almost empty and the girls on the reception desk were packing up for the night. She said, 'I think he's fallen for someone.'

'Yes,' Laura said.

'I think,' Emmy went on, taking no notice, 'that he's *really* fallen. That he's smitten. Completely – crazy.' She looked at Laura as if she might cry. She said in a whisper, 'I've never known him like this. I – I – Laura, I don't know what to do.'

———

Tyler, Rose could not help noticing, had bought the latest copy of *Country Life*, and was studying the pages of property advertisements with far more than just idle curiosity. He looked very relaxed, sitting there in one of her armchairs, his legs crossed and the magazine propped casually along his thighs, but he was concentrating in a way that made her feel, for the first time in the months that she had known him, a distinct twinge of tension.

Lunch had gone well. In fact, lunch had gone remarkably well. Prue had been not just affable to Tyler but almost flirtatious, if someone now so resolutely impervious to the attractions of the opposite sex could ever be so described. Rose had watched her responding to Tyler's questions about her past career, and felt a surge of pride in both of them for quite different reasons, and later, assembling a coffee tray despite Tyler's offer to do it for her, a swell of sheer optimism that Prue, at least, might be seeing not just something of what she herself saw in Tyler, but was also feeling a straightforward pleasure in seeing Rose so happy. When she said goodbye to Prue, she took her sister in her arms for a proper embrace and thanked her warmly for coming. Prue, zipped up stoutly in her padded coat, and slightly flushed with both lunch and the comparative heat of London, allowed herself to be hugged but merely said, 'Stay in touch, Rosie. OK?' and went up the mews towards Harley Street with the same determined gait that she used for the Sussex Downs.

The moment she was gone, Tyler said, 'Was I all right?'

Rose nodded. Then she smiled and kissed him.

'You were. You so were. She really liked you.'

'I liked her. I was impressed by her. D'you think she was reassured that I don't have unprincipled designs on you?'

Rose nodded again. He caught her as she went past him.

'I really don't,' he said. 'You do know that?'

She paused.

'I do.'

'If you really don't want a ring . . .'

'I'd love a ring.'

He took her chin in his hand. 'Really?'

'Really.'

But now he was looking at *Country Life* with a different kind of focus, almost detached from her, as if he had a purpose that didn't need her consent, or even her approval. He was wearing a denim shirt, open-necked, under a soft grey tweed jacket which was exactly the colour of his hair. He looked, as Prue had described him, personable. Highly, attractively personable. But . . .

Rose took a breath.

'Tyler.'

'Sweetheart,' he said at once, his gaze still on the magazine.

'Could – I ask you something?'

He put a hand flat on the magazine page to mark his place. 'Anything.'

'I don't want to ask it. I feel rather . . . shy, asking it.'

He smiled at her. 'Ask, Rosie. Ask whatever you want to.'

'How . . .' She stopped.

'Go on.'

'How would you pay for a ring?'

He laughed. He said, 'With money, my darling.'

'But – have you *got* any money?'

'Rosie. Sweetheart. I have money to buy a ring.' He picked up the magazine with both hands and gave it a little shake. 'I have money to contribute to a cottage. You will never find me embarrassing you about money.'

She sat down on the arm of the companion chair to his. She said, playing with the earpieces of her reading glasses, 'I just don't quite know – where your money comes from. What you have. I hate talking like this. I really do. But . . .'

'Prue told you to ask me?'

'No,' Rose said, 'Prue didn't mention how you might be fixed for money.'

'Really? All my life, people have talked about money, asked me about money, boasted how much more money they have than I do and what clout it gives them.'

'Tyler.'

'What?'

'Please stop,' Rose said. 'Don't. That's just what I was afraid of, that you'd feel insulted or threatened or misjudged.'

'I don't,' he said. He was smiling again. 'I don't in the least. But I promise I have enough money to buy you a ring.' He threw the magazine on the floor. 'Did you, now I think of it, tell Prue that I am so far from being mercenary that I suggested you sell this house and give most of the proceeds to your children?'

Rose looked down at her reading glasses.

'I did.'

'And?'

'She didn't really react.'

'Didn't she?'

'No,' Rose said, 'she just asked me how such a suggestion made *me* feel.'

Tyler waited a moment. Then he said quietly, 'And?'

She sighed. She swung her spectacles by one arm, and then she put them on and looked at him through them.

'To be honest with you,' she said, 'not good.'

———

Laura made a bed up for her sister in the little room on a half-landing at the back of the house that she used as a study. It had a built-in desk, and a bank of sockets above it for Laura's laptop and phone chargers, and a hard-cushioned sofa which extended into a bed, filling the whole room so that Laura's office chair was rammed under her desk. She found a spare duvet, and pillows, and a pair of soft old pyjamas of hers, and a new toothbrush, still in its packet, and put all these on the pulled-out sofa bed for Emmy. Then she went back down to the kitchen.

Emmy was sitting by the table, with Angus, drinking wine. Laura and Angus did not drink wine in the week, or if Laura was working at weekends, but Angus had wordlessly put a wine glass on the table when he saw Emmy, and taken a bottle of Chilean Muscadet out of the fridge, and she had drunk two thirds of it. She had also, round mouthfuls of one of Angus's weekday specials of salmon steaks cooked in soy sauce and ginger, cried a good deal. She admitted that although she hadn't seen Jess Ballantyne perform live, she had Googled her and found a clip on YouTube of her singing 'Over the Rainbow' in an Edinburgh Festival Fringe cabaret, and she was both hot-looking and had an amazing voice. In fact she was, said Emmy between sniffs, something of a stunner, and if Emmy then met her and discovered that she was nice as well – Nat obviously couldn't be trusted to be any kind of judge of that – it would just add to the misery of everything.

At some point Angus, who often marvelled at how different two sisters could be, said,

'But Em, love, surely all this has occurred to you before? I mean, it might just as well have been you as Nat. Surely by your age you've been through all this?'

'Twenty-seven isn't old!' Emmy said indignantly.

'No, but by twenty-seven, most people have had at least one major relationship.'

'Not us,' Emmy said. 'Not me. Not Nat. Sure, we've had friends that were a bit more than that, but we always talked about it, we always asked each other what we thought, we kind of never let *go* of each other, whatever else was going on, and this time Nat has just gone ahead and plunged in without even telling me he was seeing her, not a word, not a single word until he suddenly wants to show her off to me as if – as if I'm supposed to *congratulate* him.'

Laura said, 'It is his life, Em, you know. One or other of you, it was bound to happen.'

'You always think that,' Emmy said crossly. 'You always do this tolerance, live-and-let-live thing. But you aren't a twin. You don't *know*.'

'I know enough,' Laura said, 'to predict that if you don't embrace this relationship of Nat's, the only person who'll suffer is you.'

Emmy sighed. 'I know. It's just so much, all at once.'

'What is?'

Emmy looked at them both across the table. 'All this romance,' she said. 'All this falling in love stuff. All this "can't you be happy for me" nonsense. First Mum, and now Nat.' She looked down at the smeared plate that had held her salmon. Then she said, 'And you know what I'm thinking, don't you? I might as well say it out loud, seeing as you are both so priggishly, thoroughly, married. So. What about *me*?'

CHAPTER NINE

Rose said she knew nothing about Berkshire. She'd never even been there. Well, she'd been through it, of course, on motorways, but she'd never stopped in it or looked at it or considered it. Sussex she knew a bit, East Sussex because of Prue and her school in Lewes, and now her cottage in Wivelsfield Green, but Berkshire was as unknown to her as . . . well, as Pembrokeshire or Cumbria were. So looking at this admittedly charming-seeming cottage with its thatched roof and views to something called Bucklebury Common was as strange to her as if Tyler was proposing they consider a Scottish castle or a Cornish cave.

Tyler said he understood. He completely saw how she felt. It was a huge change, but then their meeting and falling for each other was bound to create change in itself, wasn't it, a change from being alone, from being directionless, from fighting the world without an ally? And you couldn't expect change not to disconcert you, particularly if you were over the age – as they both definitely were – when change was only exhilarating.

He took her hands. She noticed that whenever he needed reassurance about anything, he touched her. He was always warm, when he touched her, always a robust physical presence who could be relied upon for his good humour as much as for his perpetual positivity. He held her hands and fixed her with his steady but unforceful gaze.

'I just want to look at the cottage, Rosie. I just want *you* to look at it, to start getting your head round living somewhere else.'

Rose wanted to say, 'Don't say that,' and didn't. She looked back at him.

'Wood Cottage,' she said, and her tone sounded mocking to her.

'Wood Cottage,' he said, seriously. 'Three bedrooms, an inglenook fireplace, beamed walls, a conservatory kitchen . . .'

'What does that mean?'

'It means that it's bigger than it was, and modernized, and light.'

'All that garden . . .'

'I thought,' Tyler said, 'that you loved a garden. I know you're a good gardener.'

Rose said frankly, 'I'm scared.'

'What of? Living with me?'

She glanced round her. 'No. Living – away from here.'

He brought her hands up to his mouth and kissed them.

'That's only because you never have. It's a radical notion, I grant you, but that's why I want to start getting your head gently, gently round it.'

She said nothing. He laid her hands against his chest and covered them with his own.

'Sweetheart. Rosie. This isn't *the* cottage. It's just the first cottage we look at. That's all. Think of it as a kind of – liberation.'

'Liberation!'

'Yes,' Tyler said. His hands on hers were warm and supple, not imprisoning, just there. 'Freedom from all these decisions about lawyers, from struggling to afford to stay here, from worrying about what the twins think. You'll be released, Rosie. A released woman.'

She looked at him.

'Will I?'

'Of course you will. Plus you'll have the companionship of me. Someone to make the bed with. Someone to go on holiday with. Someone, sweetheart, to do nothing with at weekends. You can teach me to garden.'

'Tyler . . .'

'Yes.'

'Tyler,' Rose said, 'I love the idea of us doing nothing together.'

'There you go.'

'But I don't quite get this thing about liberation.'

He pulled her hands up to encircle his neck, and then slid his own round her torso to embrace her. He laid his cheek next to hers.

'Let's take it step by step,' he said. 'You sell this house and you give three quarters of the proceeds to Laura and Nat and Emmy, so that they have their own assets from your estate twenty-five years before they were expecting them. So they're happy, and you're happy because you don't have to go down all these legal asset-protection byways. And then, with the quarter that's left from the sale of the house, plus whatever I can get out of America, we buy something like Wood Cottage – I know, I know, it's only a first idea, a sort of *metaphor*, if you like – and it can be in your name only so the asset is always yours, and we live there, in a new community that only knows us as a married pair, happy ever after and unencumbered by any anxiety that the children might have. See?'

Rose was gazing over his shoulder. Her eyes came to rest on a painting she had bought at the Affordable Art Fair in Battersea Park five years before, an abstract of freesias in a glass vase against a dark background. It was, oddly for a flower painting, both mysterious and slightly dangerous. It represented some particular kind of release in Rose's life, some taking charge, pleasing herself, buying something with money she had earned, on a whim. She blinked. No doubt the painting would look as strong and as significant on the half-timbered walls of Wood Cottage. Wouldn't it?

She said, 'I love the idea of giving money to the children when they don't expect it.'

He tightened his hold slightly.

'Yes.'

'And I love the idea of living with you.'

She could hear that he was smiling.

'Early-morning tea,' he said. 'Toddles round the garden when we get home from anywhere else. Evenings in front of the inglenook.'

She was laughing.

'Stop it,' she said. 'You make it sound so elderly.'

'I only meant to sound a contrast to being on our own, rattling about waiting for the next wave of life to pick us up and carry us somewhere.'

She took her face gradually away from his.

'I know,' she said, 'I'm teasing.'

He regarded her almost fiercely. 'I love you.'

'I know,' she said again.

'And I want you to be happy and free from worrying about what anyone thinks.'

'The twins—'

'The twins,' Tyler said, 'will have enough money to pay off their mortgages. Laura and Angus can buy a house with a garden big enough for those boys to play cricket and football in.' He dropped his arms to link his hands behind her waist. He said tenderly, 'All because their lovely mother is so generous.'

Rose smiled at him.

'It would make me such a happy mum.'

'Of course it would.' He kissed her nose. 'They are so lucky to have you.'

She looked up at the ceiling, leaning back luxuriously in his embrace.

'I love giving them things,' Rose said. 'Don't you think giving your children things is the best feeling in the world?'

'No,' Tyler said. 'Even if I love that you do.'

She tipped her head back. 'You're so generous to me.'

'Don't know about that.'

'Tyler,' Rose said, suddenly focusing, 'Tyler. Enough about me and what would be nice for me. What about you? What would you like to happen?'

He smiled at her. Then he let her go and put his hands in his pockets.

'Me?' he said. 'What would I like to happen? Well, Rosie, what I would really like to happen next, and soon, is for you to get this house valued.'

———

Mallory was packing. She had decided to leave behind almost everything she had brought from America, and to return with only the things – clothes, jewellery, books, a Victorian hand mirror she had found in Camden Lock – that she had acquired during her four months in London. They had been an impressive four months in the sense that they had impressed themselves distinctly on her; the theatre, her flatmates, her theatre friends, Kilburn with its half-in, half-out-of-central-London feeling, its big-city vibe coupled with its strong sense of self. Gathering stuff up around the flat made Mallory feel emotional and nostalgic, as if she was saying goodbye to a powerful and vivid life experience that she wouldn't readily know again, and to a particular kind of autonomy that you can only have in a community to which you don't belong. Disentangling scarves and sweater sleeves from random piles of clothing – Jess Ballantyne especially had a completely communal notion of ownership – made her feel unsteady and tearful, as if she was saying goodbye to something whose absence she would feel keenly and for a long time.

And then there was Tyler. There was no getting round the fact that Rose was a lovely lady and that Tyler was besotted with her. There was also no avoiding his palpable relief at being back home in England, where his instincts were to understand what was going on and he shared the national sense of humour. Mallory had always prided herself on her irony, her cool and sceptical view of human frailty, but irony like hers was two a penny in England. She longed for something essentially American again, but at the same time dreaded it, dreaded seeing it from a newly Old-World perspective, dreaded not being in London any more, dreaded not being part of the company, settling her stage wig nightly over her red hair, extracting her nose stud and putting it in a chipped china egg cup patterned with a painted chicken, for safety.

'When I'm gone,' Mallory thought, folding black leggings and black T-shirts with a carelessness that would have exasperated her mother, 'will I ever have been here? Will they forget all about me, the American actress with the English father who chose to stay behind? Will anything I've done really matter, in the long run? Will my being here have made the smallest difference to anybody?'

Tyler had tried to ring her. She'd had four missed calls from him, two without a message and two – the last two – asking her to ring him back. The final message also said that he wanted to take her to the airport to see her off, so would she please tell him her flight details. He'd sounded almost peremptory in the last call, exasperated, even, and part of her – the more adult part – couldn't blame him. She was, after all, not returning his calls deliberately. She confessed to herself that she didn't want to, so she wasn't. But at the same time, she didn't want to trail out to Heathrow airport on her own, and join the shuffle through security burdened with the isolation of anonymity. Tyler, she told herself angrily, needed to know that as a father, he had got his priorities all wrong even if she was ultimately the one who suffered.

It was no good expecting any of her flatmates to see her off either. Two of them were already focused on their next jobs and had adopted a manner of lavishly affectionate but fundamentally distracted behaviour towards Mallory, embracing her with one arm while checking their phones with the other. As for Jess, with whom Mallory, as her understudy, believed she had established a real rapport, she had become as elusive as a shadow once she had embarked on her relationship with Nat Woodrowe. She was *amazed* at herself, she said to Mallory. He was in every way completely, utterly not her type; a City boy from just the kind of middle-class, conventional background she had been brought up to despise so thoroughly. He might even, she said, rolling her eyes as if she had been beguiled by enchantment into falling for an acknowledged monster, vote Conservative. But here she was, madder about him than she ever had been about anybody. She gave a peal of self-deprecating laughter, as if her feelings for Nat Woodrowe were nothing to do with choice, and therefore no responsibility of hers whatsoever, and drifted out of the flat, leaving sheer black stockings discarded in the shower and a breath of scent and cigarette smoke in the air.

Mallory sat down abruptly on the bed. It was ridiculous to feel like this, ridiculous. She was, after all, more than used to her own company, to fending for herself. Even if her mother had still been alive, she had never been the kind of mother you could call to say you felt a bit lost, a bit sad, a bit lonely, and who could be relied upon to say consoling and cosy maternal things in return. Cindy had been cool in every sense, in the way Mallory had always prided herself on being cool. Until now, that is. Until it came to going back to New York, leaving her palpably happy father behind in his home country.

Mallory scrolled through all the contacts on her phone, all the hundreds of people and services that had been added by her over the years. She couldn't remember half of them, she realized, couldn't recall why she had had the momentary need to be in touch with Maharani Taxis or someone called Beau Tiranti. One day, when she either had absolutely nothing else to do or was in the mood for some ferocious editing of her life in general, she would apply herself to some serious deleting. One day. She spun on rapidly through the numbers and the names. One day that was, most definitely, not today.

Then she halted. There was Emmy Woodrowe, Nat's twin sister, whose name she had added that weird evening in the hotel courtyard bar, when they were all swapping phone numbers in a pathetic show of extended-family solidarity, to please Rose and Tyler. Rose, she remembered, had looked haunted. Emmy, sitting as close to her mother as she could without actually sitting on her lap, had looked furious. A pretty girl, with her long brown hair held off her face with combs, but a furious pretty girl who pointedly had hardly looked at Mallory's father. She had drunk two large glasses of wine, Mallory had observed, just casually knocking them back in the English way, as if wine and water were indistinguishable. And then, Jess said, laughing it off as if it were nobody's loss but her own, Emmy had refused to meet her twin brother's new girlfriend. Well, not exactly *refused*, in so many words, but just not responded to the request, in a way that made it perfectly clear what she felt about Nat reordering the female priorities in his life.

Almost before she knew what she was doing, Mallory had dialled Emmy's number. She sat there, on the edge of the bed above Kilburn High Street, and held her breath. She would let it ring five times. No. Six. She would let it ring out, and then she would end the call. She wouldn't leave a message. Or perhaps she would, perhaps she would just say she'd rung to say goodbye—

'Hi,' Emmy said. Her voice was flat, without a question in it, slightly indistinct.

Mallory took a breath. 'It's Mallory.'

There was a pause and then Emmy said, as if carefully enunciating, 'Wow. Is it? I didn't look.'

Mallory said courteously, 'I hope it isn't too late?'

'No,' Emmy said. 'Not. Too late, mean.'

'Are you OK?'

'Mm.'

'Emmy,' Mallory said, sitting upright on the bed, 'what's the matter?'

There was another pause and then Emmy said, 'Don't know.'

'Are you drinking? Emmy, are you drunk?'

'Maybe,' Emmy said.

'Are you at home? Are you in your apartment?'

'Oh yes.'

Mallory glanced at her watch. She said, 'I'm coming over.'

'No.'

'Yes. Yes, you – you shouldn't be on your own. And,' she suddenly felt full of courage, 'nor should I.'

'What?'

'Emmy,' Mallory said, standing up, 'Emmy. Don't drink any more. Don't. What are you drinking?'

'Oh,' Emmy said, as if the question was of no consequence. 'Vodka.'

'Well, stop. Stop drinking vodka. I'm on my way to you.'

'Why?' Emmy said. 'Why would you care?'

'I do. I get it. I *get* it.'

'Yeah.'

'Please, Emmy. Please let me come.' She looked down at her open suitcase, at the sad disorder of it. 'Please,' Mallory said again.

She heard Emmy sigh. She remembered one of her drama

teachers in New York telling the class, 'Trust your instincts. *Trust* them. Don't overlay everything with reason, give your intuition its head.' Did that sigh mean a surrender or merely that the vodka had removed Emmy's capacity to decide?

'OK,' Emmy said at last. She sounded infinitely weary. 'OK. Bring soup.' And then she laughed, a short bark of laughter that had, Mallory thought with her new and awe-struck knowledge of Shakespearean English, nothing of real mirth in it.

———

Seth Masson had enjoyed replying to Emmy's post on his Facebook page. Yuhui, who was of a grave and meticulous bent, had researched the word 'pedant' for him – possibly old Italian via even older French – and he'd had a happy time devising a reply and weaving into it the suggestion that Emmy might be a person over-fond of making superfine dis-tinctions, and been momentarily disappointed when she appeared to have tired of the sparring match already by fail-ing to respond. He mentioned it to his father in one of their infrequent phone calls, and his father, ever disposed to make light of anything potentially troublesome, said to forget it, it was an English thing – a kind of tease to cover a feeling of awkwardness.

'Awkward?' Seth said. 'Why the hell should she feel awk-ward?'

'Because you are about to be related by marriage, and you've never met.'

'But,' Seth said, '*she* messaged me. She started it.'

Tyler said, 'But she's English,' as if that explained every-thing.

Seth waited a moment, and then he said, 'You sure about this marriage thing? You sure you need to get married, again?'

'Very sure.'

'Daddy, Yuhui and I are in it for the long haul but we don't feel the need to get married.'

'Then I'm different,' Tyler said genially. 'I do.'

'Uh-huh,' Seth said. His mind was slipping off his father's plans in England, his father's fiancée's daughter's incomprehensibility, and returning to the familiar and happy haven of baking. He could sense a palpable relief in his brain, a thankful abandonment of a stony and inhospitable mental terrain for the welcome landscape of the known.

'Daddy,' Seth said, his voice gathering momentum, 'I've been approached by a packaging-giftware company. They have an idea for Doughboy gift packs, a box containing some of our sourdough starter, plus a disposable panibois and a dough scraper and a Doughboy apron and some hessian gloves. Under twenty-five bucks, they're suggesting. What do you think?'

Tyler said, too heartily, that he thought it sounded a splendid idea. And an excellent price. Seth then told him that business was so good, they needed to hire another baker, someone who understood gluten-free, someone to whom they could offer possibly twenty thousand dollars a year. What did Tyler think about that, for evidence of success? Tyler appeared to think nothing. He failed to respond.

'Daddy?' Seth said. 'Pa? Did you hear me?'

'It's Mallory,' Tyler said. 'I can't get hold of Mallory. She's flying back and I want to see her off and she won't answer her phone to me or respond to my messages.'

With difficulty, Seth pulled his mind back from sourdough.

'Mallory?'

'Yes,' Tyler said. 'Have you spoken to Mallory?'

'You know us, Daddy,' Seth said, 'we're lucky if we call each other on our birthdays.'

'You're no use, are you?' Tyler said cheerfully. 'No use to anyone except the bread fanatics like yourself.'

'He called me a fanatic,' Seth said later to Yuhui. 'Like I was a jihadi or something.'

She looked at him with her steady, serious Japanese gaze.

'He doesn't understand you, Seth.'

'No.'

She came to stand next to him. 'We have a *calling*.'

'Yes.'

'We are feeding minds and souls.'

He regarded her with respectful affection. He said, 'He can't find Mallory. She won't return his calls.'

Yuhui began to untie her Doughboy apron.

'She'll have her reasons,' she said.

———

Emmy said that Mallory should certainly ring her father. She said it with mock seriousness, wagging a finger, and Mallory made a face and said, squirming, that she really, really didn't want to. They had made a kind of pact together, over a lot of wine in Emmy's apartment, a defiant and happily infantile pact involving their both being abandoned children, children who were deeply disappointed by the selfish self-absorption of their parents (and brothers, Emmy added) and must henceforth make their way alone, like babes in the wood.

Mallory had slept the night on Emmy's sofa, her head pillowed on a mirrored cushion from India that left her right cheek printed with tiny indentations, and in the morning, hazy from the night before, they had agreed that Emmy would take time off work to come out to Heathrow with Mallory the next day, to be, she said, her send-off crowd. They also made a plan that Mallory would go back to Kilburn to collect her suitcase, and then return to Emmy's flat for her final night in London.

Emmy paused in front of the mirror, arranging her hair in long curls over her shoulders. She said, to the reflection of Mallory, sitting behind her on the crumpled sofa eating muesli, 'We didn't think we liked each other. Did we?'

Mallory put her forefinger into her mouth to dislodge a raisin from her teeth.

'Nope,' she said. 'We didn't.'

'And now,' Emmy said, twisting her hair, 'look what a little misfortune and a lot of alcohol can do.'

'Sugar,' Mallory said, 'I'm kicking myself for not realizing.'

Emmy began to giggle.

'About your father?'

Mallory made a wide gesture with her cereal spoon.

'About *you*, dollface. That you were cool.'

Emmy turned round to face her. 'We are united by misfortune.'

'Sure are.'

'But you will ring your father?'

'Um . . .'

'For *you*, Mallory, even if not for him.'

Mallory eyed her. 'And you'll meet Jess Ballantyne?'

'Not sure.'

'Yes you will, cupcake. If I will, you will.'

Emmy stooped to present a lightly clenched fist to Mallory.

'Sistah . . .'

Mallory touched Emmy's fist with her own.

'Sistah.'

'Wish you weren't going.'

Mallory put her bowl down and stood up. 'You come to New York.'

'I might.'

'I know a wonderful bar. In fact, several.'

'You have to ask yourself,' Emmy said, 'if they'd notice.'

'Who? What?'

Emmy picked up her jacket and began to slide her arms into the sleeves.

'Our families.'

'Does it matter?'

There was a pause. Emmy finished pulling on her jacket and picked up her bag. She said, not looking at Mallory, 'I've got an awful headache. And yes, I think it does.'

CHAPTER TEN

The young man Tyler had summoned from an estate agency to assess the value of the mews house introduced himself as Sherif Yilmaz. He wore an immaculate suit and his accent was as English public school as his haircut. The hand he extended to shake Rose's emerged, she noticed, from a beautifully laundered double-cuffed shirtsleeve. He glanced round the hallway with approval.

'Mrs Woodrowe. This is an exceptional property.'

Rose inclined her head. It struck her that if she had been able, somehow, to clasp the walls in her arms, she would have liked to do so. Standing behind her at the respectful distance dictated by her ownership, rather than his, Tyler said, 'It has a garage. And a garden. All in central London.'

Sherif Yilmaz had a clipboard in his hand and a smart-phone. He gestured with the latter.

'Would you mind if I took some pictures, Mrs Woodrowe?'

Rose didn't look at Tyler.

'Yes, I would, actually. As this is only a first visit.'

Tyler didn't speak, and Rose didn't look at him. She said to Sherif, 'This is just an assessment, you know. There is a lot to consider.'

'Rosie—'

'Houses,' Rose said firmly, 'are far more to us than just an investment. I know they are the biggest investment any of us makes in our lives, but very few of us can see them only as piggy banks.'

Sherif regarded her soberly. 'Absolutely, Mrs Woodrowe. That is the main reason for my going into the business.'

Tyler put a hand lightly on Rose's arm. 'Rosie . . .'

She didn't turn. She said, 'As long as that's understood.'

'I thought—'

'Shall I show you round, Mr Yilmaz? Or would you prefer to explore on your own?'

He put his phone in his pocket. He said, with elaborate courtesy, 'If you would permit me to look round alone, Mrs Woodrowe, I can make a better assessment.'

She turned away and made for the sitting room.

'Help yourself.'

Tyler followed her, having watched Sherif climb the stairs at a speed he was sure Rose would consider over-expedient. She was standing by the French doors looking at the garden through the glass.

'Sweetheart,' he said, 'I'm sorry.'

Rose went on looking. He came to stand behind her, not touching, merely standing.

'I'm sorry,' he said again, 'I really am. I shouldn't have said anything. I probably shouldn't even *be* here. This is none of my business. Are you angry that I organized him to come?'

'No,' Rose said.

'Are you – angry with me, somehow, anyway? Or are you just upset about the house?'

'That,' Rose said shortly.

'But—'

She spun round.

'I didn't think I'd be. I am so happy and excited about some aspects of the future, but for some reason, this is hard. Very hard. It's ridiculous. It's only a house, for God's sake.'

Tyler took her hands. 'Yes.'

'I don't know what it's about. Really I don't. But I feel all jangled up, having that boy here, knowing he's upstairs *appraising* it all, for what it's worth in money, for Christ's sake, only money. I kind of hate it even while I know it makes sense. Of course it does. Of course I want to be able to give money to the children, of *course* I do. But somehow it frightens me at the same time.'

He leaned forward slightly, holding her hands.

'What does, Rosie?'

She pulled her hands free. 'I don't know. I just feel frightened.'

'Of me? Surely not of me. The last thing I want or intend on this earth is for you to feel anything but utterly safe with me.'

She looked at him uncertainly.

'No. Not you.'

'Who then?'

'I don't know. Life, perhaps. Or myself. Perhaps I'm frightened by myself.'

He took a step closer. He said, 'That's what I'm here for. To see you are never frightened again. To make sure of it.'

'Tyler,' Rose said, 'we can't undo our lives up to this moment. We are as we are. We are what we've become. So I might not *want* to feel scared about selling this house, but I find that I am. Very. So I have to try and deal with that, and so do you. You've never lived anywhere that mattered to you, after all, have you?'

He said energetically, 'I'm longing to.'

'I get it. I understand that. I know it makes you want to get on with things. Well, I'm the reverse. I don't want to sell this house; I don't want to live somewhere else, however much I want to live a new life with you. I'm torn. I'm really torn. And you will simply have to be patient with that; you will have to go along at my pace rather than yours.'

He put his hands on her shoulders. 'Why?'

She looked at him directly.

'Don't make me spell it out.'

'Because you have more money than I do?'

She said nothing. He tried to smile.

'How sad,' he said.

'In what way? Sad that it should be so or sad that it isn't more romantic?'

'Both,' he said. He dropped his hands. 'Why can't we decide everything *together*? Do everything *together*?'

She reached out and laid a hand on his chest.

'I've had seven years of doing and deciding on my own. I can't flip the switch of those seven years just like that.'

'How long do you think it will take?'

'I have no idea. I'm still getting used to falling in love, after all.'

He said seriously, 'You *are* in love?'

'Oh yes.'

'Rosie . . .'

'What?'

'Sweetheart, I'm sorry. I'm sorry for rushing you. I don't want to rush you. I don't want you to do anything you don't want to at a pace that doesn't suit you. I want you to be safe and happy. I want you to feel like you've never felt before, in all your life.'

There was discreet throat-clearing from the doorway. They both glanced up. Sherif Yilmaz stood there wearing the expression of one who has consciously seen and heard nothing.

'I wonder,' he said, 'if I might look at this room and the kitchen? And the garden possibly?'

'Of course.'

'I have to say, Mrs Woodrowe, that from what I have seen so far, this is, as I said before, an exceptional property.'

'Oh,' Rose said. 'Yes. I know.'

'How very gratifying it will be,' Sherif said, advancing into the room, 'to be marketing such a gem.'

'If you do.'

He gave a little half-bow. 'Of course.'

Rose did not look Tyler's way. She gestured towards the kitchen.

'As long as that's understood, then. Please. Help yourself.'

———

'It'll be my dad,' Nat said to Jess Ballantyne. 'It's my turn for the Sunday morning call. Except he's playing golf or something so it's Saturday night instead.'

They had just come back from supper in a tapas restaurant with a whole crowd of Jess's friends. Nat was an exotic in such a circle, cherished for his preppy weekend clothes and mocked for his work with – ugh – *money*. He was blithe about the latter. As he said to Jess, handing over his credit card for yet another meal or round of drinks, he had the dignity and the freedom afforded by having the means to pay for what they had just consumed. Didn't he?

Jess had been amazed by his flat. The first time he took her back, she had looked around her in astonishment, and then tiptoed round it touching surfaces in awe as if, he said affectionately, she was used to living in a squat. Or a cardboard box.

'I practically do,' she said, gazing at his bathroom as if she had never seen such a phenomenon before. 'You wouldn't believe where I've lived. I'd never let my mother anywhere near where I lived. She'd have a fit.'

'I think,' Nat said, trapping her against a doorframe, 'that you exaggerate in an actressy way to make a drama.'

She tipped her head back. 'Maybe.'

He kissed her neck. 'That's a yes, then.'

She laughed her throaty theatrical laugh, and put her arms round his neck.

'Show me,' she said, 'where your bedroom is.'

Now, of course, she was living there. The bathroom, which previously had only contained the shower gels and facial scrubs of Nat and his male lodger, became a – to Nat – seductive chaos of cosmetics and discarded scraps of lingerie. He adored being unable to find his razor, or toothbrush, in the disorder round the washbasin as much as he enjoyed the male ritual of grumbling about it. His sheets smelled of her perfume, her hair clogged up his shower, there was purple nail varnish by the coffee maker and lipstick-smeared cigarette butts – appalling and thrilling in equal measure – in cheap glass ashtrays that she had half-inched from outside tables at bars, and brought back to sit beside his carefully sourced items from Alessi. He was electrified by all of it, from her presence in his flat to the evenings in her friends' voluble company. He had never, he thought, felt so alive.

But there was a problem. It wasn't a big problem, but it was there. That, and the other thing. The Emmy thing. Nat reckoned that the Emmy thing would iron itself out in time, but the first problem was something he needed to talk to his father about, and it was his turn for his father to ring from Melbourne, and report on another extraordinary and flawless Australian sunrise.

Nat indicated to Jess that he was going to take the call into the bedroom. She was already lolling on the sofa with the TV on, and merely blew him a kiss for encouragement. He had said that he needed to talk to his father about his mother, and Jess had worn her caring and respectful expression in response.

'Absolutely, babes. You do what you need to do.'

Nat closed the bedroom door and sat down on the edge of the unmade bed. He would never, in the past, have left his bed unmade, but Jess was encouraging him to *live*, to obey his impulses, not to give in to thinking ahead all the time, planning for eventualities that might never happen, exhausting himself with pessimistic apprehensions.

'Dad,' Nat said. 'How's Oz?'

'Well,' William said, his voice pained with the obligation to be honest, 'it's raining. Of course, we desperately need the rain. The cattle and sheep farmers are really suffering.'

'Mm,' Nat said. His eyes strayed to the crumpled pillows, to a wisp of black netting that might be what passed for underwear in Jess's wardrobe.

'Otherwise,' William said vigorously, 'all more than well. Job good, health excellent, everything splendid. And you?'

Nat lay back on the bed and pulled the scrap of netting out of the folds of the duvet. It was underwear. He laid it on his forehead and closed his eyes.

'Dad,' he said, 'it's fantastic. Fantastic, here.'

'Good Lord,' William said, 'you sound as if you're in love.'

'I am. Completely.'

'Right,' William said. 'Right. Splendid. It was bound to happen. Who is she?'

Nat put a hand up to his forehead and opened one eye.

'She's an actress. She's called Jess Ballantyne. A serious actress. She's just been in an Ibsen and is waiting to hear about an audition for the Young Vic.'

'An actress.'

'Yes, Dad. I had no idea Shakespeare was so brilliant. I've been to some auditions now. He knew about *everything*.'

'You did Shakespeare at school,' William said repressively.

'Yes, but *Henry V* and battles and all that. Boy stuff. Not all this wonderful insight into the human psyche, you know?'

'Well,' William said. 'Good. Always good to widen one's horizons.'

'The thing is, Dad, I want to ask you something.'

'Ah.'

'I – kind of want this flat to myself now. I mean, just Jess and me. You know? I'd quite like Tim to go. Tim, my lodger. I mean, he's fine and out a lot and pretty unobtrusive, but I really want it to be Jess and me.'

There was a pause, and then William said, 'But Tim pays the mortgage.'

'I know, Dad.'

'So if Tim's contribution goes, what will make up the shortfall?'

Nat closed his eyes and laid his hand flat on Jess's underwear.

'I was hoping – you might.'

'Me!'

'Well, the flat's yours, really, isn't it, so I thought you would think it was in your interests . . .'

'No,' William said.

Nat opened his eyes and sat up, dislodging the underwear.

'Please, Dad.'

'Nat,' William said weightily, 'I can't afford it. I can't afford any more help. I've done my bit by all three of you as far as property is concerned, and I can't do any more. Ask your mother.'

'Mum?'

'Yes,' William said, his voice gathering energy, 'ask your mother. She's the one with a valuable property. She's the one who apparently wants to kick over the traces and marry again, for God's sake, so ask her. When did you last see her?'

Nat was suddenly bewildered.

'I don't know, maybe a couple of weeks ago.'

'I thought you went with her to see a solicitor?'

'I did. I–'

'Well? I gather the solicitor was pretty clear.'

Nat picked up the black netting again and crushed it in his palm.

'She was.'

'And your mother didn't like it.'

'No.'

'Of course she didn't,' William said triumphantly. 'She didn't like being told she couldn't indulge a whim. A mere whim. Any more than you do. She doesn't want a pre-nup and you don't want a lodger. Well, Nat, sorry but we can't always have what we want.'

Nat shouted suddenly, 'How dare you!'

A second later, the bedroom door opened. Jess stood there, adorably, insanely, wearing only one stiletto. She mouthed at him, 'You OK?'

He patted the bed beside him, indicating that she should limp across and sit down. He put an arm round her and pulled her close.

'I shall ring off now,' William said in a stately voice, 'I shall conclude this call, and leave you to reflect a little.'

Nat pressed his mouth into the side of Jess's head. He dropped his phone onto the bed beside him and from it, from Australia, came the sound of William's voice, comfortingly ridiculous in its disembodiment.

'Goodbye, Nat. Take some time to calm down. And give my love to your sisters.'

———

Mallory had gone to stay with a friend who had a basement flat in Brooklyn, and with her laptop open on the friend's cluttered table against a backdrop of famed posters from the Cuban Revolution, she Skyped Emmy in London.

'Miss you already,' Mallory said.

It was the evening and Emmy was lying on her sofa, her laptop balanced on her stomach.

'We're mad,' Emmy said. 'We wasted all those months. We could have been friends all along.'

'Better late than never.'

'Come back.'

'No,' Mallory said, 'you come here.'

'I'd love to.'

'Come!'

'There's less and less to keep me here.'

'Em,' Mallory said, 'have you met Jess yet?'

'No. And you didn't let your father come to the airport.'

'But *you* did. Come, I mean. And I called him. I called him from Heathrow and I called him from here.'

'Was he miffed?'

'No,' Mallory said. She was eating what looked like a bagel while she was talking. She added, round a mouthful, 'He only wanted to talk about cottages.'

'Cottages!'

'He and your mother are planning to go live in the country in a cottage.'

'*What?*'

Mallory wiped some cream cheese off her lower lip. She said, 'Why don't you ask her?'

'Mal . . .'

'Why don't you ask her,' Mallory repeated, chewing her bagel, 'what she and my father think they're doing?'

Emmy said sadly, 'I wish you were here.'

'Are you coming on to me?'

'No,' Emmy said, still sadly, 'not like that. I just need an ally in all this.'

'Nat and Jess—'

'Them too.'

'Then get your ass over here,' Mallory said, leaning towards the screen.

'I can't afford to.'

'Sure you can! I'll find you somewhere to stay.'

'I haven't got leave left, at work. I haven't got the fare.'

'Sugar,' Mallory said, 'ask your mom.'

'What, for an airfare?'

'Sure. Why not?'

Emmy squirmed a little.

'I can't. She's always been – so generous. I can't ask her for more.'

Mallory leaned back. She screwed up the bag her bagel had come in and that she'd been using as a plate. Emmy watched her aim for a bin in the room behind her.

'Gee,' Mallory said. 'Missed.'

'Whose flat is that?'

'It's called an apartment here, Em. It belongs to someone who used to teach fight movement at my drama school. Mostly, he's with his boyfriend in Queens. You could stay here. Yes! Come stay here.'

'Oh I wish!' Emmy said. 'I *wish.*'

Mallory leaned so close to the screen that her mouth was almost touching it. Emmy watched her with fascination.

'Ask your mom,' Mallory said again. 'What's to lose? *Ask* her.'

———

'Oh,' Emmy said.

She looked past her mother into her mother's sitting room where Tyler sat, in an armchair, looking very much at home.

'What, darling?'

Emmy shrugged.

'I thought – I kind of thought it'd just be you and me. When I rang. I thought, when you said come round, that it would be like it used to be here.'

Rose gave her a second kiss.

'Sometimes it is, Em. But not this evening. Tyler's here for supper and . . .' She stopped and then she said, 'And now *you* are. I've made a prawn curry. You know, one of those aromatic Thai ones.' She turned and called to Tyler, 'Emmy's here!'

He got up at once and came across the room, smiling broadly. Then, despite Emmy making no indication that she would welcome an embrace, he put his arm round her and kissed her warmly on the cheek.

'How lovely,' Tyler said. 'A daughter. And one who can tell me all about mine.'

Emmy stood there in his embrace. Then she said, 'She said she rang you.'

Tyler didn't take his arm away.

'She did. She did indeed. And she said that you were there to see her off.' He gave her shoulders a squeeze and dropped his arm. 'As long as someone was there, you know.'

Rose said carefully, 'I don't think you should disguise how hurt you were, Tyler.'

He smiled genially. 'I wasn't hurt, exactly.'

'You were.'

'Well,' he said, shrugging, 'I did think it was a bit odd, just leaving like that after these months together. I mean, I wouldn't even have *come* to London if it hadn't been for Mallory. And then' – he glanced at Rose – 'I never would have met your mother again.'

Emmy let a beat fall, and then she said, 'Exactly.'

Rose walked quickly across the room, saying over her shoulder, 'I'm just going to check on my prawns.'

Tyler looked at Emmy. He said quietly, 'Are you and Mallory determined to play aggrieved teenagers over this forever?'

Emmy didn't look at him. She looked over his shoulder instead. She said, 'Woodrowes are used to talking frankly to our mother, about everything, so it's taking us a little time to adjust to her having secrets from us.'

'*Secrets?*'

Emmy moved away from him towards the sitting room. 'This cottage idea . . .'

'Yes?'

She halted and looked pointedly at the slew of papers and brochures on the carpet around the chair in which he'd been sitting. She said, in an accusatory voice, 'Mallory says you are planning to buy a *cottage* together.'

He laughed. He said easily, 'Emmy, that's no *secret*.'

'Then why hasn't Mum told me? Us? Why are there suddenly all these plans we don't know about?'

Rose appeared in the kitchen doorway, untying the apron she wore – had always worn, Emmy thought, with a rush of bitter nostalgia – while cooking. She said, almost too brightly, 'I love that you can get everything you ever want in London, however exotic. I'd never even *heard* of sumac a few years ago.'

Tyler said, 'Emmy didn't know about us looking for a cottage.'

Rose began to fold her apron with elaborate care.

'Darling Em, it's just an *idea*. No more than that.'

'Mallory knew about it.'

'I told Mallory,' Tyler said. 'I'd have told her a whole lot more if I'd only had the chance to see her.'

Rose said to Emmy, 'We're just thinking about the future. Trying ideas out, that kind of thing.'

'Sweetheart,' Tyler said, 'I think it's all got a bit further than that, don't you?'

Emmy was staring at Rose's hand. 'What's that?'

Rose, encumbered still by her apron, immediately clasped her left hand with her right, as if for protection.

'It's my ring. It's a present from Tyler.'

'It's an engagement ring,' Tyler said proudly. 'A nineteenth-century aquamarine, which, amazingly, has survived all this time, because aquamarines aren't as hard as diamonds. Isn't it pretty?'

Emmy looked pointedly at her mother.

'An engagement ring?'

'Yes, darling.'

'Mum. What are you *doing*?'

Rose lifted her chin.

'I am looking to my future, darling. I am living my life in a way I grant you is unexpected, but it is both real and very exciting.'

Emmy sat down abruptly on the sofa. Tyler bent over her solicitously. 'Would you like a drink, Emmy? Anything. We've got it all, brandy, vodka, wine . . .'

Emmy said, flustered, 'No, nothing, I don't want a drink, yes I do, yes, could I, I don't know what . . .'

Tyler said helpfully, 'I'll make you a vodka and tonic.'

Emmy began to cry. Rose dropped her folded apron on the carpet and hurried to sit next to her, putting her arms round her daughter.

'Darling. Darling Emmy. Don't cry. Please don't cry. There's nothing to cry about, really there isn't, there's just plusses ahead of us, everything will be better than it has been – happier, more settled . . . promise you, darling.'

Emmy found a balled-up tissue in her sleeve and blew her nose into it.

'It's a shock,' Rose said. 'Of course it is. And there've been a lot of shocks recently, haven't there?' She smoothed Emmy's hair back from her forehead, and then she said, almost conspiratorially, 'Have you met Jess?'

Emmy sniffed into her tissue.

'Who?'

'Jess,' Rose said. 'Nat's Jess.'

Emmy gave a shuddering sigh.

'No,' she said, 'no. Not yet.'

'Nor me. He seems – very smitten.'

Emmy inched out of her mother's embrace.

'Yes.'

'Don't think,' Rose said, trying to reach Emmy's hair still, 'that I don't know how hard that must be for you, Nat being with someone.'

Emmy said nothing. Tyler came back into the room with a tumbler clinking with ice cubes.

'There,' he said, handing it to Emmy. 'Vodka, tonic and lime slices.'

She took it wordlessly and put it on the carpet by her feet.

'Darling,' Rose said. Her voice was pleading. 'Darling. Please look at me.'

Emmy glanced at Tyler for a second.

'Thank you for my drink.'

He said gallantly, 'My pleasure.'

Rose reached out to put a hand on Emmy's arm.

'What a lot to take in, darling. Don't think I don't understand.'

Tyler had resumed sitting in his armchair, but on the

edge, leaning towards them with his elbows on his knees. He said, 'I'm so glad you're in touch with Mallory.'

Emmy nodded.

'Actually,' he went on, 'it's exactly the kind of friendship we'd hoped for. Isn't it, sweetheart?'

'Darling,' Rose said to Emmy, 'what can I do to make you feel better? What?'

Emmy said, 'I'm OK.'

'No, you're not. I can see you're not.'

Emmy looked at the carpet, past her drink. 'I talked to Mallory today.'

'Did you? How lovely.'

'On Skype,' Emmy said.

'How was she?'

Emmy stuffed the tissue back into her sweater sleeve.

'She was fine. In a friend's apartment in Brooklyn. She starts rehearsals next week.'

Tyler said, 'So I imagine she's learning her lines?'

'She didn't say. She wants me to go over.'

'Well, do! Of course! Wonderful idea.'

'I can't,' Emmy said flatly.

'Why not, darling?'

Emmy stared at the carpet. 'Don't ask, Mum.'

'But of course I must ask.'

'Why d'you think?'

Tyler said, 'Is it the money? Is it the cost of an airfare to New York?'

Emmy looked at Rose and gave the smallest nod of her head.

Tyler was smiling. 'Is that all?'

'All?' Emmy said.

'Yes,' he said. He looked at Rose. His smile was very broad. 'If it's just a question of money,' Tyler said, 'I think we can help with that. Can't we, sweetheart?'

CHAPTER ELEVEN

Wood Cottage had a lovely garden. Rose could see that, could see how lovely it was and, more importantly, how it could be made lovelier. It faced south, it had enough trees, and there was a terrace outside the conservatory kitchen that was both wide and deep, and segued gracefully into the lawn without the need for steps. Tyler watched her going round the garden, noticing the planting, working out the amount of upkeep needed, squinting up at the angle of the sun. He imagined himself on a ride-on mower, making immaculate stripes on the tidy parts and cutting curving paths through the more casual ones, among the apple trees. Their apple trees. The thought of owning apple trees and a ride-on mower induced in him something close, he thought, to ecstasy. He wondered in amazement, thinking back, at how he had spent all those years of his marriage to Cindy living in houses of her father's choosing, stepping out into gardens – yards – rigorously controlled by Moses. Looking back, he thought he must have been sleepwalking. If the existence of Seth and Mallory hadn't been there to contradict him, he might have believed that he had spent thirty years simply dreaming. But he wasn't dreaming now. He was looking at a house and a garden that might very well be his. A place he could put up shelves and clear guttering and cut the grass. He knelt down and brushed his hand reverently over the grass. The possibilities of ownership broke over him in a sudden flood of joy.

But the house. It was plain, from the moment she entered the house and saw the copper jugs shining in the over-restored brick fireplace, and the too-bright rugs on the improbably glossy floor, that Rose wasn't going to like the house. The owners had replaced the original windows with diamond-paned double glazing in sturdy plastic frames. The conservatory kitchen was kitted out in stridently varnished wooden units, with fancy handles in antiqued metal, and fretwork cornices. There were jokey notices on the toilet walls and herds of whimsical china animals on the windowsills. Rose grew very quiet.

'It's just décor,' Tyler said gently. 'Surface stuff.'

'The windows aren't.'

'The windows are a pity,' Tyler said. 'I'll give you that. But this room' – he gestured round the master bedroom, which he was trying manfully not to furnish in his mind's eye – 'is great. Big enough, double aspect, bathroom off it—'

'A *pink* bathroom,' Rose said.

'Which could easily become a white bathroom, sweetheart. Quite a big bathroom, actually. With a window.'

Rose said, in a whisper, as if she didn't want to hurt the room's feelings, 'I don't like it.'

'But you liked the garden.'

Rose looked about her.

'I like most gardens. I like the *fact* of gardens. On principle.'

He came closer. 'We can change the décor, you know, completely. We can change everything. Even the windows.'

She looked at him directly.

'I don't like it, Tyler.'

'Could I ask . . .' he said, and stopped.

'What?'

'Could I ask if you aren't actually going to like anything? Because – because of selling the mews?'

She said robustly, 'Hang on, darling, this is the first house.'

'It's a lovely house. In a lovely setting.'

'I thought you wanted to go at my pace, whatever that turned out to be.'

'I do,' he said firmly.

'Well, it doesn't sound like it. This is the first house we've seen and you want me to love it at once and decide to buy it. That's *your* pace. Not mine.'

He looked at her. Then he sighed, and smiled.

'Yes,' he said.

It occurred to Rose to say that, looking back, she knew she had acquiesced too much in her marriage to William, that it wouldn't be inaccurate to describe William as a bully, and that experience had made her very resistant to any kind of pressure subsequently. But looking at Tyler, eager and shamefaced all at once, softened her. She reached out to take his hand. She shook it slightly.

'It's the *first house* we've looked at,' she said softly.

He grinned at her.

'I know. I'm an idiot. I was, in my mind's eye, already on a mower out there.'

She smiled back.

'You'll get your mower.'

'It's as if thirty years of pent-up desire for ownership, possession, *happy* certainties are suddenly flooding out of me.'

'I know.'

'I never got it, before,' Tyler said. 'I never understood about place, about somewhere *belonging* to one, about the idea that you could close a door on your own kingdom.'

'Steady on!'

'I mean it,' Tyler said earnestly. 'I mean it now. If I hadn't met you, I might never have understood about home. Not properly, anyway. I'd have had a vague idea of England, a kind of acceptance of other people's aspiration and pride and satisfaction in where they lived, but I wouldn't have understood it, as I do now. I wouldn't have wanted to join *in*.'

Rose squeezed his hand and let it go. She said, 'The zeal of the convert, maybe.'

'Probably.'

She looked round the room again.

'It isn't the décor, Tyler. It's the feel of this house, the atmosphere.'

'OK.'

She made a face at him. 'Sorry.'

'Me too,' he said. 'We've a lot to learn.'

She went out onto the landing where sunlight fell onto a deeply tufted small rug and a triangular stool with barley-sugar twisted legs. She looked back at him. She had been about to add to his last remark, 'About each other as well as ourselves,' but checked it. That was, she told herself, two instances of self-censorship in ten minutes. Was that new? Had she got used to freedom in that respect too?

She held out a hand to him.

'It's OK,' Rose said. 'This was our trial run. We'll do better next time. Won't we?'

———

It was, Nat realized, almost three weeks since he had seen his mother to speak to, face to face. It was about the same length of time since he had seen Emmy, but that, being altogether a more delicate and tricky situation, was something his mind shied away from even more comprehensively. But Rose – he was rather horrified with himself that he hadn't seen Rose in all this time; had hardly seen her, in fact, since their visit to the solicitor. It wasn't like him, he told himself, to neglect his mother and sisters. He had always prided himself, since William left, on being the man of the family, the rational, experienced broad shoulders that could bear the brunt of the less attractive aspects of modern life. He couldn't but marvel, really, at the effect Jess Ballantyne had had – was having – on him, and how completely he had plunged into a relationship with her, to the exclusion not just of all else, but of all else that once constituted the backbone of his life. One minute his mother's intention to re-marry and all the fall-out from that had filled his horizons; the next, it felt to him, it was Jess, Jess, Jess.

'Don't blame me,' Jess said, lounging against him on the sofa. 'You're a big boy. Big boys choose to surrender, if that's what they do. It is *utterly* unreconstructed to think that I have witchy wiles of some kind.'

He'd kissed her nearest shoulder. He quite agreed with her, even if part of him rather liked the idea of witchy wiles, of being the victim of some alluring and dangerous magic spell. In fact, he felt sorry for all those poor people out there who weren't absolutely in thrall to a Jess Ballantyne, even if – as Jess had teasingly suggested – he couldn't equate what he was feeling to what his mother might be feeling herself. What was absolutely natural and legitimate for him was somehow viscerally squirm-making when it came to her. It was still much easier to think about her financial protection than her emotions. In fact, when he tried to nerve himself to think about her emotions, his mind simply slammed to a halt.

'I cannot go there,' he said to Jess. 'Yuck. I can't.'

And Jess, curled up in one of his armchairs reading Shaw's *Major Barbara*, had laughed. He had pounced on her, tried to take her reading glasses off, and she had resisted him completely, never taking her eyes off the page, dementing him with her indifference.

'God,' he'd said to her, 'what am I to do about you? What?'

She said, still reading her text, 'Go and see your mother. *Go*.'

So he did. He bought a bunch of early peonies, as smooth and tight as little pink cabbages, and went round to the mews house after work one day. Rose was alone, wearing the old corduroy trousers she kept for gardening in, and was entranced to see him.

'Nat! Oh Nat, how lovely, how unexpected, what a—'

He kissed her cheek firmly.

'Enough, Mum. I haven't risen from the dead.'

'Darling, I'm allowed to be pleased, surely?'

He pushed her gently down the hall towards the sitting room.

'Yes, just not all this return of the prodigal amazement nonsense. You look great.'

'I am great,' Rose said. Her hair was ruffled and her cheeks were rosy. 'And so, I gather, are you. Hm? Hm?'

He felt a helpless smirk cross his face.

'Actually . . .'

'Yes?'

He spread his hands. 'I'm – blissful.'

She smiled at him. 'I am so happy for you, darling.'

'She's – fabulous. Just fantastic.'

'Can I meet her?'

'Of course!'

Rose said, 'Has Emmy met her?'

Nat looked out at the garden.

'Not yet.'

'Don't you think—'

Nat held up a warning hand.

'All in good time, Mum. *And*, may I say, none of your biz.'

'But if it's Emmy, it is.'

'Shh,' Nat said, smiling. He gave her shoulders a quick squeeze. 'All OK, Mum?'

She nodded. 'Very much so.'

'Laura says,' Nat said, 'that you are looking at cottages and wearing a ring. Where is the ring?'

Rose patted a trouser pocket.

'In here. For gardening.'

'Can I see it?'

'You don't want to see a *ring*.'

'Mum,' Nat said, 'I want to see your ring and I want to hear more about this cottage thing. I thought we'd agreed that you wouldn't decide anything without talking to me. To us.'

Rose extracted her ring from her pocket and held it out. 'There.'

Nat picked it out of her fingers and inspected it. Then he held it out to her.

'Very pretty. And all paid for, I presume, by Mr Masson? Now then. This cottage idea?'

'It's only an idea.'

'Funded by?'

Rose gestured to the sitting-room walls. 'This.'

'Selling this!'

'Uh-huh,' Rose said.

'Jesus,' Nat said. 'Some cottage this would buy.'

'Only a little bit of this.'

'What? Would buy a cottage?'

'Yes.'

Nat stared at her. 'And the rest?'

Rose slid the ring back into her pocket. She said, 'Let me make you some tea. Or a drink. Would you like a drink drink?'

'Mum,' Nat said warningly.

Rose said, 'It's only an idea so far. The cottage thing. Selling this. I'm just – thinking about it, as a plan for the future, for mine and Tyler's future.'

Nat sat down in the chair Tyler usually occupied and crossed his legs. He steepled his fingers together, his elbows on the chair's arms.

'OK,' he said. 'OK. Just let's suppose, for now. If you decide to sell this, and you and Tyler buy a cottage somewhere – this would all have to be signed off by lawyers, you know, you do understand that? – what happens to the surplus left from selling it? *Please* do not say the words "joint account" to me.'

'I wouldn't,' Rose said. 'Nor would Tyler. No, the current thinking is . . . Actually, I mustn't say. I mustn't tell you something to your advantage that I haven't properly told the girls.'

Nat sat up straighter, unlocking his fingers. He looked suddenly alert, his hands pressed flat against the chair's arms.

'Advantage?'

Rose nodded, reluctantly.

'You mean . . . ?'

'Please,' Rose said, 'no more. I shouldn't have said what I've said. I shouldn't even have hinted at it.'

Nat stood up. He said warmly, to his mother, 'You're lovely.'

She flapped her hands at him self-deprecatingly. 'No, no.'

He moved towards her. He was beaming.

'Mum,' Nat said. 'This is heaven sent. It really is. There was something, something about money, that I was nerving myself to ask *you*.'

———

It was a constant surprise, really, what Aunt Prue was aware of. You could suppose that she was immersed in her Sussex village life, going for constitutional walks, reading improving books, having sufficient social intercourse to be stimulated but not distracted, involving herself very much on her own terms with community demands, but it was far harder to visualize her acuity about her relations in London. Emmy knew that the sisters spoke on the phone infrequently but regularly and she also knew that Rose was very measured – guarded, even – in what she said. But for all that paucity of information, Aunt Prue seemed to know things and sense things, and this was a constant source of amazement.

'Honestly,' Emmy said to her aunt on the telephone. '*Honestly*. How do you know I haven't met Nat's girlfriend yet?'

'I'm guessing,' Prue said. 'And I'm right. You are both, you and Nat, for different reasons, as reluctant as each other.

And of course you are not at all used to not coming first with him. Are you?'

Emmy said, 'I really *really* don't want to be ticked off about this.'

'You sound just like your mother.'

'Who ticks *you* off?' Emmy demanded.

'Oh my dear,' Prue said, 'I do it to myself. All the time. I shall probably be very severe with myself after this call, and then I'll go and walk it off.'

'You ought to have a dog.'

'Don't change the subject. When are you going to meet Nat's girlfriend?'

Emmy said unhappily, 'I don't know.'

'Fix a meeting. Fix it with her, not him.'

'Can't.'

'Yes, you can.'

'Please don't bully me, Aunt Prue.'

'Do it. You'll thank me.'

Emmy tried another deflection. She said, 'I've got a new friend. Actually.'

'Ah,' Prue said. 'A man or a woman?'

'A woman. Mallory Masson. Tyler's daughter. We kind of got together at the last minute, just before she went back to New York. But we Skype. Or FaceTime. She wants me to go over.'

'To New York?'

'Yes.'

'Well, you should go. I first went to New York when I was younger than you, and it was astounding. Formative.'

'Mm,' Emmy said.

'Meaning?'

'Meaning that I had a weird conversation in Mum's house about it. She was trying to stop Tyler offering to pay for my airfare, as far as I could see. I certainly don't want a single penny from *him*. I think he got over-excited about me and Mallory being friends, or something.'

'Let me get this clear,' Prue said. 'Your mother's fiancé – yes, I'm afraid that's what he technically is, however much you dislike it – offered to pay your airfare to New York to see his daughter?'

'Sort of. I couldn't quite work it out. Maybe he's come into some money, or something. Maybe it was just an impulse. Whatever it was, Mum didn't want him to say any more.'

There was a silence from Prue's end of the conversation.

'Are you there?' Emmy said.

'I think,' Prue said in a tone of renewed briskness, 'that I had better talk to your mother again.'

'It's all we do, isn't it, talk and talk and analyse and discuss—'

'No,' Prue said, interrupting. '*No*. We act. Or at least, some of us do. And you are going to act now, Emmy. You are going to make a plan to meet Nat's girlfriend, and you are going to do it *now*.'

——

'I don't think,' Jack said severely to Rose, 'that you are a good granny.'

She looked immediately stricken.

'Oh, darling.'

'I mean,' Jack went on, pursuing his advantage, 'some people at my school get collected by their grannies *every day*.'

'Yes,' Rose said, chastened.

'And I don't think you've been to my school since I was *three*.'

Rose took a deep breath. She held a copy of *Gangsta Granny* that Jack had insisted he wanted as a bedtime story, and had then, because of his constant interruptions, not listened to.

'I don't think you want me to read this book to you, do you? Would you like another book or do you just want to criticize me?'

He regarded her, sitting up in bed in his Kylo Ren pyjamas, his hair still damp from the bath.

'What's criticize?'

'It means,' Rose said, 'in your case, finding something wrong with me.'

'Well,' Jack said, spreading his hands wide, 'where *have* you been?'

Rose put the book down on Jack's duvet.

'I've been taking some time, darling, to do things just for myself. Doing what I want to do.'

'And have you finished now?'

She smiled at him.

'Isn't it enough that I'm here now? That I came to see you and Adam and gave you your bath?'

'I don't like having a bath with Adam. Sometimes he pees in the bath, you know.'

'I expect you did too, darling.'

'A lot,' Laura said from the doorway. 'Remember? Adam's asleep. He's brilliant at it. Put him down, thumb in, eyes closed, flip over onto his knees, bingo, gone.'

'I bet he doesn't have many things to think about,' said Jack.

'Unlike you, darling?'

Jack nodded soberly. Laura came into the room and bent over him in a tucking-in manner.

'I'm taking Grandma Rose downstairs now.'

'But she didn't even read me one page.'

'Because you didn't let her. We are now going to test you to see if you can stay in bed and go to sleep on your own.'

Jack said, 'When I'm five.'

'No,' Laura said, 'before that. When you are still four.'

Rose got up and stood looking down at Jack.

'If you can't, darling, I'll—'

'He *can*, Mum,' Laura said firmly. 'He can. He just has to make himself.'

Rose bent to kiss him and he lurched up to cling round her neck with sudden vehemence. Then he subsided back onto his pillow and turned on his side.

'By the way,' Jack said, his face to his bedroom wall, 'I don't like that lumpy blue thing on your hand.'

———

'Wine?' Laura said to her mother, holding up a bottle by the fridge.

Rose shook her head. Laura put the bottle back in the fridge and extracted a filter jug of water instead.

'This is so rare,' Laura said, opening cupboards in search of tumblers, 'Angus out and me in. D'you mind pasta? I haven't been shopping this week – or, more truthfully, Angus hasn't been shopping. Goodness knows what Justine gives the kids although, being Belgian, she can cook and is really inventive. I wonder why English girls seem to pride them-selves on not cooking? I mean, I'm not half the cook Angus is and I practically boast about it.'

'Perhaps you wouldn't,' Rose said carefully, 'if you didn't earn more than he does.'

Laura clattered ice cubes out of the front of the fridge door and dropped them into two glasses.

'Probably not,' she said, untroubled. Rose watched her pour water on top of the ice cubes and decided not to suggest a slice of lemon as well. Laura held a tumbler out to her.

'Cheers, Mum.'

Rose took the glass. 'Cheers, darling.'

'And whatever Jack says, I think that's a very pretty ring.'

Rose made a huge effort not to glance at her left hand. 'I can't quite get used to wearing it.'

'No.'

'Will you be honest with me?' Rose said. 'Will you tell me frankly what you feel about me wearing an engagement ring?'

Laura smiled at her. 'Fine.'

'Really? Really fine?'

'Mum,' Laura said, 'he's a nice guy. And he makes you happy. Both of those things make a ring from him to you fine by me.' She crossed the kitchen to a row of tall jars lined up on a metal shelf. 'It really will have to be pasta, Mum.'

Rose said politely, 'I like pasta.'

Laura took down a jar of farfalle and held it against her. She said, in a different tone, 'Mum . . .'

Rose took a swallow of water. 'Yes.'

'Ring fine,' Laura said, cradling the jar, 'Tyler fine. Situation fine in general. But what is all this about selling the house and buying a cottage?'

Rose traced a pattern on the nearest countertop with her forefinger.

'It's – nothing settled. It's just an idea.'

'Really? I heard you went to look at a cottage somewhere. I heard you were going to give Nat some money so that he and his new hottie can have an exclusive little love nest mortgage free.'

Rose looked up. 'Laura! You sound quite heated.'

'I am,' Laura said. She banged the pasta jar down on the central table. 'I *am*.'

Rose moved towards her. 'Darling, you never get worked up!'

'Well,' Laura said, staring down at the pasta jar, 'I am now.'

'Look,' Rose said, coming nearer and trying to put her arms round her daughter, 'if I decide to sell the mews – *if* – you three would get exactly the same amount; it would be completely fair, I would just divide two thirds of the profit three ways.'

'No!' Laura shouted.

Rose gazed at her. Laura stepped back so that her mother couldn't reach her.

'It's not that,' Laura said furiously. 'It's got nothing to do with fairness or sibling competitiveness or anything. It's – oh God, Mum, it's just that you shouldn't be doing it at *all*.'

'But I thought,' Rose said in bewilderment, 'that you liked him, that you thought he was good for me.'

'I did. I do. But you've got to keep your money as *your* money.'

'He isn't interested in money. In fact, he was the one who suggested I should give you three—'

'*Mother!*' Laura shouted again.

The kitchen door opened. Jack stood there, his hand grasping the knob. 'You're making a lot of noise,' he said.

Laura said nothing. Rose crossed the kitchen and took his hand. She said firmly, 'I'm taking you back to bed.'

'No!'

Laura looked up. She said in her usual voice, 'Do what Grandma Rose says. And do *not* get out of bed again.' She picked up the pasta jar and began to carry it back across the kitchen. 'I can't cook this, Mum. Not even pasta. I'm going to ring for a takeaway. Indian OK by you, or would you rather have Chinese?'

Rose stood in the doorway, holding Jack's hand. Then she bent and lifted him into her arms.

'Either,' she said. 'Honestly.'

'Mum,' Laura said.

Rose waited, holding the weight of Jack clumsily against her.

'I'm not cross,' Laura said. 'I'm not cross with *you*. I'm just . . .' She paused and pushed the back of her wrist up against her nose. 'I'm just frightened for you, Mum. That's all.'

CHAPTER TWELVE

It was Jess who did the telephoning, in the end. She sent Emmy a text which read, 'Hi, this is Jess. Time we met!' and then, the next day, she rang while Emmy was on her lunch break in the Strand and looking at an off-the-shoulder top in Topshop

'I can't hear you,' Emmy said, putting the top back on the rail, where it immediately slipped from its hanger and fell to the floor. Rose, she knew, would have expected her to bend and retrieve it, and put it back on the hanger.

'Go somewhere quieter then,' Jess said.

'I'll ring you back.'

'Straight back. I've got a rehearsal.'

It struck Emmy that she could retort, 'And I have work,' but she said nothing. She stooped and picked up the top and slung it across the dress rail, ignoring Rose's voice in her head telling her to put it back on the hanger. Then she went out of the shop, and crossed the Strand to find the relative peace of the courtyard round the crypt entrance to St Martin-in-the-Fields.

'Hi there,' Jess said, answering her phone at once. She

sounded warm and friendly. 'I should have rung before. We should have met.'

Emmy leaned against a set of ornate iron railings and thought of Mallory.

'We should.'

'Well, now we can.'

'OK.'

'Without Nat. Don't you think?'

'OK,' Emmy said again. Mallory had said, 'You'll like her. You can't not like her. She's a lovely person, kind of confident, you know, but not arrogant. Don't set your face against liking her just because of your brother.'

Emmy had said, 'You don't know about being a twin unless you are one,' and Mallory had done her thing of leaning right up close to the screen and saying 'Blah, blah, blah' with a mouth like a fish, which was, Emmy thought, like closing your eyes and sticking your fingers in your ears and singing loudly in order not to have to acknowledge something someone else had just inconveniently said.

Now, Jess was saying, 'What about breakfast? Say, a ten o'clock breakfast?'

'At ten o'clock,' Emmy said, 'I'll have been at work for an hour.'

'Okaaaaay,' Jess said, dragging the syllables out as if she was thinking. 'After work for you, then. After rehearsal for me.'

'Come to supper,' Emmy said, to her own amazement. She'd had no intention of saying such a thing, not the slightest intention, and then she found herself adding, 'At mine. On Friday.'

There was a brief pause and then Jess said, 'Goodness. At yours.'

'Yes. It's just down the hill. From your – from Nat. Two minutes. One if you run.'

'Thank you,' Jess said politely.

'Is there anything you can't eat?'

'Nothing I can think of. Are – are you sure?'

Emmy watched a young man with a rucksack lope past, a dog obediently trotting at his heels. There was a tin mug hanging from the rucksack and the boy, who was fair, had his hair in elaborate cornrows, the ends finished with blue beads. She pushed herself upright from the railings.

'About having you to supper? Yes, I'm sure.'

'Thank you,' Jess said. 'What if Nat wants to come in the end?'

Emmy began to walk back to the Strand. The boy's neat plaited head was still visible, moving purposefully through the crowd ahead of her. How did you train a dog to follow you, even in London crowds and traffic, like that?

'He can't,' Emmy said. 'Even if he thinks he'd like to come, tell him I don't want him to. OK?'

———

Angus said to Laura that he didn't mind. He genuinely did not mind, he said, doing the big weekly shop, remembering to put the rubbish out, hearing Jack's reading practice, emptying Adam's disposable-nappy container, organizing Justine for the week, ringing the council about the rats in the empty house next door, but he *did* mind if, after all this maintenance of their daily lives, Laura was absorbed in something that made her cross. He was, he pointed out, used to her being absorbed in something else, but he wasn't used to her being cross. Absent-minded, fine; snappy, not fine at all, especially snappy with him who was doing everything in his power to make the wheels of their life run smoothly.

Laura didn't look at him. She was in her study, staring at her laptop.

'Sorry.'

'Sorry's not enough, babe. Turn that effing thing off and look at me.'

He was holding Adam in his arms, and Jack was leaning interestedly against his leg. Adam was eating. Adam ate all the time, if he had the opportunity, and he was clutching a miniature box of raisins.

'Laura!' Angus said loudly.

She gave a little jerk and gasp. Jack said helpfully, 'You should do what Daddy says, you know.'

The screen on Laura's laptop went black. Very slowly, she turned her swivel chair round to face them. 'There.'

'What's the matter, Laura?'

Laura reached her arms up to take Adam. He settled on her knee, glued to his box of raisins. She sniffed his hair.

'He even smells sticky.'

Angus leaned on the door jamb and folded his arms.

'Come on, Laura.'

Jack imitated his father's pose on the opposite door jamb.

'Yes, come on, Laura.'

Laura said, ignoring Jack, 'It's Mum.'

'What about her?'

Laura gestured. 'Not in front of the boys.'

'Oh,' Jack said airily, 'don't mind *us*,' mimicking his parents.

Angus said, 'Is she having second thoughts, then?'

'No,' Laura said. 'No. That would be easier in lots of

ways.' She looked up at Angus. 'It's . . .' She stopped and then said with careful exaggeration, 'I'll have to spell it out. Ell. Ess. Dee. I think that's the problem.'

'What?' said Jack.

Angus didn't look at him.

'It's medicine,' he said and then to Laura, 'But I thought a solicitor had sorted all that?'

'It's a new idea,' Laura said. She smoothed Adam's hair back from his forehead. 'He's even got raisin in his hair. It's something that I kind of gathered from the twins. Mum and I had a bit of a showdown—'

'What?' Jack said again.

'—last night. The new plan is to sell up, give us three a chunk of the proceeds, and buy a – a smaller rural property together.'

'Jesus,' Angus said.

Jack stood upright and unfolded his arms. 'Is that a bad word?'

Angus put a hand briefly on his son's head.

'I shouldn't have used it. Black mark, Daddy. Laura, this sounds crazy.'

She nodded. 'Made worse by the fact that the twins seem to be all for it.'

'No!'

Laura looked up at him. 'Oh yes,' she said. She got to her feet clumsily, holding Adam who was now tearing his raisin box to pieces in search of the very last one. 'One wants not to have a lodger any more on account of his current nonstop sex life and the other wants to go to America.'

Adam began to roar. He cast his tattered raisin box to the floor and strained towards his father.

'You can't be hungry,' Angus said, heaving his son into his arms. 'You've been eating solidly since dawn. Put your thumb in.' He picked up Adam's sticky left fist and plugged the thumb into his mouth. Adam subsided against him at once, heavy and drowsy. Angus said to Laura, over his head, 'I thought the twins were the ones so opposed to Rose having any kind of relationship.'

'Grandma Rose?' Jack said.

Laura smiled at him.

'Yes. Grandma Rose.' She glanced at Angus. 'They were.'

He let his breath out on a long sigh. He said, 'I want to say another very bad word.'

'You shouldn't,' Jack said kindly. 'You'll only get in trouble.'

Laura said to Angus, 'I shouted at Mum.'

'You never shout at anyone.'

'I did last night. And I might well do some more.'

'Not at me, I hope.'

'No,' Laura said, 'not at you. You just got caught in the crossfire.' She put a finger out and pressed it into Adam's nearest cheek. 'I was just figuring out the best way to see the twins. And make it plain what I think.'

'Of them?'

Laura took her finger away from Adam's cheek and leaned in to kiss him instead.

'You bet,' she said.

———

Nat was used to the women in his life being a priority. Ever since he could remember, he'd had a personal pecking order of important if not crucial women relations, with Emmy coming first, closely followed by Rose, and then Laura. He had never been a laddish boy, or even especially clubbable; he had never derived satisfaction or confidence from being included in an all-male group. At school, he had had separate and particular friends, rather than gangs of them. As his father – once an ardent rugby player – ruefully noted, he had been the kind of boy you might find alone on a climbing wall, or practising serves on a squash court, rather than being commended for being a valuable member of a team. When he announced to Rose that he had chosen a man as a lodger, when he first moved into his flat, she had been taken aback.

'A man! Goodness. I thought you were looking for a girl to share with.'

Nat was looking at his phone. 'I didn't think Emmy would like it.'

Rose had kissed him, in a deliberately congratulatory way. He heard her later on the telephone telling Laura how mature the twins were being, not living together in a flat, and now how sensitive Nat was being about the gender of person he let his second bedroom to. Emmy hadn't wanted a second bedroom. She said that if she couldn't live with Nat – they had made a solemnly announced decision together – she didn't want to live with anyone. He had been very touched. Now, he was outraged. Outraged and hurt and bewildered. What was Emmy playing at, asking Jess to supper and telling him he couldn't come, that she didn't *want* him to come?

And Rose wasn't much better. Rose, who had always been, even when creating a difficulty, so transparent, so easy to read and influence. He mightn't have approved of this liaison, as he termed it to himself, or the speed of it, or her conduct in the solicitor's office, but he could see, despite his own exasperation, what the internal battles she was fighting were. And then, she half offered him enough money to transform his life, and seemed immediately to think better of it. One moment she was talking openly about some kind of advantage for him and Emmy and Laura attached to the sale of the mews house, and the next she was in a flurry of retraction, begging him to ignore her, obliterate their conversation from his mind. She became, he thought indignantly, as mulish as she'd been after seeing Grace Ashton, almost covering her ears while she insisted, loudly, that she had spoken out of turn and should never have opened her mouth.

Nat rang Laura. Her phone went to voicemail – she'd be taking evening surgery of course – and he decided, angrily, not to leave a message. Even if he had requested – or, in his present mood, demanded – that she ring back, she probably wouldn't. She wouldn't deliberately, she would simply fail to get round to it. Surgery would finish, she would drive wearily home and domestic life would suck her in and use her up to such an extent that if she did remember about his message, it would be days later and Nat wanted a reaction *now*. Right now. He wanted someone from his inner circle of women to empathize with his current state of mind and tell him that he was completely justified in thinking that his sister and his mother – and even, painfully, his girlfriend – were behaving in a way that wasn't just puzzling and arbitrary, but plain *wrong*. He wasn't interested in being a victim of incomprehensible behaviour, he just wanted to be acknowledged as in the right. He nodded to himself, even though no one was watching. He was indisputably right.

Laura rang back in ten minutes.

'Nat? You OK?'

'I'm amazed.'

'I'm in the car. On the way home. I saw you'd rung. Are you all right?'

Nat looked up at the ceiling.

'Seething. But physically fine.'

'Oh God,' Laura said. 'What now?'

'You don't want to know.'

'No,' Laura said, 'I don't. But I'll have to. So tell me.'

'I'm alone!' Nat said, in the tone of one who couldn't believe what they were saying.

'Yes?'

'Laura,' Nat said, 'I'm alone in the flat because' – he began to enunciate with exaggerated clarity – 'Jess is having supper with Emmy and Emmy told Jess to tell me that I was not wanted. That's what she said. Not wanted. Emmy didn't want me to come.'

There was a pause.

'Laura?'

'Come and have supper at ours,' Laura said.

'No, really, I'm—'

'*Come*,' Laura said.

'Thank you.'

'Honestly,' Laura said, 'the way some people drive! Why are they all so *ratty* all the time? Actually . . .' She stopped.

'What?'

'Actually,' Laura resumed, 'I'd like to see you. I'd like to see you anyway. There's something I want to talk to you about.'

—

Emmy hadn't cooked. She hadn't made a deliberate plan not to cook, she just hadn't got round to planning what to buy, to shopping for food, so when Jess turned up, below the open windows of her studio flat with her arms full of flowers, Emmy felt flustered. She looked down at Jess – long purple-velvet coat over trousers tucked into knee boots and a wide smile – and said, 'Do you want to go away again? I haven't done anything about supper.'

Jess was laughing. 'I'm not here for the food.' She held up the flowers. 'Tulips,' she said unnecessarily. 'For you.'

Emmy went to let her in. It was a wrong-footed start, not to have food, to be brought tulips by someone in a purple-velvet coat. Someone smiling. Why had she asked her to supper? Why had she asked her and been horrible to Nat and not bought anything to eat? Why, Emmy thought, crossing her sitting-room space and noticing the copy of a gossip magazine that was lying against the crushed cushions and that was so obviously not a copy of something by James Joyce or Proust, do I get myself into these situations?

Jess was wearing a hat. Not a beanie or something sensible to keep the rain off, but a big-brimmed, glamorous, swooping sort of hat, in which she looked – well, wonderful. And effortless. She looked completely natural in her hat, as she did in her boots, which were slouchy, with turned-down cuffs, like pirate boots. She stood on Emmy's doorstep like a dancer, slightly on one hip, and held out the sheaf of white tulips.

'Hello,' Jess said. 'Hello, Nat's sister.'

Emmy stared.

'What?'

'We can be friends, can't we?' Jess said. 'We can get along, at least. Let's go down to the pub.'

So they went to the pub. Emmy left her tulips in a sink full of cold water and collected her bag and her khaki drill parka – eclipsed immediately by the purple velvet – and accompanied Jess obediently to the pub. Or mindlessly, she told herself, glancing sideways at the way Jess walked, at the bag hanging on her shoulder that looked as if it had been made and embroidered in an Afghan village – probably, Emmy thought churlishly, as part of some worthy charitable project.

'At least,' Emmy said, trying to pull herself together as they approached the pub, 'let me buy the wine.'

Jess halted by one of the outdoor tables and dropped her bag off her shoulder onto it. She gave Emmy her wide smile. 'Lovely.'

Emmy looked at her.

'Aren't you coming in?'

Jess settled gracefully into a chair. She said, still smiling, 'Can't smoke inside.' She began to rummage in the embroidered bag.

'Nat hates smokers,' Emmy said.

Jess stopped rummaging. She glanced up at Emmy from beneath the brim of her hat.

'Not all smokers, it seems.'

They held each other's gazes for a moment. Then Emmy said, 'Red or white?'

Jess drew out a classy dark-red cigarette pack with a label on it that read: 'Smoking seriously harms you and those around you.'

She said, 'Oh, red. Every time. You don't mind, do you?'

'What?'

'If I smoke.'

'I'd rather you didn't.'

'So would I. So would Nat. But there we are.'

Emmy pushed her way into the pub. Australian Jake was behind the bar with his red bandana tied round his head and the single earring shaped like an anchor. Emmy had initially thought he was very attractive, but an endless evening of stories about bunking off school to go surfing had severely dimmed his appeal. Close up, he could also be forty. Maybe even more. But he was still good for giving her a bottle of trade-price Beaujolais on a tray with two glasses and two bags of salt and vinegar crisps, and his breezy well-honed pub banter was reassuring in its familiarity. Emmy carried the tray back outside and put it on the table beside Jess's bag. Jess was on the telephone. Something about her phone attitude, her air of having a delicious intimacy of some kind, made Emmy think that she was talking to Nat. She poured wine – a lot of wine – into one of the glasses and held it out.

'Yours, I think,' she said loudly.

Jess took the glass with the hand holding the cigarette, and went on talking, smiling, into her telephone. Emmy sat down in the chair opposite with a bang, and took a big gulp of her wine. She counted to twenty. Then another twenty. Then she stood up.

Jess blew a kiss into her phone, clicked it off and swung round. She raised her glass.

'Cheers. Why are you standing up?'

Emmy said, 'I was leaving.'

'Were you? Why?'

'You were on the phone.'

Jess put her wine glass on the table and leaned back. She took a long and thoughtful drag on her cigarette.

'Oh, Emmy.'

'What?'

'You are so like Nat.'

Emmy wanted to say, 'And you are unbearable,' and didn't.

'Please sit down. I'll turn my phone off. Right off. Please don't go.'

Emmy didn't move. Jess took off her hat and tipped her head back to shake her hair free. She said, staring up at the sky, dim with London's not-darkness, 'Does it actually matter?'

'What?'

Jess brought her head slowly forward to look at Emmy. 'If we like each other or not. Obviously Nat would prefer it, if we did. Shall we try again?'

Emmy looked at the table, at the wine bottle and the glasses and the crisp packets and Jess's dark-red carton of cigarettes. She took a deep breath.

'I don't think so,' she said. She took a step away. 'Ring Nat again. He can come and collect you.' She bent to push the wine glass towards Jess. 'He can drink my wine.'

———

Prue rang Rose to tell her that she was coming to London to see her on Wednesday. Rose said that Wednesday wasn't very convenient, so Prue said steadily that that was fine, she would change her podiatry appointment and come on Thursday or Friday, whichever Rose preferred. And no, she didn't want lunch or even coffee, she didn't even want to come to the mews house, she could say what she needed to say in a coffee shop, so why didn't they meet in John Lewis on Oxford Street, and then Prue could buy the mattress topper she was after from the bed-linen department, after they had finished.

Rose said, 'Must you be so portentous? Can't you tell me what this is all about?'

'The children.'

'*My* children?'

'Of course,' Prue said. 'Who else's children really concern me?'

Rose was aware of Tyler in his armchair across the room.

'Couldn't we have a conversation about whatever it is, now?'

Prue was looking out of her kitchen window, and noticing that her wisteria was beginning at last to show signs of coming into flower.

'I've always found,' she said to her sister, 'that face to face is far better in every way than the telephone. I need a mattress topper; John Lewis is five minutes from your front door. What is so difficult or momentous about meeting me there for half an hour next Thursday.'

'I just always feel as if I am about to be reprimanded.'

'Nothing to do with me,' Prue said.

'Well . . .'

'See you Thursday,' Prue said. 'I have to fill the bird feeder. You wouldn't believe the mess they make, especially the goldfinches.'

Rose put the phone down and sighed.

'What?' Tyler said.

She shrugged. 'Nothing. Just the usual. She said it was about the children this time.'

Tyler rose from his chair. 'Your children? What business of hers are your children?'

She smiled at him. 'I only ever feel brave enough to think that when I'm off the telephone.'

Tyler said seriously, 'Your children are very, very lucky.'

She sighed again, and gave him a fleeting smile. 'You're biased.'

'Yes. I'm biased in thinking they are lucky to have a mother like you, maybe. But they are lucky to have been born into affluence, to have had good educations, to be—'

'Being lucky,' Rose said, interrupting, 'doesn't always make you happy, though, does it? Especially if people keep telling you how lucky you are, telling you to count your blessings.'

'I won't do that, Rosie, ever. I might count my own, but I'll never ask you to count yours, or what the outside world sees as yours.'

She moved across to him and put her arms round his neck.

'I know.'

He regarded her. He said, 'I don't want you ever to feel *obliged* again.'

'Thank you.'

'I mean it.'

'Yes,' Rose said. She kissed him. 'I know,' she repeated.

'You aren't obliged to Prue, you know. You aren't obliged to your children. You aren't obliged to me.'

She loosened her arms a little.

'There's something in me, then,' she said, 'that feels obliged to all of you, in some way.'

'Your invention, sweetheart.'

Rose took her arms away and folded them.

'We had this conversation, didn't we? That we are, by this stage, as we are.'

'Yes.'

'Tyler,' Rose said, standing in front of him, arms folded,

head high. 'Tyler, I'd like to move forward a bit, I'd like to make plans.'

He put his hands in his pockets, and smiled at her. 'I'm waiting.'

'Can we make an appointment to see another cottage?'

———

Nat rang Laura and said he wouldn't be round for supper after all. There was a lot of noise in the background, jolly pub or restaurant noise, Laura thought, and he sounded a little shifty, as if the reason he was giving for not coming over for supper wasn't the real reason at all. He said that Emmy had had a change of plan, something to do with work, he wasn't at all clear what was going on, but the upshot was that he and Jess were now going to be together for the evening after all, so sorry for the change of plan, but he was sure Laura understood.

Laura looked at the three sea bream that Angus had got out of the freezer and that were thawing on the kitchen table, on a baking sheet. She had a Friday night glass of wine in her hand and the telephone in the other against her ear. Angus, perched on the edge of the table with his own glass of wine, was listening, his eyes on Laura's face.

'Bring her,' Laura said. She took a swallow of her wine.

'What?'

'Bring Jess to supper,' Laura said. 'We've got enough fish for four. I'd like to meet her. We both would.'

Angus put his glass down on the table and stood up. He went across to the freezer and stood by it, his hand on the door, looking questioning.

Nat said, sounding caught off guard, that that was really

sweet of Laura and they'd have loved to, but there were other plans.

'Other plans?' Laura said. 'But I thought the original plans had just gone haywire, so you were free?'

'I was,' Nat said. 'But now – I'm not. There's – well, there's new arrangements. After it all fell through. With Emmy. Laura . . .'

'What?'

'It's so nice of you to ask us round but I think we're – we're meeting up with some people.'

Laura gave Angus a wink.

'What people?'

'Um,' Nat said, 'friends of Jess's.'

'But,' Laura said, persisting, 'they can't be very concrete plans because you were coming here, and Em and Jess were going to have supper together. Right?'

Nat was silent. Laura could hear merriment and laughing in the background. She said, 'Nat. Where are you?'

'In the pub,' he said lamely.

'What pub?'

'Our pub.'

'Yours and Emmy's pub? Where's Emmy?'

There was another silence and then Nat said reluctantly, 'She's gone home.'

Laura shook her head at Angus and he returned to the table and his wine glass. Laura put her own glass down. She said, more severely, into the telephone, 'Nat. What is going on?'

'Nothing.'

'Has there been trouble? Has there been trouble between Emmy and Jess?'

'No,' Nat said miserably.

'Ah,' Laura said. 'And if I were to ring Em, would she say the same thing?'

'Please don't.'

'Look,' Laura said, 'I have something, a family thing, that I want to talk to you about. Irrespective of what Em and Jess did or didn't do. So please come here, as invited, and bring Jess if she'd like to come. She can talk to Angus while I talk to you.'

She could hear Nat's discomfiture down the phone line.

'Sorry,' he said.

'Just come.'

'I can't,' he said, 'I really can't. I've promised.'

'Even if I tell you that I'll ring Emmy? And Mum? I might well ring Mum too.'

'Ring who you like,' Nat said recklessly.

Laura took the phone away from her ear and looked at it. Then she put it back under her hair and said, 'Bye Nat,' into it and dropped it on the table. Angus looked at it.

'Poor guy,' he said.

'Boy solidarity.'

'No,' he said, 'situation solidarity.' He looked at the sea bream. 'Can you eat more than one fish?'

She picked up her wine glass. 'Probably.' Then she looked at him. 'Emmy didn't like Jess, did she? I wonder if I will.'

CHAPTER THIRTEEN

Mallory flew to San Francisco for the weekend, to see her brother. It was no good hoping to stay with Seth and Yuhui, she knew – it would have meant the couch as her bed and accepting their inflexible, all-absorbing routine round Doughboy – so she contacted her old high-school friend, Carmen, and arranged to sleep on Carmen's futon instead.

Carmen worked for the San Francisco Museum of Craft and Design, which was housed in one of the old grey industrial blocks on 3rd Street, in Dogpatch. Carmen, who had been wild and experimental at high school, had become a disciple of modern craft, and posted on Facebook very serious photographs of exhibitions of sculpture in cardboard and conceptual metalwork. She lived in a cramped apartment high up on Potrero Hill, with a narrow view between buildings to the bay, and the Bay Bridge. The futon in her living room, which doubled as a couch when folded up, was, she said, at Mallory's disposal. Any time.

Seth's reaction to the news that Mallory was coming was completely neutral. He had had exactly the same 'Uh-huh' reaction to the news that she was going to drama school in New York, to the news that she was going to be on stage in London, and to the information that after four months in England, she was now back in New York. Mallory was not to know that Yuhui had spoken very earnestly to Seth about the significance of family, and of Mallory and Seth being of great consequence to one another, especially if their father chose to stay in London, and Seth, who listened to Yuhui, had been chastened. Not chastened enough to call his sister back, or go to the airport to meet her plane, but sufficiently chastened to make time for Mallory on Sunday morning, after the weekly yoga class which Yuhui insisted was crucial to their mental, as well as physical, wellbeing.

Yuhui did not come to the brunch Seth and Mallory had together. She made a quiet, emphatic point of not coming, but sent, via Seth, a present of a small Japanese teapot and a packet of green tea decorated with cherry blossoms. She much looked forward, she told Mallory in an accompanying card, to their meeting again when the time was right. Her handwriting, in brown ink with an italic nib, was small and regular, and she had added two kisses under her signature. Seth watched Mallory unwrap her teapot and read her card with the satisfaction of one who cannot possibly be disappointed.

'She's a doll, huh?' Seth said to Mallory.

Mallory turned the teapot round in her hands. It was black and delicately grooved, with a bamboo handle threaded with a single stripe of scarlet.

'She sure is.'

'I just marvel that someone like Yuhui wants to spend her life with me. *Me!* What you eating?' Seth said.

Mallory was still looking at her teapot.

'French toast, I think.'

'Good choice. They bake their own bread here and slice it thick for French toast. As it's Sunday, I'm going for the fennel sausage, and the chilli cheddar cornbread with jalapeño jelly.'

Mallory glanced at him. 'Not sourdough?'

Seth took no notice. 'And drip coffee. You want drip coffee?'

'I want,' Mallory said, 'to talk about Dad.'

Seth put the menu down.

'Dad?'

'Yes,' Mallory said. 'Our father. Our English father who looks as if he's discovered his roots again as well as Rose Woodrowe.'

Seth made a face.

'What's she like?'

'Nice,' Mallory said. She took a swallow of iced water. 'Very nice. Very English.'

'Blonde?' Seth said.

Mallory got her phone out of her pocket and scrolled to find her photo gallery.

'Brown. Brunette-ish. Kinda blondey brown.' She held her phone out. 'There.'

Seth squinted at the phone. 'She looks OK.'

'She is,' Mallory said, 'and Dad is in the same state about her as you are about Yuhui.'

Seth grinned. '*Dad* is?'

'Yes,' Mallory said. 'You know he is. You've heard him on the phone.'

'I'm not always concentrating on the phone.'

'You amaze me,' Mallory said sardonically.

Seth looked at her, as if seeing her properly at last. He said, in a much gentler tone, 'What's up, Mal?'

She shook her head and put her hand briefly up to her eyes. 'I don't know.'

Seth reached across the table and squeezed her forearm. He said, 'Is it him wanting to marry again?'

Mallory sniffed.

'I don't think so. I mean, it isn't as if he and Mom were ace at marriage, for God's sake. They lived in the same house, sure, and they didn't get divorced, but that's about it, isn't it? Why should I care if he wants to try getting it right this time? But . . .'

'But what?'

'But there's never been space for us, for me, in either of their lives. Has there? I know I could have made more of an effort to be with him after Mom died, but I had my own stuff to deal with, I couldn't take the risk of asking for too many details of how he was.'

'In case he told you?'

Mallory looked at her brother in surprise.

'Yes.'

'To be honest with you,' Seth said, moving the holder of paper napkins an inch to the left and then moving it back again, 'I'd probably feel just as you feel, if it wasn't for Yuhui.'

'And sourdough.'

He gave a small grin.

'OK. And sourdough.'

'I thought the theatre would sort it for me. And it did. It really did. But then it didn't kinda fill the horizon the way it did at the beginning. Like I said to Emmy—'

'Emmy?'

'Rose's daughter. I only found her at the end. I could kick myself. I said to her that whatever we do in life, we need to know we are loved. That we are lovable.' She looked at him. 'Don't we?'

He nodded slowly. 'Dad too.'

Mallory picked up her water glass again.

'Sure,' she said, 'Dad too. But before there was her, there was us. Wasn't there?'

Seth looked at the menu once more.

'If we're going to have this kind of conversation,' he said, 'I need to eat. So I'm gonna order. OK?'

———

Prue indicated the mattress topper in her capacious Liberty-print holdall.

'Very pleased,' she said. 'Left over from the clearance sale so only half of even the sale price. Have you had breakfast?'

Rose nodded. 'A banana.'

'Not what I'd call a proper breakfast. I usually make porridge. Why don't you try porridge, Rosie?'

Rose looked down at her coffee. The barista had swirled a palm-tree pattern into the foam, which was very pretty but would not manage to make any of it taste more interesting. She made a non-committal noise.

Prue had chosen peppermint tea and a redoubtable scone with an improbably glossy top. She gestured at it.

'Share my scone?'

Rose shook her head. 'No, thank you all the same.'

'What is it, Rosie?'

Rose didn't raise her eyes.

'You tell me. You're the one who asked for this meeting.'

Prue sliced into her scone and gave an exclamation of disgust. 'Look at that. As dry as a desert.' She pushed the scone plate to one side. 'I'm not eating that. I'm not paying for it, either. I'll have it out with them later. I wanted to talk to you, Rosie, because of money and the children. I've spoken to Emmy.'

Rose put a teaspoon into the foam palm tree and broke up the pattern.

'Did you?'

'Yes. Don't pretend you don't care. I rang Emmy.'

At last Rose raised her head.

'Why?'

'Because,' Prue said weightily, 'I thought it was time she got over herself and met Nat's girlfriend.'

Rose's expression didn't alter. 'She has just met her. And it wasn't a success.'

'Well,' Prue said, 'and is that a surprise?'

Rose sat up straighter. 'What do you mean?'

'Was Emmy ever going to like a serious girlfriend of Nat's? Any more than she was going to like anyone you had more than a cup of tea with?'

'What are you trying to say?'

'That Emmy needs a distraction. Emmy won't grow up until she is diverted from the emotional ties of her child-hood.'

Rose said, almost thoughtfully, 'I want to tell you to mind your own business.'

'Your children, my nieces and nephew, are my business, Rosie. They always have been, as you well know, and they always will be. I wanted to see you because Emmy said something about possibly going to New York to see Tyler's Mallory and I wanted to talk to you about that. About, as I said, money and the children.' She leaned forward and put a hand on Rose's nearest one. She said, in a much lower and more sympathetic tone, 'I know you don't want to sell the mews. I know how you feel about that house. I know what it represents to you. So I don't think you should feel you have to sell it in order for Emmy to be able to go to America, and the others to have their share too. So I wanted to see you to tell you that I am perfectly prepared to buy Emmy a ticket to New York, and to give the others an equivalent amount. I suppose I could have told you over the telephone but that seemed to me a bit impersonal. So here I am, Rosie, saying that Emmy can go to America and you don't have to sell the house to help her.'

Rose looked at her sister's large, capable hand lying on her own.

'Oh, Prue.'

'Don't thank me. I can't bear being thanked.'

'I'm so touched,' Rose said, 'I really am.'

'Then let me do it.'

Rose turned her own hand over so that she could give her sister's hand a squeeze before she let it go. Then she said, smiling at Prue, 'You are so lovely, Prue, but it's fine. It really is. I've got my silly head around selling the mews now, I really have. And I'm thrilled to be able to give the children some money, thrilled. Laura's been so sweet and anxious about it all on my behalf, but I think she is reassured now, I *think* she is. I did my best to help her see that I'm doing what I want and that Tyler is possibly the least mercenary man she will ever meet. It was just a shock, I expect, when he

213

first suggested selling the mews, and I had to get over that shock, but I have now, I have, and Emmy can go to America.'

Prue said nothing. She regarded her sister steadily and in silence.

Rose picked up her coffee cup in both hands and took a neat swallow. She said, 'I know I didn't like that first cottage we looked at.'

Prue said inexorably, 'Nor any of the subsequent ones.'

'No. No, I know.' Rose glanced at her. 'They were none of them right. I didn't get that "This is the one" feeling about any of them. But Prue . . .'

'What?'

'We're going to see another one on Saturday. In Hampshire. In Jane Austen's bit of Hampshire. And whatever I've felt about any of the others, I don't seem to be feeling about this. It's brick. Eighteenth-century brick. With a wonderful garden. Look, I'll show you.'

She held up her phone. Prue shook her head.

'No, thank you, Rosie.'

'But—'

'Do you know,' Prue said, her gaze scanning the cafe for someone to whom she could complain about her scone, 'I just can't get my head round this cottage scheme of yours, I just can't. Even in Jane Austen's Hampshire.'

'Are you offended that I declined your very generous offer to help Emmy?'

Prue lifted the scone plate and indicated it forcefully to someone across the room.

'Not in the least,' she said. 'I reserve offence for sizable social and cultural issues. And I would like to believe you when you say you are doing what you want to do. The trouble is, Rose . . .' She paused and then she said, 'I just can't.'

———

Emmy was cooking. She had determined to turn over a new leaf and get a proper grasp on daily life, so she had bought, as a first step, onions and prawns and mange tout peas (a pity that two of those items had been flown into the UK using expensive and undesirable air miles) and was, with the addition of a pot of Thai green curry paste she had found in her cupboard, making supper. The recipe said that the preparation would take fifteen minutes, and that it would serve two people, which meant, Emmy thought with satisfaction, that supper for tonight and tomorrow would be catered for. Two evenings of home-cooked supper and no booze was a commendable start to what she was determined would be a different way of living. Of being.

The recipe said it needed coconut milk. Emmy didn't have coconut milk in the cupboard. She turned out what she did have – cereal bars, a jar of crystallized ginger, a squeezy bottle of lemon juice, boxes of rice and polenta, a bottle of Greek olive oil, a packet of dried chillies – and found, at the back, a small tin of coconut cream, dated 2014. She looked at it. Where had it come from? She had only just bought the flat in 2014. Did it matter, for the curry, if it was cream, not milk? And did it matter, being two years out of date?

She yanked at the ring pull on the top of the can and peeled it back a little way. The coconut cream was very white and looked like plastic, lying in a smooth crust round the top of the can. Emmy pushed a finger into it and her finger went through the top crust of the cream and into the coconut liquid underneath. She pulled it out and put her finger in her mouth. Then the doorbell rang.

Still holding the can, Emmy went across to her entryphone. There was no screen beside it, so she picked up the handset, holding her sticky forefinger well away, and said, 'Hello?' questioningly into it.

'Hi,' Laura said. 'It's Laura.'

Emmy was amazed.

'Laura! What on earth are you doing here?'

'I've come to see you,' Laura said. She sounded, Emmy thought, older-sisterly. 'Angus has the children and I've come to see you. I came on the tube.'

'Why?' Emmy said.

'Let me in. Let me in first, Emmy.'

Emmy put the handset back and pressed the downstairs-door release. Then she opened her own front door and stood beside it, still holding the can of coconut cream.

Laura came briskly up the communal staircase. She was wearing what Emmy thought of as her doctor clothes: a shirt tucked into tailored trousers, and a blazer. Her hair was in a ponytail and her capacious bag was on her shoulder. She reached Emmy's landing and took her sister by the shoulders to kiss her.

'Em.'

'I am very surprised. You never ever—'

'Well, I have now. What's that?'

Emmy gestured with her can. 'Coconut cream. It's two years old. Can I use it?'

'Sure,' Laura said. 'It'll be fine. Just maybe not so nutritious as it once was. What are you making?'

'Prawn curry.'

'Enough for two of us?'

Emmy looked at her. 'Could be. I just can't get over your being here.'

Laura went past her into the flat and dropped her bag on the floor. Then she shrugged off her jacket.

'I'll help you with the curry.'

Emmy said, not moving from beside the door, 'Is there a crisis? Has something happened?'

Laura began to unbutton her cuffs and roll up her shirt-sleeves.

'There was just a bit of a list, Em, a list of things building up. Things I want to talk to you about. And Angus said why didn't I just come and surprise you.'

'It's a surprise all right.'

'If it had been planned,' Laura said, 'you might have prepared yourself, mightn't you? Or you might have gone out.'

'Only if what you were going to say was very uncomfortable.'

Laura looked at her. Then she moved across and took the can of coconut cream out of Emmy's fingers.

'It's not uncomfortable, Em. It's just so I can get my head round some stuff. What's this going in?'

'What stuff?' Emmy said.

Laura carried the can across to Emmy's kitchen section. She touched an open iPad with her free hand.

'Is this the recipe?'

'What stuff?' Emmy repeated, and then, 'Yes. Yes, it is.'

Laura bent over the iPad. 'Have you chopped the onion?'

'Not yet.'

'We'll get this going, then we'll talk. Have you got a frying pan?'

Emmy crossed the room to open a drawer by Laura's knees. 'There. Laura, what is it?'

Laura laid a chopping board on the worktop. Then she turned to face her sister.

'I want to know about Nat's Jess. I want to know what happened that night. And even more, I want to talk about Mum.'

'Mum!'

'Yes,' Laura said. She pulled the only knife off the magnetic rack that Emmy used as a parking place for scissors and her bike keys and the metal tag for supermarket trolleys. 'Mum. What's all this about you going to America?'

Emmy said defensively, 'It was just an idea.'

'Why?'

'I wanted to see Mallory.'

'Tyler's Mallory?'

'Yes. She asked me. She asked me to go and stay with her in New York.'

'For a holiday?'

'I s'pose so.'

Laura stopped peeling the onion and turned to face her sister. She said, 'You don't need a holiday, Emmy. Look at me. *Look* at me. Aren't you just wanting to go to New York because you can't immediately think of what else to do, and you want a distraction?'

Emmy said lamely, 'I *like* Mallory.'

'What's that got to do with anything?'

'Why shouldn't I go to New York? Why shouldn't I go and stay with Mallory? Aunt Prue is all in favour of my going.'

Laura put down the knife and the onion. Then she said, 'Leave her out of it. Leave everything out of it, even what you think you want and the reasons you think you have for wanting it. And think about Mum.'

Emmy looked at the floor.

'I *do* think about Mum.'

'Listen, Em. *Listen*. Mum has got this scheme in her head, she's kind of convinced herself that it's even what she wants. You know about this scheme?'

'Sort of.'

'This plan to sell the mews and give us all this money and then buy a cottage somewhere with Tyler?'

Emmy nodded.

Laura said fiercely, 'It's insane.'

'Not if it's what she wants. You always said that if she wanted to live her life that way, then she should be allowed to, that it was *her* life.'

'But I don't believe it *is* what she wants. I think it was, it really was, at the beginning, when it was all such an adventure, so exciting and head-turning, but I don't think it's that any more.'

Emmy raised her head. 'Don't you?'

'No,' Laura said, 'I don't. Not any longer. I think she doesn't want to disappoint him now. Or let him down. You know what she's like. She always thinks she *owes* people.'

Emmy said with sudden resolution, 'She doesn't *owe* me a single thing.'

'Exactly.'

'I couldn't bear her to make some sort of sacrifice because she thinks I'd like the money.'

'Ah,' Laura said. She turned back to her onion. 'That's better.'

Emmy came to stand very close to her sister.

'Don't you think she's OK, then?'

Laura was chopping. She said carefully, 'I think she's OK mostly, yes. And, if you want to know, I think he's fine in lots of ways. I think he really does adore her.'

'But?'

'There's just something,' Laura said.

'What kind of something?'

'It's hard to put my finger on. Too romantic, maybe. Even too Mum-obsessed. Something missing, something about background, family. And there's money. I don't think he's at all greedy or anything, I just think he's a bit – hopeless, I suppose. Impractical about money. Just a vague sort of unease I have about him, that he's a kind of impractical dreamer.'

Emmy leaned against the counter close to her sister.

'What does Angus think?'

Laura scraped the onions into the frying pan.

'Nice guy. Plainly mad about Mum. But why hasn't he any money?'

'Hasn't he?'

Laura flicked her a glance. 'Have you seen any evidence? One rented one-room flat here and apparently nothing to sell in America?'

Emmy said cautiously, 'Does it have to be about money, in the end?'

'Not if it was you. But if it's Mum, and she's sixty-four, yes.'

'I hated the idea of Tyler at the beginning. So did Nat.'

'Because of Dad?'

'Oh no,' Emmy said with emphasis. 'Because of Mum.'

Laura picked up the jar of curry paste. 'This?'

'Yes.'

'So,' Laura said, 'you know where I'm coming from.'

Emmy nodded vehemently. She said, 'So what do we do?'

Laura spooned curry paste into the onions.

'You start,' she said, 'by not going to New York. And Nat starts by not throwing Tim out of his flat. Where's a wooden spoon? I'm almost done.' She turned to look at Emmy. 'Which brings us neatly to the other thing on my list of topics to talk with you about. What happened that evening between you and Jess?'

———

Tyler heard from Seth that Mallory had been to San Francisco. It was an unsatisfactory call, because although Seth was very friendly, he was also very preoccupied because a new batch of sourdough starter had grown a mould which Seth had never experienced before and which, even though it was to be immediately discarded, was a matter of grave concern. He wanted to explain to his father that although the mould wasn't deep into the starter, and the whole culture could probably be revived with proper feeding at the right temperature, he couldn't, with public health concerns, take the risk. So when Tyler wanted to ask specifics about Mallory, and the reasons for Mallory's going to San Francisco, and the content of any conversations Mallory might have had with Seth, he was unable to give his father any more than the briefest of replies. Yes, she looked fine, he thought, and seemed OK and had work lined up after the show she was in, but no, he had no idea when he'd see her again – jeez, Dad, it was surprising enough to see her as it was!

Tyler rang Mallory. There was no reply. He left a message to call him. Then he sent her a text and a second text, and considered ringing Rose's Emmy to ask if she had spoken to Mallory recently, but something held him back. It was the something – not quite definable – that always afflicted him when it came to Rose's children. He liked them. He was very sure about that. He liked them all, and he admired Laura. Laura was doing the kind of professional job that benefitted her fellow man and thus was deserving of real respect. And those twins of Rose's were both in paid employment and were likeable and personable. But – and there was a but in Tyler's mind – he wasn't making progress with any of them. He might like them, and they might show no sign these days of not liking him in return, but he wasn't getting anywhere with any of them.

So, quite apart from wanting to know why she had suddenly flown to San Francisco, Tyler wanted to talk to Mallory about Emmy, ask if there was anything he should know about her, if there was anything he was doing that offended her, or troubled her. Because he really didn't want that. He really – and he was aware of his own earnestness as he thought about it – wanted to improve his relationships with Rose's children. He liked them and he wanted them to like him. He wanted, he realized, for them to feel that they were all part of his and Rose's future. He wanted them to be more than just there. He wanted them to participate.

He tried Mallory's phone again. It would be early evening in New York, well before evening theatre performances began.

'Hi,' Mallory's message said, 'this is Mallory's phone. I'll call you back.'

Please do, Tyler thought. He wouldn't leave another begging message. Please do.

CHAPTER FOURTEEN

'I've been thinking,' Tyler said.

They were sitting in a Hampshire pub, before their appointment to see the brick cottage, eating, in Tyler's case, a ploughman's lunch. It was a very substantial version of a ploughman's lunch and included generous wedges of English cheese, as well as little heaps of walnut halves, and dried cranberries, and apple chutney in a separate miniature pot. Rose had eaten two of the walnut halves and a sliver of cheese but said that she wasn't really hungry; certainly not hungry enough to merit her own order.

She paused, a single cranberry in her fingers.

'Have you?'

'I think,' Tyler said, 'that we should throw a party.'

Rose put the cranberry down on a paper napkin.

'Goodness.'

'Don't you think? I mean, surely you've given lots of parties in your time?'

'But not for ages. Years. In fact, I think the last proper party I gave was when I was still married to William. We used to have open house on Christmas Eve – but you don't want to hear about that.'

He smiled at her.

'I'm fine with hearing about you and William giving parties. Of course you gave parties. How could you be married all those years and not give parties?'

Rose had a fleeting memory of those Christmas Eve parties, of the noise in the festively decorated house, and the tension caused by William always being late, arriving in a blast of bonhomie and universal sympathy for the nobility of his work that had occasioned his lateness, when the reality – a pre-Christmas assignation with Gillian Greenhalgh – had been so very different. She looked briefly at her aquamarine.

'A party . . .'

'Why not?' Tyler said. 'Your friends, my English friends, such as they are. I've met your children, after all, I've met your sister, but I haven't met your friends. I'd like to. I'd *like* to meet your friends.'

Rose smiled, as if to herself.

'I'd like that too.'

'Would you? Would you really?'

She glanced at him. 'Why do you ask?'

Tyler put down a chunk of granary bread. He said, seriously, 'I ask because I don't want to pressure you into doing anything you don't want to do. I may want to have a party, but I don't want you to have one against your will.'

She said seriously, 'It wouldn't be.'

'It could be *our* party. Our first party. As a couple.'

'Yes,' she said. 'It could.'

'In fact, I know a wine merchant. I was at school with someone who now has his own wine business.'

She nodded. 'Good.'

'Rosie. What is it? Would you rather we didn't have a party?'

'I'd love to have a party. I want to have a party.'

He held the ploughman's plate out to her. 'That's wonderful. I'm so glad. Have some more cheese.'

She shook her head. He lowered the plate to the table again.

'Honestly,' he said, 'you live on air. I take you out to lunch and you eat half a tomato and a tadpole.' He looked at his watch. 'Ten to two,' he said. 'Shall we move?'

'A party,' Rose said. 'A party! It's so long since I even thought about a party.'

Tyler reached out to give her hand a quick squeeze.

'Cottage first. Then party. We can talk about both, going back to London. Rose . . .'

'Yes?'

'Do you . . .' He stopped.

'Do I what?'

'Do you feel OK about this cottage, about seeing this cottage?'

She stood up and wound the scarf she was carrying round her neck.

'Don't hold me to it,' she said, 'but I feel fine about this cottage. More than fine, actually. In fact, I feel that this cottage might be the one. And,' she added, picking up her bag and threading it onto her arm, 'I am up for this cottage, *and* a party.'

—

Nat ran Tim to earth by his coffee machine. Tim had been for an early morning run, and was preparing, as was his wont, to cycle to work in his running gear and shower at work before donning the suit and shoes he was carrying in an ergonomically designed backpack. He was making himself, as he often did, a double espresso before his ride.

Nat leaned on the counter beside him and folded his arms across his bare chest. He had left Jess asleep and climbed into a pair of pyjama trousers on his way to the door. There had been a time, not so very long ago, when he and Tim had done an early-morning run together and in unspoken competition. Tim had not commented on this friendly habit having ceased any more than Nat commented on the nutritional unsuitability of following a ten-kilometre run with a double espresso. He simply yawned a bit and ruffled his hair back and forth and watched Tim drop coffee capsules into the machine's mechanism.

'Want one?' Tim said. His hair stood up in sweat-soaked spikes but his shorts and T-shirt, fashioned out of some miracle modern fibre, looked both cool and dry.

Nat yawned again and extracted something from a back tooth.

'No ta, mate.'

Tim put his favourite mug – commemorative, designed for the 2016 UEFA European Championship – under the spout of the coffee machine and pressed the start button.

'Don't tell me not to drink this.'

'Wouldn't dream of it.'

Nat eyed the mug. It was thick and white, with a red-cross football on it, and, in deliberately amateur lettering, the slogan 'C'mon England'.

'Been meaning to ask you something.'

'Mmm?'

'Now that me and Jess . . .' He stopped.

Tim glanced at him. 'Am I in the way?'

Nat raised an arm to scratch between his shoulder blades. 'No, mate. Not really. Not exactly.'

Tim was watching his coffee drip into the mug. 'Seems to me,' he said, 'that I leave the bathroom in a much more civilized state than she does.'

Nat grinned. He said proudly, 'Wouldn't be difficult.'

'But you'd like me out?'

'It's more,' Nat said, 'that we'd like the place to ourselves.'

'So I'm in the way. Like I said.'

The coffee stopped dripping. Tim switched off the machine and picked up his mug. He looked at Nat again.

'What about the mortgage?'

Nat pulled a face. 'Tricky. There might be a solution, but I'm not counting on it.'

Tim was qualified as an accountant. He raised his mug briefly in Nat's direction, as if making a toast.

'Don't you think you'd better be sure before you decide finally? What'll you do with a second bedroom anyway? Or maybe I'd better not ask.'

'Look, mate,' Nat said, 'no offence. Honestly. I'm just kind of – sounding you out. Telling you what's on my mind.'

Tim took a swallow of coffee, screwed his eyes shut, took another and banged his mug down.

'That's better. Nothing like endorphins followed by caffeine.' He bent to pick up his backpack. 'Love seems to be catching in your family right now.' He hoisted the backpack onto one shoulder. 'I'll look for another room, OK?'

'It's not that you're not welcome, mate.'

Tim took flexible sunglasses on a rubber lariat out of a

zippered pocket in his backpack and put them on. Then he turned his head, suddenly transformed into that of a giant insect, and clumped Nat on his shoulder.

'I'm cool with it. I am. I'll ask around. See ya.'

After he'd gone, Nat wandered to his laptop, which he'd left on the glass table he'd been so proud to own until Jess told him that it wasn't so much cool as suburban, and switched it on. He bent over it, yawning, and noticed that among the emails which had relentlessly arrived during the night, there was one from his sister, Laura. It was short, as Laura's emails – uncharacteristically for a woman – usually were.

> Hi Nattie – can we meet? Something I need to
> discuss with you. Supper here at the weekend?
> Girlfriend very welcome. L xx

Nat sighed. Being in rehearsal, rather than performing, Jess would be free at the weekend, in the evening. And of course she and Laura should meet. Needed to meet. Laura, he told himself, was not like Emmy, and in any case, he was far from averse to showing Jess off. But if Laura met her then of course Rose would be next. Which meant, these days, Tyler too. He straightened up and ran his tongue round his teeth. What a pity, he thought, what a terrible pity that you couldn't hold on to that first, utterly thrilling and entirely private mutual ecstasy of a new relationship for more than a moment before the world crowded in, peering and asking questions and making judgements. He glanced at the closed bedroom door. At least, even if he couldn't think how the mortgage was to be afforded without Tim, he could tell Jess that he had put Tim in the picture. He had started the ball rolling, which in turn had started off several other balls. Jeez, he thought, heading back to the coffee machine, why does anything so wonderful have to come at such a price?

———

Rose lay in the bath. There was a glass of wine balanced on the edge, brought by Tyler, and a big towel within reach for when she got out of the water, also left by Tyler. Tyler was, at this moment, downstairs with a Lebanese cookbook and the beginnings of supper. As the bathroom was just above the kitchen, she could hear the rumble of radio news and the odd clash of a saucepan, and through the west-facing window of the bathroom, she could see a late-spring sunset streaking a duck-egg-blue sky with streaks of coral and apricot. She closed her eyes for a moment and swished the water pleasurably across her stomach with her right hand. This, she thought to herself, is contentment: deep, satisfied contentment. It might not have the insane fervour of a new or sudden passion, but it has so much that is both steadier and more profound instead.

Behind her closed lids, she took herself through the rooms of the Hampshire cottage. They were pretty rooms with eighteenth-century proportions and panelled shutters at the windows. Nothing was very big, certainly, but there were good ceiling heights and a couple of carved fireplaces and a magnificent and unexpected landing, like an extra room, with a sash window looking over the garden. Standing at that window, Rose had gazed not only at the garden but at the lane beyond it, and, beyond that, at a field full of decorative Jersey cows, stands of mature trees in brilliant new leaf, a collection of haphazard tiled roofs, and a church tower with a weathervane on one pinnacle that had caught the sun with a flash of fire.

The cottage had four bedrooms, one of which could easily be made into a second bathroom, two reception rooms and a kitchen with a solid-fuel cooker installed in a substantial chimney breast. Outside there was a paved terrace, a greenhouse, flowerbeds, a vegetable garden, lawns and apple trees. The present owner had waxed the floors, eschewed curtains in favour of the shutters, and painted all the exterior woodwork white. In the bathroom, a cast-iron, claw-footed bath stood in the centre of the room and there were white cotton rugs on the floor either side of it, and a painted table at the head end on which stood a pottery soap dish, a stack of books and a patterned jug of white lilac.

'Well?' Tyler had said softly, from behind her.

She'd been speechless. In truth, from the moment the agent had opened the door to the front hall, flooded with light from the landing above, Rose had capitulated. Whatever optimism she had – or hadn't – concealed from Tyler before they actually saw the cottage was unleashed to an overwhelming degree the moment she stepped under the white-painted lintel and onto the cider-coloured floorboards. It was a moment of recognition, a sort of homecoming, an exultant feeling of not wanting to live in such a house so much as just needing to.

In the garden, Tyler had put his hands in his pockets and surveyed the apple trees.

'We could have hens.'

Rose swallowed. 'I've never had hens.'

'Nor me. But it can't be that difficult. Bantams, perhaps, with feathery feet.'

'Tyler . . .'

'Yes?'

'It's – wonderful. Isn't it?'

He took one hand out of his pocket and put an arm round her shoulders.

'Do you think so? Do you really think so?'

She nodded vigorously. He gripped her shoulders. She said, 'Is it mad?'

'Is what mad?'

'Is it mad to fall for a house so suddenly, so completely?'

'I wouldn't say so.'

'I thought,' she said, 'that I wouldn't like anything in the country. That I wouldn't like the country.'

'I know.'

She glanced at him. 'Were you just waiting?'

He squeezed her shoulders a second time and let her go.

'I was hoping,' he said. 'Put it that way.'

'I want it. I'm a bit frightened by how much I want it. Suppose lots of other people want it too?'

He smiled.

'It's been on the market for over six months. I don't think we'll be fighting off too much competition.'

'Oh, Tyler!'

He folded his arms. He said, teasingly, 'Sober up, Rosie. Offers and surveys and checking the Land Registry and all that first. Suppose there's a pig farm next door, or someone has permission to build a whole estate of houses—'

'Stop it!'

He smiled at her again.

'Just teasing. I'm thrilled to see you so happy. I was longing to see you happy . . .' He stopped.

She blew him a kiss.

'I know. It just had to be the right house, the very house.'

'Sweetheart. Can I ask you something?'

'Of course,' she said, turning to look at the greenhouse, at a toppling stack of terracotta flowerpots, at the open kitchen door.

'Would this cottage, if we can get it, compensate you for having to sell the mews house?'

She stopped turning, to look at him. Her expression was suddenly grave. 'Oh yes,' she said.

Oh yes, she thought now, lying in her bath. To exchange her London bath, even with its window, for that bath in the centre of the room with the lilacs and a copy of Shakespeare's sonnets was what Prue would call a no-brainer. Prue would love the cottage. The children, surely, would love the cottage, would completely understand why the relationship with Tyler made absolute sense in such a setting, especially if she could be generous to them a good twenty years before any of them were expecting it. To live somewhere like that, on an acre of Hampshire earth as so many generations had done before her, would represent a resonance, a continuity, a sense of belonging and perpetuity she had never known before, never thought of as desirable or necessary.

She opened her eyes and slowly sat up, feeling the water shivering down her skin. She reached for her wine and took a grateful swallow. There was so much, suddenly, to look forward to, so much to plan, to relish. She put the wine glass down and got to her feet, reaching for the towel, and stood there in the water holding the towel against her, overcome with a flood of thankfulness. Without Tyler, without meeting

Tyler again, none of this would be happening, none of it. Surely everyone, in the end, would understand that?

———

Emmy had flung herself, quite apart from the cooking, into work. There was no defined hierarchy in her office but a pecking order had inevitably emerged for all the insistence on first names and open plan and casual dressing, and the man who was nominally in charge of Emmy's team noticed a significant and effective difference in her performance. Emmy was in to work half an hour earlier each morning and remained every evening to finish tasks that she would previously have left until the following day. She pulled off, in addition, various coups, including making an advertising campaign for a small artisan gin distillery into enough of a story to attract the attention of – and consequent coverage in – a national tabloid. The two brothers who had started the distillery with a loan from their father, in his garage, came into the office to be lauded by everyone, and to meet Emmy. The managing director, who was called Matthew and had ginger stubble and a propensity for lumberjack shirts raised his glass of celebratory Prosecco and made a speech which was partly about gin, but mostly about Emmy.

The brothers said that there had been a fifteen per cent increase in sales since the media coverage, and two bars in Shoreditch and one in Hoxton were now taking the gin. They said that the bottling company they used were also now treating them with a measure of respect rather than as yet another pair of naive amateurs. They looked at Emmy and asked was that her real name because they wanted to incorporate it somehow into the new raspberry-flavoured gin they were planning, as a tribute.

Emmy felt suddenly shy. She looked at her glass of Prosecco and said that actually her name was Emma. She'd been christened Emma.

'Emma!' Matthew said, as if making an announcement. 'What does it mean?'

'Whole,' Emmy said to her wine glass. 'Or universal, or something. The first Emma in England was Edward the Confessor's mother.'

Everybody laughed, even though Emmy hadn't said anything witty. The gin brothers made their way through the crowd and said that they were sure some bright idea of how to incorporate her name into the label on the new gin would come to them, but in the meantime, thanks a million, it was brilliant. Emmy hooked her hair behind her ear with her free hand and said that they were welcome and she was just doing her job. But she was glowing. She glowed all the way through the rest of the party and found herself, while walking up to Shaftesbury Avenue from work to get the bus home, ringing Rose.

'Darling!' Rose said, and then, as she always did, 'Where are you? Is everything OK?'

'I'm fine,' Emmy said. 'On my way home.'

'Lovely.'

'From – well, from a bit of a celebration actually, at work. A celebration about me, in fact. Something I did.'

Rose sounded, Emmy thought, a little distracted. She said, 'Oh! What? How wonderful!' but she said it in a slightly constrained way, as if she was holding something back. Emmy climbed onto the bus and made her way to a seat at the back, next to an olive-skinned boy who seemed to be utterly asleep, his head propped against the glass of the window.

'I got free publicity for one of our campaigns in a national paper, Mum. It had an effect at once. The boys who make the product want to name their next idea after me.'

'What is it?'

Emmy lowered her voice. 'Gin.'

'What?'

'Gin, Mum. Gin. As in gin and tonic.'

Rose sounded bemused.

'I see.'

'I don't think you do, Mum. And the gin isn't important. What I was ringing to tell you is that I've had a bit of a suc-cess, at work.'

Rose's voice was warm. 'That's wonderful. It really is. Very proud-making.'

Emmy looked sideways at the sleeping boy. His eyelashes were blue-black on his cheeks and as thick as fur. She said, 'It's kind of nice, to be praised for a work thing.'

'You deserve it.'

'Well . . .'

'Emmy. Darling, have you got a moment?'

'Sure,' Emmy said, 'I'm on the bus.'

'There's something,' Rose said, 'that I want to tell you. To say to you.'

The bus had stopped, and the boy woke and slipped out of his seat and off the bus in a single, seamless movement. Emmy shifted across so that she was by the window, and could see the boy running up Museum Street towards the British Museum. Where on earth was he going at such speed? She said, into her phone, 'I'm here, Mum.'

'I think,' Rose said, her voice gathering energy, 'that you'll be able to go to New York soon.'

Emmy frowned out of the bus window. 'What are you talking about?'

'Darling,' Rose said, 'I thought you wanted to go to see Mallory in America.'

'I did,' Emmy said, 'for about ten minutes. When Nat – oh, never mind. I thought I needed a break, a change of scene or something. And then Mallory said—'

'Mallory?'

'Yes. We were FaceTiming. Mallory said why didn't I try just putting my back into work for a start. Instead of getting hung up on things I couldn't change. So I have. And honestly, Mum, I never thought there'd be results so quickly, I never thought something would happen almost at once. I mean, I only took on this account two weeks ago, and I had this idea about the family angle – you know, two brothers, their dad's garage—'

'Emmy,' Rose said, cutting across her, 'Emmy, listen. If you want, still, to go to America, I think you can.'

'Mum. Are you listening? I don't want to go to New York just now. I did, but now I don't. Because of work. I've rung you to tell you that work has turned a corner, that I feel differently about work, that – that maybe work can become much more than just being something that pays the bills while I wait for a big something else to happen. I thought – for God's sake, Mum, I thought you'd be pleased!'

There was a silence and then Rose said, without complete conviction, 'I am.'

'Well, why are you going on about New York then?'

There was a pause. Then Rose said carefully, 'Emmy, something's happened.'

'A good thing?' Emmy demanded. 'A thing I'll be pleased about?'

Rose's voice gathered enthusiasm again. 'Oh yes, darling. Yes you will. You can't fail to.'

Emmy felt a sudden small lurch of suspicion. 'What? What is it?'

Rose said in a voice full of barely contained rapture, 'We've found a house!'

'You what?'

'On Thursday. Yesterday, was it? Heavens, yes, only yesterday! We saw the most heavenly little house.'

'Mum . . .'

'It's basically eighteenth century. Brick, very doll's house, utterly charming. It stands in an acre of the most lovely garden with apple trees, and there's a church across the fields, and cows, and a free-standing bath . . .'

'Mum!' Emmy said loudly.

'It's so sweet.'

'What,' Emmy said fiercely, 'do you think you are *doing*?'

She could hear Rose give a little gasp.

'Sorry,' Rose said, 'that was all too much of a gush. I know it was. But I love it. I loved it as we drove up, it was quite extraordinary, to just *know* about a house in one's guts, somehow, even before I'd stepped inside.'

The bus was approaching Rosebery Avenue. Emmy stood up and began to make her unsteady way between other passengers' knees and then down the aisle.

'You can't do this, Mum.'

'What can't I do?'

'You can't just sell up in London and decamp to the country like this. You can't just – fling one life aside and seize on another as if there weren't any consequences.'

'The consequences, may I remind you, are very much to your advantage,' Rose said.

The bus had stopped. Emmy stepped out onto the pavement, her phone still held to her ear.

'But I don't want the money, I don't want—'

'Emmy,' Rose said, interrupting yet again, 'this is just more of the same, isn't it?'

'The same what?'

'You haven't changed,' Rose said. 'Have you? You haven't changed since I first met Tyler again. At bottom, darling – and you will always be darling to me – you just can't bear me to be fond of anyone but you children. Can you?'

CHAPTER FIFTEEN

Nat was startled when Jess appeared from the bathroom, ready to go and have supper with Laura and Angus. She wasn't wearing any of her customary exotica, but jeans and a checked shirt, and her hair, usually a cascade of long curls, was held back with the big butterfly clip she used to keep her hair off her face in the bathroom. She planted herself in front of him.

'OK?'

He stood up and peered at her. He said, uncertainly, 'Great. Fantastic. Always fantastic.'

She said, 'I didn't want to put a second sister off.'

'You couldn't.'

'I wasn't going to risk it. And I wasn't going to risk comparative possessiveness, either.'

Nat thought fleetingly of Emmy, and with a distinct pang. He hadn't seen Emmy in more than a fortnight now, which was one of the longest stretches of not seeing her in all their lives together, if you didn't count their gap years where he had tried to feel useful building a primary school in Tanzania, and Emmy had wept over the plight of street children in São Paulo. They had come home sobered and distressed by the endlessness of the world's problems to find Rose in her own state of dismay, having been confronted by William's revelations about Gillian Greenhalgh. Nat remembered them all sitting round the circular table in the Highgate kitchen with an ill-advised bottle of cachaça that Emmy had brought back from Brazil, and with which she had made caipirinha cocktails. It had been a most confusing homecoming, with the relief outweighed by the disclosure, and the familiarity of two of the three women he loved most in the world severely tempered by what they had seen and what they were going to have to go through.

He took Jess's hands.

'It'll be OK with Em. In time. I know it will.'

Jess licked her lips. Her face, Nat noticed, was almost clean of makeup, her mouth undefined by the red lipstick he usually found so dangerously confident and exciting.

'Maybe.'

He kissed her forehead. 'Laura's very different, anyway. You'll see.'

'Mm,' she said. 'The doctor and the actress. Not sure.'

When they got to Laura's house, Angus was upstairs settling the children and Laura was on the phone. She waved to them affably and gestured at the fridge and made bottle-tipping movements with her free hand, and then she wandered out of the kitchen and continued her conversation in the passage beyond.

'I think she's talking to a colleague,' Nat said. 'It doesn't sound like a patient. Usually it's a patient; she's *always* talking to patients.'

Jess examined the boys' paintings, attached to the fridge door with magnetic letters in primary colours.

'How many children?'

Nat looked over her shoulder.

'Those'll be by Jack. He's four. Very articulate.'

Jess indicated a purple handprint. 'And that?'

'Adam,' Nat said. 'He's twenty months. Just grunts. Grunts and eats.'

Jess glanced at him. 'You adore them. Don't you?'

Nat opened the fridge. 'S'pose so. Beer? Wine?'

'Why can't you admit that you adore them? And Emmy? Why can't you admit that your family mean the world to you?'

Nat stared into the fridge. 'Dunno.'

'I'll have a beer,' Jess said.

'OK.'

'One of the things I like about you is that you *feel* things. You really do. I don't know why I screwed up with Emmy. I don't know what devil got into me.'

'Or into Emmy,' Laura said, coming back into the kitchen. 'Em's good at devils of her very own. We all are. It's the human condition. Hi,' she said to Jess, 'I'm Laura. I hope Nat's getting you a drink.'

Jess took Laura's briefly outstretched hand.

'I like the boys' pictures.'

'Thank you.'

'Your beer,' Nat said, holding out a bottle.

Laura looked at him.

'Take the top off for her, Nat. Just take the top off. Honestly.'

'If you give me the gadget . . .' Jess said.

'No. No. He can do it. He knows he should do it.'

Nat eyed his sister.

'Am I in for a hard time? Are you going to tell me off as per usual?'

Laura considered him. She put her head slightly on one side.

'Not exactly. But when Angus comes down, I need to ask you about something.' She smiled at Jess. 'D'you mind helping Angus with a paella?'

'Not at all.'

'Good,' Laura said. She opened a drawer and rummaged to produce a bottle opener. She held it out to her brother.

'There you are,' she said. 'Make yourself useful.'

—

'Now,' Laura said.

She was sitting on the swivel desk chair in her study, and Nat was nursing a beer on the sofa bed, which had been folded up and was piled with a number of Jack's toy animals.

'Please don't just go for me.'

'I won't. I wasn't going to, anyway. But we haven't had the chance to talk for so long and all this stuff keeps happening.'

'Mum stuff?'

'Yes,' Laura said, 'Mum stuff.'

She took a sip from the wine glass on her desk, then she said, 'She's nice.'

Nat felt a foolish smile spread involuntarily across his face. 'Jess?'

'Of course Jess. Angus will be very happy indeed having her to slice peppers for him, never mind having someone gorgeous to show his cooking off to.'

'She *is* gorgeous.'

'Emmy thought so.'

'*Did* she? I thought Emmy—'

'It was *because* she's gorgeous that Emmy got off on the wrong foot with her, you dope. She was on the wrong foot from the get-go, and then she couldn't get back onto the right one. Which leads me . . .' She stopped.

Nat picked up a plush dolphin with exaggerated plastic eyes, and looked at it.

'To what?'

'Mum,' Laura said. 'Mum and her house.'

Nat put the dolphin on his knee.

'I'm a bit out of touch.'

'I'm afraid you can't be,' Laura said. 'However besotted you are, you can't stop focusing on Mum and the Tyler thing. You can't. And you can't blithely accept a wallop of money from Mum to have the flat to yourself, either.' She leaned forward. 'She shouldn't be selling, Nat. She just shouldn't. It's very generous and typical of her to think of giving us all money, but she can't. It's feckless. It's plain stupid. She's not at an age where she can afford to give away *anything* because, who knows? Who knows how long she'll live? Who knows whether she'll get ill or whether something unexpected will happen? I mean, supposing she was hit by a cyclist? Or fell off a bus? What I'm trying to say, what I was trying to get across to her, is that not only is the money the mews house represents *hers*, it's got to last her forever, and nobody knows how long that forever will be. So I just don't think she should be encouraged to give away a single penny; I don't think any of us should do anything other than make it absolutely plain to her that the last thing we want is any premature generosity from her.'

Nat was stroking the dolphin with a regularity that indicated he needed to do something calming.

'I asked Dad.'

'What did you ask Dad?'

'I asked him, as he paid the deposit on the flat, if he'd beef up on the mortgage a bit so that I didn't have to let the second bedroom.'

'And?' Laura demanded.

'He said no.'

'Of *course* he did,' Laura cried. 'What else did you expect? You and Em are so lucky, d'you know that? Fancy having flats, in this day and age, in central London.'

'You've got a whole bloody *house*!'

'Down payment,' Laura said calmly. 'From Angus's parents and Dad. We pay the mortgage, just like you do. Like you *have* to do, hot girlfriend or not.'

Nat flung the dolphin on the floor. He said, 'I thought you were the one telling Mum she could live as she liked, that it was her life, that she was free to choose.'

'I was,' Laura said, 'I did. And in an ideal world, I do think that. I can't bear the way everyone sits in judgement on everyone else all the time. But I realized that Mum's situation scares me. It really does. She can't throw caution to the wind, whatever she feels about Tyler. She just can't. She has got to think of her future.'

Nat took a pull at his beer. 'So?'

'We can't let her. We can't let her just do what she wants.'

'Even if what she wants helps us to have what we want?'

'Even then.' Laura said. She picked up her wine glass. 'Have you spoken to Em recently?'

Nat stared at his beer bottle. 'Nope.'

'When then?'

'Not for a couple of weeks. Have you?'

Laura put her glass down. 'Not to talk to, properly. 'She wanted to go to America.'

'Yes.'

They looked at each other.

Nat said, 'Well, if I can't, she can't.'

'She knows that.'

Nat grunted. Then he said, 'So that leaves telling Mum, doesn't it.' He looked directly at Laura. 'God, Laura. Think what it'll be like, telling Mum.'

———

Rose stood in her kitchen. She was alone because Tyler had gone out to buy a half-bottle of champagne. To celebrate, he said. He had been laughing. He said he knew drinking at lunchtime on a weekday was usually out of the question, but today, after all, was not an ordinary day, was it? I mean, he said, it was hardly commonplace to have the first person who came to view your house offer you twenty-five thousand above the asking price if you would agree to it being immediately taken off the market, now was it? He had gone whistling up the mews, running like a teenager. And left Rose standing in her kitchen. Stunned.

She wasn't, she realized, looking at anything. She knew the familiar view out into the garden was there, just as she knew that the unit against which she leaned was solid. But nothing, in a disconnecting way, felt known. She swallowed. Perhaps it was shock, simply. Tyler, wanting to waltz her round her sitting room, had been sure her dazed reaction had been shock. To have the very first viewers of the house – a pleasant Canadian couple in their fifties who said that they had spent the last three years looking for an ideal base in London to be near their daughter, who had married an Englishman – visibly fall in love and make an offer within half an hour of arriving was enough to take anyone's breath away. The Canadian husband had made his money out of a chain of auto-repair shops across Ontario, they were keen gardeners, and had begun to despair of ever finding anything in London that would be a home to their grandchildren as well as more than a pied à terre for themselves. They adored the mews house. The wife said several times that she also adored what Rose had done with it, that Rose's taste was completely in tune with her own. The young man from the estate agency who was escorting them looked as if he could scarcely contain his satisfaction at matching both buyer and seller so precisely.

Rose gripped the edge of the unit and bent forward, hunching her shoulders. Only a few nights ago, lying in the bath, she had been entirely certain that the Hampshire cottage would compensate, in every way, for having to sell the mews. But now, with their offer on the cottage still not finally accepted, and this whirlwind of a prospect on the mews, she felt dazed and slightly sick, as if some kind of happy, but safely distant, fantasy had resolved itself into a faintly menacing and immediate actuality.

She focused on the work surface between her hands. She must think. Think. Her future lay with Tyler, with being married to Tyler, living with Tyler as Mrs Masson. Yes. Yes, she was quite sure of that. And that future would be in that irresistible cottage with hens under the apple trees and Jack and Adam going out into the garden with Tyler to pull carrots and collect eggs. In addition, Laura and Angus could pay off their mortgage probably, and Nat could have his flat to himself and Emmy could fly wherever she wanted. It would all work. It would all be – wonderful.

In addition, Rose thought doggedly, staring at the worktop, facts had to be faced, uncomfortable facts that were a consequence of her relationship with Tyler. She hadn't had a lodger in months. She hadn't even looked for one. She hadn't, she had to admit, allowed herself to do anything but revel in having the whole house to herself. Tyler had somehow – inevitably, she supposed – colonized the spare bedroom as a kind of dressing room, with his clothes and shoes stored in the wardrobe, and the bed piled with his things – papers and document folders and a tangle of charger cables.

Furthermore, she had completed no translations now for almost six months. The income from the last work she'd done had just about lasted, but, now she came to face it, there had been almost no recent requests. There had been requests when she first met Tyler again, which she had blithely refused, and gradually, if she made herself think about it, those requests had all but ceased. No lodger, Rose thought to herself, no translations: no income. The bottom line is that if I don't sell this house, I will have nothing to live on, and that is entirely my own fault. I will not be able to sustain myself because I have let things slide. Or not so much slide as career madly to the bottom. Rose Woodrowe, Rose said to herself, feeling panic surge in waves in the pit of her stomach, you are a complete and utter *fool*.

She heard the front door open, and slam shut behind Tyler. He was hallooing from the hall. He came into the kitchen on a gust of outside air and buoyancy, holding the champagne in a plastic bag.

'Brilliant,' he said. 'They even had a half-bottle ready chilled. Darling, you haven't moved!'

'I couldn't, Rose said.

Tyler put the bottle on the counter and began to open cupboards in search of glasses.

'I'm not surprised. I'm really not. What an amazing stroke of perfect good fortune! It's enough to stun anyone.'

Rose said, 'But we haven't heard about the cottage.'

Tyler put the two champagne glasses on the counter. Then he came to put his arms round Rose from behind.

'We will. Sweetheart, we *will*. Is that what's troubling you?' He turned her round to look at him, peering into her face. 'My poor Rosie. It'll be *fine*. I promise you. It'll be absolutely fine. If we don't get that cottage, we'll get another, there'll be one that's even better, I *know* it.' He pulled Rose closely to him and held her. He said against her hair, 'This is such a good omen, such a wonderful start. This, my sweetheart, is where we can actually begin.'

—

Laura had asked Emmy if they could meet somewhere, soon. Emmy was amazed. Laura never made time to meet anyone, never seemed to consider that anyone else had a life that couldn't be accommodated round the uniquely demanding requirements of her own. The trouble was, Emmy thought, that Laura wasn't just OK, even as an elder sister, but she was also justified. Her life, with her job and her family, was of course more intractable than Emmy's single existence was, even if you factored in Emmy's newfound – and satisfying – commitment to work. Holding her telephone to her ear and trying not to sound exaggeratedly amazed, Emmy said, 'Wow. Gosh. Yes, that'd be lovely,' and Laura suggested a bar near Piccadilly which was, she said, both reasonably quiet and easy for them both to get to. All the same, Emmy was wary.

'What's this about?' she said.

'Nothing scary.'

'It's just that you never suggest any plan that isn't me coming to you.'

'Em,' Laura said, as if she had no idea what Emmy was talking about, 'don't be an idiot, and see you there on Thursday.'

The bar was an American bar, and deep underground, down a wide staircase carpeted in a deliberately retro pattern. Laura was already there when Emmy arrived, drinking, she said, a whisky sour because the barman had suggested it and it had suddenly seemed a delicious and exactly right idea. Her phone was, as usual, on the table in front of her, but she was in jeans rather than work clothes, and her hair was loose on her shoulders.

Emmy dumped her bag on the floor and leaned in to give her sister a kiss.

'Cocktails in a cocktail bar, huh?'

'It's yummy,' Laura said. 'I don't really like whisky but the bar guy said focus on the sour, and he's right. D'you want one?'

Emmy picked up the menu.

'I want something long, I think. Maybe a vodka and tonic?'

'He'll ask you which, out of umpteen vodkas.'

'Does it matter?' Emmy said, sitting down opposite her sister. 'If I'm going to drown it in tonic anyway?'

Laura smiled at her. 'You look great.'

'You too, actually.'

'Day off,' Laura said, tossing her hair back. 'Haircut, lunch with a friend who is nothing to do with work, drinks with you. Fantastic!'

A waiter appeared and stood, smiling, beside Emmy.

'I'll have a vodka and tonic.'

'Have something interesting,' Laura said, 'go on. Have a proper drink.'

'I want something long?'

'What about a Moscow Mule?' suggested the waiter.

Emmy looked at him. 'I've never had one.'

'Vodka, lime, lengthened with ginger beer,' the waiter said.

Laura leaned forward.

'Go on!'

'All right,' Emmy said, 'OK.' She smiled her order at the waiter and then glanced at her sister. 'What are you celebrating, then?'

'Nothing,' Laura said. 'In fact, it may be because there really is nothing to celebrate that I feel a bit reckless.'

'Reckless? *You?*'

'More I suppose – what's to lose.'

'Please don't,' Emmy said. '*Please* not you too.'

'What d'you mean, me too?'

'I mean,' Emmy said, 'Mum. I had the weirdest conversation with Mum. I was going to ring you and tell you about it, but I haven't, not because I didn't mean to, but just life—'

'Forget that. Forget intentions. Tell me. Just tell me what Mum said.'

Emmy sighed.

'I was on the bus going home and I thought I'd ring Mum and tell her about my getting stuck into work and the immediate results of that, and she was fine, she was her usual lovely self but kind of distracted, you know? As if she wasn't really listening to me, wasn't taking in what I was telling her. And then it all went a bit mad, it all poured out.'

Emmy's drink, pale tawny and clinking with ice, arrived and was set down in front of her.

'Your Moscow Mule.'

'What poured out?' Laura demanded.

'Thank you,' Emmy said to the waiter, and then, to her sister, 'All this stuff, about having found the perfect cottage, in Hampshire or somewhere, and how she was going to buy it and sell the mews and give us all a wad of cash so I could fly to New York and see Mallory, and I said but Mum, I don't want to go to New York any more, that was just a whim, before I really began to get somewhere with work, so please don't even think about giving me any money, *you* need the money and then, then, she went kind of crazy and accused me of never liking Tyler from the get-go, and setting my face against her ever having any relationship anyway because I couldn't bear her to love anyone but us three. I mean, it was *insane.*'

Laura had picked up her drink. She put it down again with a small bang.

'Oh my God, Em.'

'I should have told you. I should have rung you at once.

Now I've told you, I can't think why I didn't tell you the minute it happened.'

Laura shook her head. 'No. No, it doesn't matter, it doesn't.'

'She didn't sound like Mum, Laura, she didn't.'

'No.'

'She sounded like someone a bit mental, to be honest, like someone who cannot stand to be disagreed with without going off on one.' She picked up her drink and took a pull through its straw. 'Ooh. Yum. Now I've got that off my chest, I suppose you'd better tell me what you wanted to say to me?'

Laura looked at her, a long, direct look. Then she shook her head slightly.

'I wanted to see you. Just wanted to. And to tell you that I've talked to Nat.'

'Ah,' Emmy said quietly.

'I saw him at the weekend. He brought Jess to supper. Try not to be put off by her being so amazing to look at.'

Emmy sighed again. She looked at her drink. She said, 'What did you say to Nat?'

'That he couldn't accept money from Mum to have the flat to himself.'

'And?'

'He agreed,' Laura said. 'He's mad about Jess, but he agreed. Mum needs her money. She needs to keep her own money. For her future. For herself.'

Emmy stared at her.

'Oh my God, Laura. So we're all agreed. Except Mum.'

———

It was an impulse, to take the train to Lewes. Rose wasn't given to impulses, especially any that didn't involve Tyler, and that meant, in fact, telling Tyler the half-truth that she needed to see her sister on her own, in order to tell Prue the good news about the cottage. Also, she added, her voice warming with enthusiasm, while she went to Sussex, why didn't Tyler use her absence to plan the party, phone his wine-merchant friend, make lists?

Tyler had, as he always did, completely understood. Taking his cue from Rose, he had been measured and dignified in his reaction to the news that their offer on the cottage had been accepted. They had gone out to dinner, in a restaurant on Marylebone Lane, and Tyler had paid – in cash, Rose noticed, while hating herself for noticing – and they had toasted the future and each other, but without any giddy rapture, and Rose had felt a surge of reassuring relief. Tyler had talked gently, not urgently or excitedly, about the wedding and she had told herself repeatedly that any pressure she might feel under was entirely of her own making.

The impulse to see Prue was as unexpected as it was pressing. Prue had always given the distinct impression that she didn't care for William, and that she most emphatically did not care to be patronized by William, so for all the years that she was married to William, Rose had fallen into his reciprocal habit of mildly despising her sister, of gently mocking her for her appearance and tastes and manner, of regarding her as an overbearing caricature of herself. But gradually, without William to condition her opinion, other emotions about Prue were emerging, as if they were coming to life and vigour again after decades of being flattened and trampled on. It had been gratifying to have Prue approve of

Tyler; it was remarkable, if sometimes irritating, to acknowledge Prue's palpable concern for her and her children's
welfare; it was odd, but significant, to find that Prue's good
opinion was desirable, and her support extremely important.
And all of these new or revived feelings were inevitably confusing.

So when she found herself drinking coffee in Prue's
orderly but charmless sunroom, Rose found herself saying,
'Do you know, I don't really know why I'm here.'

Prue grunted. She had put a plate of biscuits on a
wicker stool by Rose's chair. They were the kind of biscuits,
Rose thought, that one looked at, in the supermarket, and
thought, 'I wonder who on earth would ever buy those?'
Well, someone like Prue, plainly. Someone who lived in order
and cleanliness but without style or panache. Someone
who could be relied upon to speak their minds and be on
your side, whatever. Someone who, like Prue, would always
have ex-pupils stopping her in the street to tell her that
she had changed their lives, to whom she would invariably
reply, 'Thank you, but stuff and nonsense. You did it yourself.'

'Where's the cottage, then?' Prue said, putting her cup
down. 'Have you got a picture?'

Rose produced her iPad and scrolled to find the shot of
it from the lane, symmetrical and comely with a cloud-dotted
blue sky behind. She handed the iPad to her sister.

'There you are.'

Prue looked at the screen without comment. Then she
said, 'You came to show me this, didn't you?'

'Of course!'

'It's delightful.'

'It so is,' Rose said warmly. 'It's seriously lovely in every way. I walked in and I just thought – I could live here!'

'So you're going to.'

'Oh yes,' Rose said. 'The offer's been accepted, exchange in a month, completion before the summer.'

Prue swiped the screen to find another picture.

'Ah,' she said, 'an Aga.'

'Yes!'

'And a claw-foot bath. And what looks like some original shutters?'

'And fireplaces! It's got an acre of garden and fruit trees. Tyler said we might have hens.'

Prue went on looking at the screen.

'It looks very pretty, Rosie. Very you.'

'It is. I can't tell you how much it is me. It's . . .' She stopped.

Prue looked at her over the top of her reading glasses. 'It's what, Rosie?'

Rose looked down at her lap. 'It's very – auspicious.'

Prue took her glasses off. 'Auspicious? What do you mean?'

'I mean,' Rose said, gathering courage, 'that I feel really, truly happy about it. That I felt I could live there and be me, in every way. Or even a better kind of me, if you know what I mean?'

Prue put the iPad down and laid her glasses on top of it. 'Would reassured be an apposite word for how you feel?'

Rose said reluctantly, 'Yes. Yes it would.'

'Ah,' Prue said again. There was a pause and then she added, 'May I ask you something?'

'Anything. You know that.'

'I'm just wondering,' Prue said, 'if you love this cottage more, if differently, than you love Tyler?' She regarded her sister, who had gone from staring at the floor to staring fixedly out of the window. 'The thing is, Rosie, that if Tyler means to you what I think you intend to convey he means to you, wouldn't you be happy to live with him anywhere?'

———

Jess watched television drama, or films, Nat thought, the way he watched sport: with that kind of deaf, focused attention that could not be distracted. If he sat right next to Jess while she was watching a play, and kissed her neck or tried to touch her in the most seducing manner, she took no notice at all. She didn't try and swat him away as if he were no more than an annoying insect, she simply could not feel him or be affected by him in the smallest degree. She was, he thought admiringly, completely and utterly impervious to him. Impervious, in fact, to everything but what was happening on screen. So he knew to wait until the weekend television showing of *Citizen Kane* was entirely over, before he spoke.

'Jess?'

'Mm?'

'Can – can we talk?'

She turned to look at him. 'About what?'

He fidgeted a bit on the sofa, turned himself sideways, slung an arm along the back.

'This flat.'

'OK,' she said. 'What about this flat? I think it's lovely.'

'It is,' Nat said. 'It's not the flat. It's Tim.'

Jess made a sweeping gesture. 'Tim? What's the matter with Tim? I like Tim.'

'So do I,' Nat said hastily, 'he's cool. He's a great guy. But you know we thought we'd like the flat to ourselves?'

Jess turned to regard him. Her eyes were huge.

'Did we?'

'Yes. Yes, we did. We thought how great it'd be if it could just be us, here. No Tim. So I had an idea of asking my parents if they could help, with money I mean, and – well, I'm really sorry, Jess, but they can't. I'm so sorry. Really I am. But it looks as if – Tim'll have to stay.'

Jess gazed at him. Then she shook her head. '*What?*'

'I'm so sorry, but—'

'Nat,' Jess said, smiling broadly at him. 'Whose idea was this? Was it mine? Was it? I mean' – she gestured at the living space – 'this flat is about a million times more luxy than anywhere I've ever lived, and you think I think sharing the space with Tim is a *problem?*'

'I just thought you and I might like—'

'Listen,' Jess said, leaning forward, putting her hand, to electrifying effect, on his thigh. 'Listen, babe. It is *so* cool here. It's amazing. I haven't lived anywhere like this, *ever*. But . . .' She paused, and took her hand away.

'What?' he said.

'It's lovely, being with you. I love it. Sometimes it's more than lovely, it's fantastic. But, babe, it isn't really my scene. You aren't my natural scene. I love your sister. I'm sure I'll love your twin sister in time. This is all great, *you* are great, but don't get heavy with me, don't start wanting more from me than I ever signed up for, just don't.' She leaned further forward and kissed his cheek and he caught a breath of the scent of her, warm and slightly spicy. 'Live in the moment, babe,' she said, her mouth almost touching his. 'Don't plan, don't be so *serious* about everything. What's that tag? Carpe diem? Well do it, babe, do it. Seize the day and fuck tomorrow. OK?'

CHAPTER SIXTEEN

Rose had appeared to be in no hurry to get back to London. Prue had assumed that they would have coffee together, and then Rose would gather up her bag and her jacket and start talking about the train she needed to catch, but, on the contrary, Rose had wanted to look at Prue's garden and, while staring at the ginkgo tree that Prue had grown from a cutting given to her by a colleague twenty years ago, said rather vaguely that she supposed she had better be back in London by early evening.

So Prue, ever decisive, had taken her into Lewes for lunch in her favourite cafe, where she urged Rose to have a glass of wine.

'No. No, I really don't want one. Especially if you're not having one.'

'I'm driving,' Prue said.

'Then I can't, I really can't.'

'I think you should.'

'Why? Why do you think I *need* a glass of wine?'

Prue was studying the menu. 'It will relax you,' she said.

'For heaven's sake!' Rose exclaimed. 'I don't need relaxing! What do you mean?'

Prue put the menu down. 'Just that.'

Rose gazed at her, mutely.

'Have a glass of wine,' Prue said, 'and then you can tell me what is the matter.'

Rose said, almost in a whisper, 'I don't *know* what is the matter.'

Prue grunted. 'I usually have the salad of the day here, and then a slice of apple and cinnamon cake with my coffee. Would that suit you?'

'Lovely,' Rose said absently.

'Rosie.'

'Yes?'

'You didn't answer my question.'

Rose looked past her sister, and out into the cafe.

'Which question?'

'You know perfectly well. When you were raving about this cottage and I asked you whether you were more in love with the cottage than you were with Tyler because if you were madly in love with *him*, presumably you'd live anywhere as long as you could be together?'

Rose said obdurately, 'The salad of the day sounds a very good choice.'

'I'll order two then,' Prue said. 'And then we'll wait. I can wait for a very long time, Rosie. I spent my working life dealing with children, after all. I'm very used to waiting.'

Rose sighed. Then she said slowly, 'I love Tyler. I really do. And nobody in my life has ever been as sweet to me as he is. *All* the time.'

'But?' Prue said.

Rose retrieved her gaze from across the cafe. She rearranged the cutlery on the table a little.

'I'm a bit frightened . . .' she began.

'About what?'

'About – money,' Rose said, lining up the forks. 'About being dependent again. Or maybe having someone, who isn't one of my children, being dependent on me. About not being able to control how other people – someone else – spends money or thinks about money.'

'Yes,' Prue said.

There was a silence. Then Rose said, as if she was thinking aloud, 'I suppose I've got used to my independence. And the freedom of that. I mean, I'd made a perfectly good life for myself, hadn't I? I was more than managing, I was taking a kind of *pride* in managing. And I'm not saying I wish this had never happened, I wouldn't *dream* of suggesting that this glorious thing would have been better as a fantasy than a reality, but I've just had some sobering thoughts recently, I've found myself less – well, carried away if you like. I can't seem to match his utter certainty about everything to do with the future.' She raised her head and looked miserably at Prue. 'I feel such a killjoy.'

Prue picked up the menu again.

'Men are such romantics. Far more romantic than women, when it comes to it. What woman would ever have thought that founding an empire was a good notion?'

'Prue?'

'Yes?'

'Do *you* think I am a passionless killjoy?'

'Has he said that?'

'No,' Rose said. 'He wouldn't, probably, even think of saying such a thing. But *I* think it. Fear it.'

'No,' Prue said calmly, 'I don't and you aren't. It's sense

261

and sensibility again. Most women grow out of sensibility. Less glamorous but more useful.'

Rose spread her hands and regarded her aquamarine.

'It's really unfair even to ask you this, but what do you think I should do?'

'Exactly what we're doing now,' Prue said. 'Just wait. Don't *do* anything. Just wait. And while we're waiting, I am going to order you that wine.'

—

Nat stood gazing up at the façade of Emmy's building. He had told himself that walking past Emmy's front door was on his way home from the Clerkenwell Road anyway, but he was well aware that he didn't need to stop outside and look up the dark-brick façade to the full-length double windows, behind a black-iron balustrade, that indicated her studio flat. He observed that the windows on the floor above hers were shorter and garnished with flowering window boxes, and that the ones on the floor below hers had deep pink heart shapes stuck to the glass. It was only when he looked back at Emmy's windows, on the third floor, that he realized she was standing behind them, and looking straight back down at him.

For a full half-minute, neither of them moved. And then Emmy reached up to unlatch half the window, and opened it back into the room behind. She leaned forward and put her hands on the balustrade.

'Come up,' she said.

He swallowed, still standing in the street, staring upwards. 'I was just passing.'

'Of course,' Emmy said, 'it's on your way home. I said, come up.'

'Em . . .'

She bent over the balustrade. 'We're not having this conversation in the street, Nat. Come *up*.'

Her front door was open when he reached her landing.

'No need to *hiss* at me.'

Emmy was standing in the middle of the room, holding her phone.

'I wasn't hissing. I just didn't want the whole of Crawford Passage hearing our conversation.'

'Are we going to have a conversation?'

She put her phone down on the coffee table, on a pile of magazines.

'Of course we are. Isn't that why you were standing in the street?'

He gave her a quick glance.

'I don't know why I was standing in the street.'

'Instinct?'

'Maybe.'

'Nat,' Emmy said, 'don't be such a prize muppet. You were standing there because we need to see each other. I asked you up because we need to see each other. We've got ourselves at real cross-purposes. Haven't we?'

He nodded slowly. He said, 'You look great.'

She surveyed him up and down. 'You look a bit thin.'

He grinned, sheepishly. 'Not a lot of sleep.'

'Don't want to hear about that,' Emmy said. 'Don't want to *think* about that.'

He came across the room and embraced her awkwardly.

'Sorry,' he said. 'About everything.'

She didn't fight him off, but she didn't return his embrace either.

'Me too,' Emmy said. She moved back a pace or two. 'Coffee?' she asked. 'Glass of water?'

He said heavily, 'Just water, thanks,' and then, as if remembering his manners, 'How's work?'

'Brilliant,' Emmy said, taking a plastic bottle of water from the fridge and handing it to him. She indicated the sofa. 'Why don't you sit?'

'Thanks.'

'Nat,' Emmy said, 'why don't you be normal? Why don't you stop behaving like someone I've hardly met and just help yourself to the sofa like usual?'

Nat sat down on the edge of the sofa and put his elbows on his knees, swinging the water bottle by its neck.

'Sorry.'

Emmy came to sit beside him. She reached to take the bottle out of his hand and put it on the table.

'What's happened, Nat?'

'Nothing, really. Nothing major anyway.'

'Has she dumped you?'

His head jerked round to stare at her.

'Why d'you ask?'

'Because,' Emmy said impatiently, 'you look so abject. On top of coming round here and wanting to make it up with me.'

'She hasn't.'

'What? Finished with you?'

'No.'

'What then? Work? Mum?'

Nat's head swung back again to stare at the floor between his knees.

'She just said – that I wasn't – The One. The forever and

ever one. That I was kind of fine for now, but that I wasn't really her type.'

'Of course you aren't!'

He muttered, 'I thought I was. She is, for me.'

Emmy leaned back into the sofa cushions.

'No, she isn't. She's just mind-blowingly different and exciting because she's different.'

Nat leaned back too, slowly and carefully as if he were an invalid. He said, 'I think my heart is broken.'

Emmy turned her head against the cushions to regard him.

'No it isn't, you fuckwit. It's a bit bruised, or your pride is a bit bruised, but it'll recover. There'll be other Jesses.'

'I don't want there to be. I just want her.'

'Look at me,' Emmy commanded. He rolled his head so that their eyes were a foot away from each other.

'It isn't her,' Emmy said. 'Or it isn't basically her. It's not being The One for her that's getting you.'

He said unhappily, 'How do you know?'

'I don't know,' Emmy said, 'but I'm guessing. I'm guessing that when it's The One, you feel safe as well as blown away. I've been thinking a bit, lately, about relationships and things. I've been thinking, actually, about Mum.'

'What about Mum?'

Emmy turned her head back to stare at the ceiling.

'I don't think Mum was very happy with Dad. I don't think she was *relaxedly* happy.'

'Oh?'

'I mean,' Emmy said, waving her hands for emphasis, 'he's fine and all that, and we love him because he's Dad and everything, but he was a bit of a player, always, wasn't he? And it wasn't just him being unfaithful that Mum had to put up with, it was him being so superior to her always, the great heart surgeon and the little wifey doing a spot of medical translation in her spare time for pin money. If you think about it, he was always patronizing her. And Tyler doesn't. Whatever we think about the situation with Tyler, he thinks the world of her, he doesn't ever put her down; in fact he does the reverse, he thinks everything she does and says is a kind of miracle of loveliness and cleverness. I think, Nat, she feels safe with him like she never did with Dad.'

'Mm,' Nat said. 'D'you think she knows that?'

'Not really. But maybe it explains why she gets ratty with us about this marriage thing, because she can't understand why *we* don't seem to get it.'

Nat thought for a moment, lying back against the sofa cushions, staring at Emmy's profile. Then he said, 'Good thinking, Em.'

She peeled herself upright. 'I think you'd better go home, lover boy. There'll be supper.'

He sat slowly up, beside her. 'Jess doesn't cook.'

'Ah.'

'So it's takeaways. We practically have our own Deliveroo team.'

Emmy took care not to smile. 'There you go, then. And Tim?'

Nat got to his feet. 'Tim's staying.'

Emmy stood too. She bent to glance at the time on her phone. 'Good. And I must go, anyway.'

'Go? Go where?'

Emmy shot him a quick look. She had the ghost of a smile. 'I've got a date.'

'Em!'

Emmy picked up her phone and put it in her pocket.

'Thank you for sounding so astonished. It's just Matt, from work. Ginger with a line in checked shirts. Completely not my type.' She grinned at him. 'So who knows?'

———

All her working life, Laura had been able to compartmentalize mentally. Whatever Angus might think and say about her commitment to work hovering perpetually over their domestic life, Laura had clung to the conviction that everyone in her life knew, without doubt, that when she was at work, she was at work, and when she was home, she was firmly home. It was therefore disconcerting to find that her mind these days was refusing – or was unable – to change gear as cleanly and completely as she had always relied upon it doing. Gradually, over the recent weeks, her preoccupation with Rose, and the declared prospect of Rose's future, was seeping into at least the neutral zones of her carefully constructed life, and taking over the journeys to and from the surgery or the hospital or – even – on a much-discouraged home visit. In the time it took to make one home visit, the senior partner in the practice was fond of saying, a doctor might see four or five patients in surgery.

Rose's situation was increasingly, Laura thought, like a car – or some other vehicle – whose brakes had failed and which was careering ever faster downhill and out of control. Rose had told her about the Canadian Gaffneys, who had so fallen for her house and had made an offer on the spot, which Rose, to Laura's dismay, appeared to have immediately accepted. She had also described, in lyrical terms, the

Hampshire cottage and declared that the offer, below the asking price, that she and Tyler had made had also been accepted. And to crown it all – and, Laura felt, almost the worst plan of all in its blithe gallop into sheer folly – was this party.

Laura was trying very hard not to encourage the case in her mind against Tyler, not to share Jack's dislike of Rose's engagement ring. But it was hard, she admitted to Angus, very hard. It hadn't been Rose's idea, after all, to sell the mews house or to go house-hunting for a country cottage, and it hadn't been her idea, either, to throw a party. Rose's friends were the small circle of chiefly women friends she had known in Highgate, friends made at the school gate or on the professional circuit of their husbands' lives. Those whom Laura had spoken to had been divided into the romantics and the disapproving prudent, but had been united in telling Laura that her mother's choice was her mother's undoubted choice, and had to be gone along with.

'It's no good,' Jenny Dodds had said on the phone to her, 'you three sitting in judgement and reproof. You may well be right – in fact, I personally think you are – but Rose is choosing for herself at long last, and she has the opportunity and means to do so. She'll be more than aware of what you all think, but in the end, she can do as she pleases, and unless you three go along with her, you'll find yourselves missing one of the fundamental relationships of your life. And I can tell you, having fought with my own mother all my life, you don't want that. Especially not with a mother like Rose. It would be a criminal waste.'

Jenny Dodds had accepted the invitation to the party and would be bringing her husband, Al. All the friends from the Highgate days said they would be coming, plus several of their grown-up children, who were, as one them had excitedly texted Laura, 'Busting to meet this new guy of your mother's!' Laura had felt slightly sick when she read that text, but then feeling slightly sick was a familiar sensation these days. It happened every time she thought about Rose, or her houses, or the party. It was safer, she discovered, not to let her mind even tiptoe towards the engagement ring.

'It's all very well for you,' she'd said to Jenny Dodds. 'You're a friend. You can detach yourself. But Rose is my *mother*.'

'Exactly my point,' Jenny said. 'Not worth it. He makes your mother happy and that is what she wants. End of story.'

Except it wasn't, Laura thought, because – well, because it couldn't be. It just couldn't. Her mother, who had endured so much and won her freedom so magnificently, while never maligning those who had, often deliberately over the years, caused her such pain, could not simply step out now into empty air. Of course, Rose would insist that it wasn't empty air, it was rosy clouds of possibility and happiness, but from Laura's standpoint right now, those clouds looked treacherously insubstantial.

'I'm fretting,' she said indignantly to Angus. 'There isn't a better word. I'm *fretting*.'

He moved to stand behind her as she sat gazing restively at her iPad on the kitchen table. Then he dropped a kiss on her head.

'At last,' Angus said.

'What d'you mean?'

'It gives me hope,' Angus said, moving away to clean up Adam's high-chair tray, 'that you'll fret about me and the boys when there's cause to, one day.'

Laura got up and came hurriedly over to the high chair,

laying a restraining hand on Angus's damp-cloth-wielding one.

She said insistently, 'You three have *always* been my priority. You know that.'

He didn't look at her.

'I don't know it but I'm very glad to hear it.'

'Angus!'

He pulled his hand from under hers and stood to face her.

'Let's not do this. Let's not have a row. We never have rows.'

'I don't want a row,' Laura said, 'I'm not trying to have one. I'm just – miserable about Mum. And muddled.'

'You know something?' Angus said, looking down at her. 'You are very like your father, in temperament. You've got the same focus about work, the same single-mindedness. And being a doctor means that society sanctions your single-mindedness. Actually, I think you're wonderful, but I'd like to *matter* to you more, I'd like to be at the top of your list of priorities rather than comfortably taken for granted somewhere in the middle. And if worrying about Rose is the first step in promoting me up the pecking order, then fine by me. Don't get me wrong: I love Rose. Mothers-in-law don't get much better than Rose, and I don't want her to be anything other than happy. But if she's the catalyst, then I'm pleased. Pleased and grateful.'

Laura reached to take the damp cloth out of Angus's hand and put it on the tray of the high chair. Then she looked up, not at Angus's face, but at the base of his throat.

'Sorry,' she whispered.

'Don't you want to fight back?'

'No,' Laura said. And then, 'Am I really like my father?'

'In some ways, yes.'

'Oh,' Laura said.

'Look at me.'

'I – can't.'

'I'm not angry, Laura. I'm not about to flounce off and exact some clichéd revenge. I'm just so pleased and relieved to see you worrying about Rose. What I want to say, actually, is, frankly, about time, Laura. About bloody *time*.'

Laura nodded, slowly. She didn't raise her eyes, but she lifted both hands and held Angus's upper arms.

'I *do* mind about you. I *do* know I couldn't do what I do without you being so brilliant at supporting me, at holding the fort.'

He waited, not moving. Very gradually, Laura's gaze travelled up his neck and chin and nose until she was looking at him. She said, more confidently, 'I know I take you for granted, but it isn't deliberate. I suppose I always thought of it as a manifestation of real partnership.'

'OK.'

'This whole Mum thing should have made me realize what I have in you.'

'Maybe.'

'Sorry,' Laura said again. She moved her hands up to encircle his neck. He didn't react. Instead, his tone softening, he said, 'What's the matter, Laura? What's especially the matter? These houses of your mum's?'

Laura let her hands slide until they were lying flat on his chest.

'Yes. Yes, all that. But what's bugging me in particular is this party. This – oh, Angus, this *effing* party. Everyone's coming to have a gawp at him. Of course they are! And I just feel that throwing a party and flashing your engagement ring

271

round a party kind of *locks* Mum into it all, like she's being quietly, smilingly, *herded* somewhere until the door clangs shut behind her and that's it.'

Angus linked his own hands loosely behind Laura's waist. 'You can't stop it.'

'No. *No*. If I ever could have.'

'Then you must join it. We all must.'

Laura's gaze sharpened. 'What?'

He smiled down at her. 'We all go. We offer to help. We make sure we are all just *there*.'

'Why?'

'To support her,' Angus said. 'And – well, to keep an eye.' He bent towards her and lowered his voice. 'Whatever happens, Laura, you need to see it with your own eyes. And she needs to see that you do.'

———

Mallory WhatsApped Emmy a photograph of the view from the new apartment she had been lent on the Hudson River. It was far too far up, she said, way beyond 125th Street, so the subway took an age to get to the theatre where she was currently understudying – again! – off Seventh Avenue. The view was of a huge dun-coloured stretch of water. Mallory said it was worth it all to have a rent-free river view. Emmy thought it looked very dull, and said so.

'Yes,' Mallory wrote back, 'it's dull. The theatre is dull. Waiting, even with odd walk-on parts, is dull. I AM FEELING DULL DULL DULL EMMY! I want to come back to London. I want to see you. I want to see your folks. I want to see my damn daddy. Speaking of whom – did you know he's planning to take your mom to California? To meet Seth and

Yuhui? Seth said so. Call me, pumpkin, *call* me. I am dying here.'

Emmy re-read the message several times. It was after midnight in London, so Mallory would have written it before she set off for the long trek to the theatre, in New York. She would, she thought, send a holding reply, an expression of sympathy and reciprocal affection, but she wouldn't call until she had discovered more about this plan Mallory mentioned, of Rose and Tyler going to San Francisco. It was a perfectly natural thing to do, on one level, and on another, it was – well, odd. Emmy put her phone down and stretched. Odd wasn't really that out of the ordinary just now, because plenty of other things seemed to be, too, and the world wasn't coming to an end. Or didn't seem to be. A week ago, she hadn't been on a single date with ginger Matthew, let alone a second one. And he had proved himself to be great company and with surprisingly lovely manners, ordering an Uber to take her home after an evening eating street food in Hoxton, and dancing on the pavement to an impromptu band. He'd even insisted the taxi was on his account, and when she protested, had said, 'When you earn as much as I do, you can pay for your own cab,' and then he'd kissed her cheek in a way that made her want it to be her mouth next time, and waved until the cab turned a corner.

The evening had emboldened her. It had definitely been confidence-building, as was the very fact of being asked out a second time by the same person – who was, after all, a person in authority over Emmy at work, however little he made of that, either inside or out of the office. Her evening made Emmy want to smile, and hum a little, and do a few dance steps as she sashayed across the floor towards the bath-room.

She would, she thought, do no more tonight than reply to Mallory with a brief and affectionate response. But tomorrow she would take more definite action, and she might, she thought, reaching for her eye-makeup remover, take action without checking with her siblings first. She would, she thought, ring Tyler. She never *had* rung Tyler, she had never even thought of ringing Tyler, but now she just might. She peered into the mirror and inspected her teeth. Yes, she would ring Tyler and say she had heard from Mallory who mentioned some idea of going to San Francisco and she, Emmy, was just wondering if that was true? That's all, she'd say, no big deal. Just – are you taking my mother to California, to meet your son? And wait, just wait, to see what happened.

CHAPTER SEVENTEEN

The glass doors of Rose's sitting room stood open to the late-spring evening. Tyler had hung Chinese paper lanterns in the trees, and dotted candles in glass jars here and there, and encouraged Rose to put a huge and spectacular flower arrangement outside the front door to signal to all their arriving guests that this was the party house. He had hired glasses, and organized plastic sacks of ice cubes in which to cool the wine, personally wrapped melon slices in prosciutto and topped miniature blinis with sour cream and smoked salmon. He had, Rose noticed, been humming as he worked, and every time he passed her, laden with something purposeful, he would smile at her and pause to kiss her in a way that suggested that they were in some particularly delightful conspiracy together.

She had to admit that the room and the house and the garden all looked wonderful. It had been Tyler's idea to invite the Gaffneys, and Rose could not help but feel an enormous pride, however tinged it was with anguish, at the impression her house would make on them, lit up in every sense for a party. Tyler, she thought, had remembered everything, even ashtrays in the garden for the smokers, and courteous notes to the neighbours, and had simply got on with listing what needed to be done, and then done it. She watched him for a while, hanging up the Chinese lanterns, and could not help noticing anew how thick his hair still was, how good his figure, how deft he was with his hands. She folded her arms and leaned against the doorframe. Only the last of those things, she thought determinedly, and then strictly in a professional sense alone, could ever have been said of William.

There was a new dress hanging upstairs. She had not wanted a new dress, had argued forcefully in favour of dresses she already owned, but Tyler had insisted, had taken her shopping, had refused to let her see the price on the dress she had chosen. So the new dress – silk, sleeveless, patterned in swirls of duck-egg blue and cream with a long, full skirt, an undeniably romantic and feminine dress – hung upstairs, like a picture, on the front of her wardrobe. Tyler was going to wear dark-blue trousers and a pale-blue shirt whose double cuffs would be linked with the silver knots she had given him. He had held the knots against the shirt cuffs with the same air of triumph with which he had held her aquamarine ring against the silk of the dress. His face was alight with certainty and she had felt a flash of despair with herself at not being able to – quite – surrender as not only he could, but also expected her to. He'd turned to her, still holding her ring.

'I had no idea,' he'd said, his voice full of emotion. 'All my life, my entire life, I had no idea it was remotely possible to be so happy.'

There was a beat. Then Rose smiled at him.

'Nor me,' she said.

—

Nat had told Tyler that he and his sisters would be waiters at the party. At first, Tyler had said no, no, wouldn't think of it, he wanted Rose's children to be free to enjoy themselves, but then, faced with Nat's inflexibility, had given in, if reluctantly. It became clear that he envisaged the party being run in a particular way, as a kind of showcase for Rose and her very different, very promising future, and definitely not as some kind of Woodrowe family affair. Nat heard him, with difficulty. He said, 'Would you rather we weren't there?'

Tyler looked shocked.

'Of course not. Rose would be horrified. So would I. I just don't want this to be some extension of your family parties in the past. For any of you.'

Nat said truthfully, 'It won't be. It couldn't be. But we will be better off with a job to do. All three of us.'

'I can see that.'

'The girls can hand round the food. I'll do the wine.'

Tyler glanced at the ranks of polished glasses.

'You can help me do the wine.' He gave a little laugh. 'I'll need something to do myself. Exhibit A, after all.'

Nat felt a brief softening towards him, and quelled it.

'It'll be fine.'

Tyler went on looking at the glasses.

'I so want it to be. For her.'

'Yes.'

'I – wish Mallory was here.'

'Yes.'

Tyler squared his shoulders and smiled at Nat.

'Would you like to bring your girlfriend? She'd be very welcome.'

'She's rehearsing,' Nat said. 'But thank you.'

Tyler dropped his gaze. He said to the floor, 'There's nothing wrong, is there, in loving someone more than they love you?'

Nat was startled. He said uncertainly, 'N – no.'

Tyler rallied himself instantly.

'It's very good of you and your sisters to help like this.'

'We're glad to.'

'I'd better go and see if your mother is ready.'

'Yes.'

'Are your sisters on their way?'

'Ten minutes, they said.'

'Good,' Tyler said heartily. 'Good, good. So kind. And,' he added gallantly, 'decorative, too.'

'We'll do our stuff,' Nat said. 'We're well trained.'

Tyler moved to the door.

'I'm sure,' he said. He paused, and then he said again, 'I so want it to work. For her.'

—

The sitting room was full. The terrace outside also seemed to be full, with some women guests wearing their husbands' suit jackets over their shoulders. Tyler wasn't wearing a jacket. He was in his immaculately ironed blue shirtsleeves, with Rose's silver knots in the cuffs, and he seemed to be everywhere at once, topping up glasses and smiling and smiling. Even Rose, approving of both his appearance and his hospitality skills, found herself wishing that he wouldn't smile quite so extravagantly and perpetually, and that he didn't keep directing people to look at her and pronounce on how beautiful she looked in her new dress. Passing him at one point in the crowd, she murmured, 'No need to try quite so hard, darling. Just relax a bit.'

And he had replied, whirling on past her, a bottle in either hand, 'I *am* relaxed, Rosie! I have never been so relaxed or happy in all my life!'

Perhaps, she thought confusedly, watching him, he was right and she was being oversensitive. Perhaps she should just let him be, in the way she was trying to let her children be, without constantly trying to comfort them, or congratulate them, or encourage them to make some small adjustment in their thinking or behaviour. Perhaps—

Someone put a hand on her arm. It belonged to a woman she couldn't immediately put a name to, a thin woman in an electric-blue sheath dress.

'Rose,' the woman said warmly, 'and looking as lovely as that adorable guy of yours keeps saying you do. Let me see this ring.'

———

Laura and Emmy, by mutual agreement in black dresses, had circulated ceaselessly with plates of Tyler's canapés and managed, on the whole, not to catch each other's eye when a friend of Rose's, from the Highgate days, made some comment about Tyler, or Tyler's appearance, which was designed to elicit a revealing response.

'Mum looks wonderful, doesn't she?' they had agreed they would say. 'Yes, we're all fine, getting along well. But doesn't Mum look amazing?'

Nat was behaving as he had when Rose had first broken the news about Tyler to them. He was refusing to let his sisters unburden themselves whenever they returned to the kitchen to refill the canapé plates, but was insisting, with a military precision that made them roll their eyes, that the kitchen was ordered as they went along, empty bottles stowed in the cartons they had come in, dirty glasses marshalled beside the sink. He behaved towards Tyler, as he swung in and out with full and empty bottles, with a kind of determined deference that defied mockery or challenge, and when Emmy tried to corner him over something outrageous that someone had whispered to her, said grimly, 'Later. Later. We're here to *work*.'

Laura, however, was cornered in the garden by Jenny Dodds.

'Come on, darling. I've known you since you were three, for God's sake. Very attractive man. *Very*. And your mum looks a picture. But something's not right. Is it? Something's—'

Laura held her plate of blinis between them. '*No*, Jenny,' she said firmly.

'Don't be silly, Laura. Don't try and pretend with me. He's fine. But your mother looks – is – kind of *brittle*. You know she does.'

Laura gripped her plate. She said, looking at Jenny, 'You told me to go along with whatever she decides. You told me not to jeopardize my relationship with her. Why else do you think we're doing this? For her, of course. For *her*.'

'I'll let you go in a second,' Jenny Dodds said. 'Al hates drinks parties anyway so he's been champing to leave for half an hour. It's just seeing her – and she looks gorgeous – makes me wonder if . . . well, if she wouldn't quite like to be rescued?'

Laura pushed forward, holding her plate in front of her. She suddenly felt like crying.

'Then *you* tell her, Jenny. You've known her for nearly forty years, haven't you? None of us can do any more.'

Jenny stepped back to let Laura pass. 'Of course.'

Laura didn't look at her. 'I'm going to find the others.'

'You do that.'

'Jenny . . .'

'Yes, darling?'

'Help!' Laura said in a whisper.

———

They were gathered in the kitchen. It was after ten o'clock, and a few people still lingered in the sitting room. Rose was on the sofa, her silk skirts spread around her, and Tyler was perched on the arm of the sofa beside her. They were talking to the Gaffneys and a couple who lived further up the mews, and from the kitchen, the siblings could see that the Chinese lanterns still flickered beyond the now-closed glass doors, and the group around the sofa were illumined as softly and dramatically as if they had been on stage. Quietly, saying nothing to his sisters, Nat closed the kitchen door.

He said, his back still to the room, 'Don't say anything.'

'I *have* to,' Emmy said.

Laura slumped into a kitchen chair. 'It was a big success.'

'But it was awful. *Awful*,' exclaimed Emmy.

Nat turned round. 'I don't want to talk about it—'

'We've *got* to!'

'—until I've had time to think about it. For now, we've done our stuff. We have surely done our stuff.'

Laura said miserably, 'I just want to go home. I want to get back to Angus and the boys.'

Emmy folded her arms and flung her head back to stare at the ceiling. 'None of us can go anywhere until we've talked.'

'I can't,' Laura said.

'Nor can I,' agreed Nat.

'OK,' Emmy said, still staring at the ceiling. 'Not tonight, then. But soon. This week, OK? This week.'

Laura said sadly, 'He was fine. He was really fine. He didn't show off or get all possessive, or anything. He was fine.'

Emmy's head slowly swung back until she was looking at the floor. She said simply, 'It was Mum.'

'Yes.'

There was a silence. Nat went on standing just inside the door, Laura was on her chair, Emmy was leaning against the central kitchen island. They became aware that the handle of the door that led to the sitting room was turning slowly. Nat moved away and twisted round to watch it. Noiselessly the door opened to reveal Rose herself, in her full-skirted dress with, now, smudges under her eyes. She slipped into the kitchen and closed the door behind her. Nobody spoke. Then she composed herself, linking her hands together in front of her skirts and turning to look at her children's faces, one after another. They stared back at her, dumbly.

'What?' Rose demanded.

———

Tyler said to Emmy, when she – to his delight – called, that he would like to take her out to dinner, in order to talk about Mallory. He suggested three evenings, but Emmy said that she was afraid she was busy on all of them. He then said, 'What about lunch, then?' but Emmy said she didn't really do lunch these days because work was so busy and so unpredictable, so that it was often just soup at her desk. Tyler tried for a quick meeting after work then, a drink that wouldn't eat into either her working day or her evening, and Emmy, plainly squirming at her end of the telephone, said guardedly that a drink would be fine. And then as an afterthought, she said thank you, hurriedly, like a child belatedly remembering its manners.

Tyler chose a bar in Spring Gardens. Emmy knew, the moment she walked in, that he had chosen it carefully as being a place that someone of her age would think was hip and cool. He was sitting in a purple armchair when she arrived, and the whole bar area was bathed in purple light, glowing around the polished metal pillars and falling from huge purple lampshades suspended above the bar itself.

'Goodness,' Emmy said.

Tyler leaned forward and planted an awkward kiss on her cheek.

'Lovely to see you. Did you enjoy the party?'

'Mm,' Emmy said, nodding. 'The garden looked amazing.'

'So did your mother.'

'Yes,' Emmy said, nodding again.

'Thank you for coming,' Tyler said, indicating a second purple armchair. 'And what can I get you to drink? Have a cocktail.'

Emmy sat down primly. 'Just water, please.'

'Surely not.'

'Yes, honestly. Just water.'

Tyler said sadly, 'As you wish.'

'Thank you.'

He eyed her for a moment, and then he said, 'I'm so glad you're in touch with Mallory.'

'We Skype.' Emmy said.

'It's wonderful. That you are friends, I mean. It – well, it makes me feel a lot better about the fact that she and I don't seem to be doing too well together, at the moment.'

Emmy looked at the nearest purple-lit pillar. 'No.'

'Which is very sad,' Tyler said. 'And I've spent a long time wondering what to do about it. I thought we were doing fine, and then suddenly we weren't. And that makes me very sad.'

Emmy said awkwardly, 'I really can't talk about this.'

'No. No, of course you can't. And I don't expect you to, of course I don't. I just felt I should say, somehow.'

'Yes.'

'Let me get you that water.'

'Thank you,' Emmy said unhappily.

Tyler got up and went over to the bar. Emmy didn't watch him. She sat where she was and thought how hurt and puzzled Rose had seemed to be, in her kitchen after the party, and how they had all been too tired and too wretched to be at all articulate, so she had ended by saying crossly that if they were all so exhausted, they only had themselves to blame for insisting on working at the party, rather than being guests, as both she and Tyler had wanted them to be.

Tyler came back to the table with a glass of water and a second glass full of ice cubes.

'I wasn't sure if you wanted ice.'

'I do,' Emmy said. 'Thank you.'

He sat down again in his own armchair. 'I'd have loved to have bought you a proper drink, you know.'

'This is fine,' Emmy said, splashing ice cubes into her glass. 'Honestly.'

'I wonder . . .' Tyler started.

Emmy took a swallow of her water. 'What?' she said politely.

He leaned forward and put his elbows on his knees. 'Would – would you tell Mallory something for me?'

Emmy said guardedly, 'It depends on what it is.'

'Of course,' Tyler said. 'I wouldn't ask you to say anything you weren't comfortable with. It's just – well, I wonder if you'd tell her that I'm going to California soon.'

Emmy shot a look at him. It was going to be easier than she thought.

'California?'

'Yes,' Tyler said, 'San Francisco actually. I'm taking your mother. She doesn't know anything about it yet, so don't spoil the surprise. But I want to show her all the places, all my places, in San Francisco. And above all, I want her to meet Seth.'

Emmy thought of the photograph of Seth, of his tied-back hippie hair and his Doughboy apron and his serious-faced little Japanese partner. Then she thought of Rose.

'You – you're planning to take Mum to San Francisco?'

'Of course. She's going to be Seth's stepmother after all.'

'And she doesn't know?'

'She doesn't know *yet*,' Tyler said. 'But of course she will. In good time, of course. She'd hate not knowing what to pack.'

'But you haven't discussed it with her?'

'No,' Tyler said, still smiling. 'Do you think I should?'

Emmy said emphatically, 'I certainly do.'

'Whoa,' Tyler said, raising his hands and fanning them in her direction, 'steady on! It's just a trip to California.'

'But it's a *significant* trip,' Emmy said. 'The kind of trip that should be a joint decision.'

'But I want to surprise her!'

Emmy took another gulp of water. 'And you hope that I'll tell Mallory.'

'Yes.'

'And that Mallory might think of joining you in San Francisco?'

'Ideally,' Tyler said, smiling again, 'yes.'

'Sorry,' Emmy said, 'but no.'

'No?'

'No to telling Mallory. No to telling anyone, actually. The only person who ought to be told, who *should* be told, in fact, is Mum. And she shouldn't be told, she should be asked.'

Tyler looked down at the table between them. He said quietly, 'Oh dear.'

Emmy picked her bag off the floor and put it on her knee. 'Sorry.'

'I think,' Tyler said carefully, 'that for all your undoubted cleverness, you sometimes don't understand about emotions and relationships. And what makes people happy, and feel safe. I don't want to change one single thing about your mother, except how she's been treated. I only haven't told her yet about California because I want to be able to present it to her as a whole package, a sorted, organized package about which she has to do nothing but pack a suitcase. As I did with the party. I wanted her to have nothing to do but make herself look gorgeous. Which she did.'

Emmy gripped her bag.

'Who paid for the plane tickets to San Francisco?'

Tyler didn't flinch. 'I did, Emmy. With my money. We are staying with friends of mine and will have our final two nights in a hotel. All sorted. All paid for.' He paused. 'Are you sure you can't tell Mallory for me?'

Emmy stood up and slung her bag on her shoulder. 'Quite sure.'

He looked up at her. 'Why are you angry with me, Emmy?'

She glanced at him and sighed. 'It isn't you, especially. It's – it's, oh, it's something I can't explain.'

Tyler stood up too. 'Why?'

She took a step away. 'Just something doesn't feel quite right.'

'In my seriousness about your mother?'

Emmy took a further step. 'No. Not that.'

'Then what?'

She opened her mouth as if to say something and then lost her nerve.

'I don't know,' she said eventually. 'Just a feeling. Just – something. Sorry I can't tell Mallory. And thanks for the water.'

He sketched a little bow. 'Thanks for coming.'

———

'I've found another room,' Tim said to Nat, catching him as he was about to leave for work.

Nat was looking at his phone. He had his business suit on, with a bulge in his jacket pocket indicating his rolled-up tie, and a small black rucksack hitched on one shoulder. He looked up, bemused.

'What?'

Tim was still in his running gear, grasping a bottle of energy drink. He made a face at Nat.

'Wake up, boyo. I've found another room. Not as good as this but in a great flat off Finsbury Park. Good for the journey to work.'

Nat said, 'But I don't want you to go.'

Tim gestured. 'Hey mate, I thought you said . . . ?'

'I did. But things have changed. You can stay.'

Tim looked at Nat's closed bedroom door. 'Has Jess—'

'No,' Nat said, 'she's in there. Still sleeping.'

'But I thought—'

'So did I,' Nat said.

Tim put his bottle down and laid a hand on Nat's arm.

'Hey,' he said softly, 'sorry.'

'Don't be.'

'No need to bite my head off.'

Nat put his phone in his pocket. 'You weren't to know. I wasn't to know. But the whole thing's a bloody mess right now and if you sugar off and leave me with the whole mortgage to pay, I'll probably shoot myself.'

Tim regarded him. 'Want to talk?'

'Not much.'

'OK then. I'd like to stay, if that helps.'

'It does,' Nat said shortly. He put the back of his hand briefly up against his eyes. 'Sorry, mate.'

Tim waited. Nat said, from behind his hand, 'It's my mum and money and my sisters and Jess and money again and it's shit.'

'It goes like that sometimes.'

Nat took his hand away and focused on Tim. '*Your* mum OK?'

Tim shrugged. 'She's like she always is. She's a single mum getting on with it. Works nights in an old people's home.'

'I know,' Nat said. 'I knew that.'

'So,' Tim said, 'she doesn't have a fancy mews house in central London.'

'Are you getting at me?'

'Just reminding you,' Tim said.

'My sister Laura did that too.'

'I'd like to help you,' Tim said. 'I'd like to stay here and help you. All the same.'

'Thanks, bro.'

Tim glanced at the bedroom door again. 'Is she moving out?'

Nat glanced too. 'Hasn't said anything.'

Tim looked round him. 'It's a nice gaff.'

'I'm lucky,' Nat said, 'I know I'm lucky. I'm not just quite as universally lucky as I thought I was.'

Tim picked up his bottle and took a swallow from it. 'We can all get lucky if we don't want too much.'

———

Jenny Dodds rang Rose and got her answering machine. She left a message for Rose to ring her back. Rose didn't. Jenny rang again and left another message, and then a third time, with a much more peremptory message saying that if Rose didn't ring back this time, she, Jenny, would simply come to the mews and squat there, until Rose opened the door to her. Rose rang back early the following morning.

'About time too,' Jenny said.

'You sound like my sister.'

'We have reason, your sister and I. It's adolescent not to

return phone calls. By the way, where was your sister the other night?'

'She doesn't like drinks parties. She didn't want to come.'

'Just that?'

'Of course!' Rose said indignantly. 'What are you suggesting?'

'Well,' Jenny said, 'you tell me.'

There was silence on the other end of the line and then Rose said, with obvious difficulty, 'I'm – so glad you came to the party.'

Jenny softened.

'It was a good party. The house and garden looked wonderful. So did you. And he's a nice guy.'

Rose said, too eagerly, 'Did you think so?'

'I did. Very attractive, lots of charm, clearly thinks the world of you.'

'I know,' Rose said.

'Al was fed up at how much hair your man still has. Quite sulky, going home, in fact. I should have said, at the very least, that I was used to being married to a bald guy so it no longer made any difference.'

'That wouldn't exactly have helped.'

'No. So I didn't say it. I said instead that I really valued his fidelity – or apparent fidelity, at least – but that wasn't what he wanted to hear, so he ignored me.'

Rose said, almost aggressively, 'Why did you ring?'

'To thank you for the party.'

'Really?'

'No,' Jenny said, 'not really. I wanted to ask what was the matter.'

There was a second's pause and then Rose said flatly, 'Nothing's the matter.'

'Ah.'

'What d'you mean, "ah", in that heavy way?'

'What I mean,' Jenny said, 'is that it all looked wonderful. House, garden, you, him, all fantastic on the surface, all apparently under control. But – don't interrupt me – there was something uneasy in the air, something I couldn't quite put my finger on, but it was almost as if you've got yourself up a one-way street with no exit.'

There was another silence.

'Rose?' Jenny said.

'It was the children, I'm afraid,' Rose said firmly. They insisted on being the waiting staff, not guests, as we wanted them to be, and as they'd been working all day, they were exhausted and being tired made them cross, and being cross wasn't good for the atmosphere.'

'No,' Jenny said.

Rose said nothing.

'It wasn't the children,' Jenny said, 'it was you. Something about you. You looked lovely in that dress, but you didn't look relaxed. Or serene. You looked – well, kind of *haunted*.'

'Nonsense,' Rose said.

'You said that very quickly. Too quickly, actually,'

'I'm happy,' Rose said. 'He adores me. I've got wonderful buyers for the house, and we've found the perfect cottage. I'm *happy*.'

'Right.'

'What's that supposed to mean?'

'It means,' Jenny said, 'have it your way. Think what you

are determined to think if that's what you want. What you really want.'

She could hear Rose breathing at her end of the phone, little shallow breaths almost as if she was panting.

'Rose?'

'Yes.'

'I'm just going to say one thing more. Are you listening?'

'Yes.'

'I'm not going to quote anybody you love at you,' Jenny said. 'I'm not going to mention your children. But I'm going to talk about you. *You*, Rose. You were led a terrible dance by William and since he left, you've done brilliantly. OK, you had the benefit of a classy house in an expensive location, but you've lived there, you've managed to live there and not only keep it going, but have a good life there, an interesting, satisfying life where you are beholden to no one and not distorted in any way by having to accommodate anyone else. Giving all that up for another marriage is absolutely fine as long as you really need – not want, need – to get married. You can be adored without being married, Rose.'

She couldn't hear Rose breathing any more. Perhaps she was holding her breath. Jenny counted to ten, then she said, in as gentle a voice as she could, 'That's all, Rosie. All I wanted to say. See you soon, OK?' and clicked her phone off.

CHAPTER EIGHTEEN

Prue sent Rose an email. Usually, she rang when she had something to say, but on this occasion it was an email informing Rose that she was about to go away for a fortnight to look after a fellow ex-headmistress friend, who had retired near Bridport and who was having a hip operation which would preclude her driving for six weeks. After that, Prue said, she was joining a cultural group for a tour of the palaces and artworks in Emilia-Romagna and Umbria, so she would be away, altogether, for a month. She said she hoped to see Rose when she returned and of course, she would be thinking of her a great deal while she was away.

Rose was nettled by the email. She was, she realized, indignant that Prue should have all these friends and have made all these plans without consulting her or telling her beforehand – even though, she also had to acknowledge, she didn't want to nurse anyone in Bridport or respectfully admire mosaics in Ravenna in an undoubtedly know-all and elderly cultural group herself. There was just the smallest air of reproach in Prue's email, something very slightly reproving that seemed to imply that while Rose was absorbed in her persistent folly, she, Prue, had better and more worthwhile things to do.

Rose snatched up her phone at once and rang her sister. All she got was Prue's measured voicemail message, altered this time to say that she was away with an intermittent signal for the next two weeks, and to warn callers about European roaming charges for the next two weeks after that. Rose threw down her phone in a temper, causing Tyler to stop cleaning the kitchen windows as he was doing, and ask what was the matter.

'Nothing,' Rose said. 'Just a minor irritation. I wanted to speak to Prue.'

Tyler put down the balled-up newspaper he was holding, and came across the kitchen.

'Then leave her a message, sweetheart. Tell her to ring you back.'

Rose said childishly, 'I wanted to *talk* to her. She's going away for a *month*.'

'Rosie, nobody can't be contacted these days unless, like Mallory, they choose not to be. Maybe Prue's choosing not to be. Maybe she needs a rest from us all.'

Rose didn't look at him. 'That's what I don't like.'

'I know, sweetheart. It was hurtful she wouldn't come to the party, I know it was. But she is as she is. It doesn't mean she doesn't love you like she always has. Come on, Rosie, relax a bit.'

'I don't want to.'

'What? Because Prue won't play cosy sisters, you're cross with me?'

She shook her head and stepped away from him. 'No.'

'What then? Promise you she isn't saying she doesn't love you.'

Rose held up a hand. She said clearly, looking at the shining windows he had just cleaned, 'I know that. And it isn't that, it isn't that at all. It's . . .' She paused and then she said, in a rush, 'It's more that she manages to make me not like myself at all, to feel as if I'm somehow behaving rather badly. And that, I'm afraid, makes me cross.'

———

Mrs Gaffney – 'Please call me Nancy,' she'd said to Rose – spent a great deal of time at the mews house. She wanted Rose to take her through every plant, and its history, in the garden, and to understand exactly how all the utilities worked in the house.

'Jim is amazingly impractical, especially for an engineer,' she said to Rose. 'I am the one who always fixed everything in our house in Toronto: roof, plumbing, wiring, everything.'

Rose beamed at her. 'I did a course, when I was first on my own. It was brilliant. I learned how to tile and how to hang wallpaper. And doors. Can you hang a door?'

'I'd love you to teach me. Maybe there'll be a chance to help you when you move to the cottage?'

'Who knows?' Rose said airily. 'Now you know where the fuse box is, and I'll show you the water main.'

Nancy put a hand on her arm. 'Why did you say "Who knows?" like that? Haven't you exchanged contracts on the cottage?'

Rose hesitated a moment, then she said, looking squarely at Nancy, 'No.'

'Oh, my dear . . .'

'I expect we will, though. Maybe this week.'

Nancy swallowed. She took her hand back and clasped it with her free one. 'Rose . . .'

'Yes?'

'If – you haven't exchanged contracts on the cottage, does that mean you have changed your mind about selling this?'

Rose smiled at her. 'No.'

'That is such a relief. I know it's only a house, but Jim and I have completely lost our hearts to it.'

'I know. I wouldn't dream of not selling to you.' She smiled more broadly. 'Anyway, contracts are exchanged. Legally, it's yours. In my mind anyway. I know what it means to you.'

'I don't want to pry,' Nancy said carefully, 'but if the cottage isn't a certainty . . .'

'Oh, I think it will be,' Rose said. 'There's just been such a lot going on, and the party and everything, you know.'

The front door opened and slammed shut, and Tyler called out, as he always did, 'Home, sweetheart!'

Nancy glanced at Rose. 'That is so adorable.'

Rose called back, 'In here! With Nancy.'

He came into the sitting room, a pale-blue wool scarf round his neck and a huge sheaf of purple parrot tulips in his arms. He held the flowers out to Rose.

'For you, my lovely. Couldn't resist them.'

'Oh,' Nancy said. 'So cute, so *romantic*.'

Rose looked down at the tulips. 'Gorgeous,' she said.

Tyler kissed her cheek. Then he turned and kissed Nancy's too. 'Talking stopcocks again, ladies?'

Nancy was laughing. 'How did you guess?'

Tyler cocked his head in Rose's direction. 'She's a dab hand with a plumber's wrench.'

Rose moved away. 'I'm just going to put these in water.'

'Drink?' Tyler said to Nancy. 'It's after six. I've learned to make a devilish martini.'

Nancy was still laughing. She shook her head. 'I must get back. Jim'll be finished with all his meetings by now. But thank you.' She raised her voice. 'And thank you, Rose, for another great afternoon.'

Rose appeared in the kitchen doorway holding a single tulip. 'My pleasure, Nancy. Come any time. Bring Jim.'

Nancy said happily, 'I don't think any house sale has ever been attended by all the angels the way this one has.'

Tyler sketched his little half-bow. 'That's how we like it, ma'am.'

Nancy crossed the room to kiss Rose. 'I hope you have good news on the cottage very soon.'

'Thank you,' Rose said. She watched while Tyler escorted Nancy out of the sitting room and waited, listening to their voices in the hall, and the firm click of the front door closing behind her. Tyler came back to the sitting room with evident energy, tearing off the scarf and tossing it towards an arm-chair. He said, 'Nice woman.'

'She certainly is.'

'And she adores this house. It's wonderful to be selling to someone so committed and decent who will cherish the house as you have.'

'Yes.'

He glanced at her, checked by her tone. 'Rosie? What's the matter?'

She looked down at the tulip in her hands. 'I'm not sure.'

'But something. Definitely something.' He came to stand close to her. 'Tell me.'

She didn't look up. She said quietly, 'You shouldn't have bought me these.'

He peered at her, incredulously.

'What?'

She raised her head to look at him.

'You shouldn't have bought me expensive tulips. You shouldn't have bought me an expensive dress for the party. We shouldn't have had the party.'

He tried to take her shoulders in his hands, but she stepped back into the kitchen.

'What are you talking about?' Tyler demanded. 'What's got into you? It's all paid for, dress, flowers, party, everything. I paid for all of it. With real money, cash money, not credit card never-never money. What *is* it, with you and money?'

Rose regarded him steadily, still holding the tulip in front of her as if it were somehow guarding her.

'Can I ask you something?'

Tyler spread his hands, shrugging.

'Anything. Always. You know that.'

Rose hesitated. Then she said in a rush, 'Where did the money come from?'

'What money?'

'The money for the party. The money for my dress. The money for my ring.'

'Jesus,' Tyler said. 'Anything else?'

'Well yes,' Rose said inexorably. 'The money for the rental on your flat, for living in London since January, for our meals out.' She stopped.

Tyler smiled at her.

'It was real money, I promise you. It wasn't borrowed or stolen or come by nefariously. It was bona fide money, and mine to spend.'

Rose raised the tulip a little, as if to emphasize what she was saying.

'But where did you get it? Since you seem to have owned nothing in America and you haven't sorted out your pension there, I have to ask you where you got the money you've spent the last six months.'

Tyler tried to smile at her. 'Sweetheart . . .'

'Please,' Rose said. 'Why don't you want to tell me?'

'I don't want to upset you.'

'*Upset* me?'

'You mightn't like my answer.'

Rose gave the tulip a little shake. 'Why not?'

'Because – the truth isn't very tactful.'

'To whom?' she almost shouted. 'To me?'

'Yes,' he said reluctantly.

'But why?'

Tyler drew a deep breath. He looked away, and then he looked back at Rose.

'Because, my darling and my only love, the love of my *life*, I don't think one wife – or soon-to-be wife – much wants to think that she has in a way been paid for by her predecessor.'

Rose gazed at him. 'What?'

He said simply, 'Cindy left me some money to tide me over. Cash. In a bank account. It's gone now, but it paid for the last year and especially the last six months.'

Rose glanced at her hand. 'My ring . . .'

'Yes.'

'And the party and the dress and the meals out and the flowers and the flat and—'

'Stop it,' Tyler said. 'Yes. *Yes*. But I didn't want you to know.'

'Why?'

'Because it would upset you. And it has. Look at you!'

Slowly, Rose shook her head. She whispered, 'Look at *you*.' She held the tulip out to him.

'What's this?'

'Please take it. It's yours, really.'

'I *knew* that it would upset you to know where the money had come from.'

'No,' Rose said, 'that doesn't upset me at all. Poor Cindy is what I'm thinking. *Poor* Cindy.'

'She was, in a way. That's a very healthy reaction, actually. As well as being typical of you.' He smiled at her more confidently. 'Poor Cindy indeed.' He took the tulip, holding the stalk where Rose had held it. 'She loved tulips. Any rather elegant and architectural flowers were what she liked.'

Rose cleared her throat. She said, 'Did you say that all the money has gone – the Cindy money, that is?'

He nodded. 'Pretty much. There's just enough left to cover a secret that I'm not telling you about yet but which you'll love. But it doesn't matter. The timing's perfect, really.'

'Sorry?' Rose said.

He inspected the tulip, then he looked back at Rose, his expression as open and unclouded as ever.

'Sweetheart. It couldn't be better really. I run out of funds I've been living off just as you sell this house which releases a whole lot more.'

'But . . .'

'But what?'

'The proceeds of the sale of this house are *mine*. This is mine to sell. The money is mine.'

Tyler regarded her. 'Oh dear.'

'What d'you mean, "oh dear"?'

'In my book,' Tyler said, 'and I thought in yours, who owns what isn't relevant. It completely, utterly doesn't matter. If there's money, it belongs to us both, and where it came from is of absolutely no consequence at all. I entirely respect your right to dictate how the bulk of the money from this house is spent, I've said so over and over, but day-to-day modest – *modest* – expenses are, to my mind, a joint affair.'

'Did Cindy think like that?'

'Cindy, sweetheart, was the complete opposite! It was one of the many reasons that we were so hopelessly incompatible.' He raised the tulip. 'May I put this poor thing in water with its friends?'

Rose stood aside to let him pass. 'Of course.'

'Just to go back to where this conversation started,' Tyler said, 'and reiterating what a nice woman Nancy Gaffney is – indeed, what a nice couple they both are – shall I ring the solicitor before they close and ask what has happened to the contracts on the cottage? I really can't see what's delaying a simple exchange like this.'

Rose moved to take the tulip out of his hand and add it to the vase. 'I'll do it.'

Tyler said affectionately, 'Of course. You have such a way with flowers.'

'No,' Rose said, 'I meant that I'll ring the solicitor tomorrow.'

'But I don't want you to have to do anything like that.'

'I want to,' Rose said.

'Do you? But I've spoken to them up to now.'

'I want to,' Rose said again.

'Of course, sweetheart. If you ring right now, you might just catch them.'

'Tomorrow,' Rose said.

'But we don't want to lose another day.'

Rose turned from the tulips to look at him. 'There's no hurry. I'll ring them in the morning.'

Tyler said uneasily, 'If you're sure.'

'I am.'

He came across the room to embrace her. 'You're a woman in a million. You know that? Or hundreds of millions to be more accurate. If I'd known how wonderful you'd be about Cindy's money, I'd have told you at the beginning.' He looked down at her and tenderly brushed a wisp of hair out of her eyes. 'Now, wonder woman, can I make you a wicked martini?'

———

At three in the morning, Rose remembered something Tyler had said the previous evening, and that she had been too overwhelmed by other disclosures to follow up. He had mentioned a secret, a secret plan that he was joyfully certain she would love. But she had omitted to ask him anything further because – well, because the evening had been difficult enough as it was, stilted from the moment she had declined the martini, strained all through supper and unsatisfactory television to the final shame of pretending to be asleep – something she had not done since the declining years of being married to William – when Tyler came to bed. She had been conscious of him studying her face before he turned the light out, of the toothpaste scent of his breath and then the unbearable gentleness of the slow kiss he planted on her nearest cheek. She turned to look at him now, while he slept, his face just visible in the glow from her clock radio, turned on his side towards her as usual, his expression sweet and sanguine as it invariably was. He was wearing a white singlet and blue-plaid boxer shorts and he looked clean and cared-for and healthy. It was impossible, Rose thought; everything was impossible, whichever way she turned. And so, at three o'clock in the morning, she was thinking about the children. If she thought about the children, panic surged in her stomach and up her throat, boiling up in waves that engulfed any thinking in uncontrollable surges of anxiety.

She turned over onto her other side so that she didn't have Tyler's sleeping face to reproach herself with. She remembered her desperate misery the night of their first quarrel and how hysterical with relief she had been when he had simply said, on hearing her sobbing down the telephone, 'Thank God you rang, Rosie. Thank *God*. I'll be round as soon as I've dressed.'

And he had been. She had opened the door to him, completely dishevelled and distraught, and he had taken her in his arms and held her against him wordlessly, and she had felt that she would never, ever, have to face anything in life alone again. She had clung to him, *clung*. She stared into the dimness of her bedroom. Now she was lying with her back to him and she had chosen to do so. It wasn't just a tiff, this time, either. Was it?

Quietly, in order not to disturb him, she slid out of bed and onto the carpet. Then she got silently to her feet, found her dressing gown where she had draped it over the stool by her dressing table, and let herself noiselessly out of the room. It was, she knew from long practice, five paces along the landing and then nine steps down the stairs, and she held the bannister rail as she went – the bannister rail that would soon be sliding under the Gaffneys' hands.

She didn't put any lights on. The London night sky was glowing above her, bluish and reddish, and as her eyes adjusted, the furniture in the sitting room and even the terrace beyond the glass doors, swam gradually into sharper focus. She crossed the room to look out into the shadowy garden at all her planting, at the new growth on the shrubs, and the white plumes of the inherited lilac bush, and thought of Nancy Gaffney out there, conscientiously tending to everything she had taken over, putting bird seed out, watching rain splashing onto the stones. I feel sad, Rose thought, but I don't feel utterly bereft at the thought of Nancy Gaffney being here instead of me; I don't feel, oddly, that I am being replaced against my will. I feel, rather, that I am handing something I have made myself on to someone who appreciates its value and who may alter the details but probably not the essence. I feel OK about Nancy and Jim Gaffney being here and letting their grandchildren help fill the bird feeders. I really do. Even at three in the morning, I feel OK about that.

She pressed her forehead against the cool of the glass doors and fixed her gaze on an irregular line of cement between the paving stones on the terrace. She had, she noticed, pulled her dressing gown tightly around her, crossing her arms as if she was cold. She wasn't cold. She wasn't, now she came to think of it, panicking any longer either. She felt, instead, sad but resolved, and the flutters of apprehension that disturbed the resolve were definitely there, but were not overwhelming.

Better not to over-plan, she thought; better not to try and anticipate too much. Just a step at a time, as William used – maddeningly correctly – to say; just do one thing, make one decision, and then reassess. She peeled her forehead away from the glass and stood straighter, relaxing the grip on her dressing gown. She would ask Tyler what the secret was, the secret that he had been so sure she would love, but first she would do something else, whatever the consequences. As soon as the solicitor's office opened in the morning, she would ring them and tell them that she was very sorry, but the offer on the cottage was being withdrawn. They would not, Rose would tell the solicitor, be proceeding with the sale. There would be no exchange of contracts. Thank you, she would say, and our apologies to the vendors. And then she would, somehow, tell Tyler what she had done.

CHAPTER NINETEEN

'I'm here,' Mallory said on the phone to Emmy.

Emmy had only just woken. She had slept intermittently in any case, after an excited night following an evening in which Matthew had told her that he thought he was in love with her. He had kissed her – kissed her a lot, in fact – but declined to come home with her.

'Plenty of time for that,' he'd said, 'when you decide what you feel about me.'

'Where?' Emmy said dazedly into her phone.

'At Heathrow,' Mallory said. 'I came on the red-eye. I'm coming to yours. As you would say.'

Emmy sat up a little more. 'But I'm going to work. It's Friday.'

'Not for more than an hour,' Mallory said. 'I'll be there before then.'

'Mal,' Emmy said, 'what are you *doing*?'

'I couldn't stay,' Mallory said. 'It was as simple as that. I didn't fit any more and I couldn't stay. I couldn't think about anything but you guys and it was driving me nuts.'

Emmy began to get out of bed.

'Have you told your father?'

'Not yet.'

'So he doesn't know you're here?'

'Nobody knows but you – now,' Mallory said. 'I didn't tell anyone. It was just that when I thought of coming, I kinda *had* to. So I have.'

Emmy looked round her. The sofa where Mallory would expect to sleep was scattered with the rapturously discarded clothing of the night before. She remembered high-kicking her shoes off and now she could only see one of them.

'Mal,' Emmy said, 'if you can get here by eight, I'll be here. Otherwise, you'll have to sit in a coffee shop all morning.'

Mallory laughed.

'And ring your father,' Emmy added.

Mallory stopped laughing.

'I mean it,' Emmy said. 'Being back means accepting what we can't change. Even if we don't want to.'

There was a small silence and then Mallory said, 'Dickhead. Why d'you think I've come back then?' and rang off.

———

Something had happened to the routine of William's weekly phone calls to his children. He was extremely indignant about this as he regarded his own even-handed regularity as a manifestation of fairness and generosity on his part, but in turn, every one of his three children had texted him to say that the Sunday-morning call wasn't going to work this weekend, sorry Dad, hope to be able to speak soon. And then they had been difficult, or impossible, to get hold of, and the reliable routine of the past appeared to count for nothing. William sent a – to his mind, only mildly – chiding email to all three of them, to which there was no response whatsoever.

He tried telephoning and was met by three voicemail messages. As a last resort – he told himself that he had been left with no other options – he rang Rose.

She was very startled.

'William!'

'Yes,' he said. 'Yes, it's me. I am trying to ring the children – it would be Laura's turn this weekend, as a matter of fact – but I can't get hold of them. I haven't, actually, been able to speak to any of them for over two weeks.'

Rose said, sympathetically, 'Oh dear.'

'Can you explain it? I mean, what is going on?'

Rose looked at the carpet. 'Nothing, William.'

'What do you mean, nothing? Of course there's something! You set the cat among the pigeons with this whole marriage insistence—'

'Please stop,' Rose said. 'Don't waste a long-distance phone call going over old ground. There's no point, and anyway, whatever I do or don't do is actually none of your business any more. Was there something you wanted to say to the children, something you'd like me to tell them?'

William sounded slightly mollified. 'Well, yes, actually. There is.'

Rose waited. She had a picture in her mind of the spacious bungalow where William lived in Melbourne, with Gillian Greenhalgh, to which she had mentally added a huge tropical garden full of avocado trees and squawking macaws.

William cleared his throat. 'I have something to announce, Rose. Something you should know about as well as the children.'

'You aren't *ill*, are you?'

'Ill?' William said. 'No, of course I'm not ill. In fact, this announcement is the reverse of my being ill. I'm – getting married.'

'Heavens,' Rose said. 'No need to ask to whom.'

'No.'

'I thought you didn't believe in second marriages. I thought you thought marrying a second time was idiotically impractical and unnecessary.'

'Hm,' William said.

'I see,' Rose said, 'I get it. You would be quite happy never marrying again, but *she* wants to be Mrs Woodrowe. That's it, isn't it?'

William said, in a stately tone, 'I would like my children to be present.'

'In Australia?' Rose said. 'You expect them to come to Australia to watch you marry Gillian Greenhalgh? And you think I'll pass that message on?'

William said crossly, 'I imagine you expect them to come to *your* wedding.'

'My life,' Rose said, 'is no concern of yours. In any case, whatever I do or don't do will be of my own free will.'

'Meaning?'

'You know perfectly well what I mean.'

'None of this changes my wish,' William said, 'to have my children at my wedding.'

'In Australia?'

'Naturally. In Australia.'

'And how are they going to get there? Who is going to pay for their flights to Australia? Six tickets, if you count Laura's boys?'

'I shall make arrangements.'

'William,' Rose said. 'Stop being so pompous. Just think.'

'What I'm thinking,' William said with sudden energy, 'is that I don't know what's got into you. You were so docile once, so easy and sweet and now – well, now the word virago comes to mind.'

'Yes,' Rose said.

'For God's sake, you sound as if you're smiling!'

'I am.'

'All I can say,' William said furiously from Sunday evening in Australia, 'is God help the poor bugger you're marrying. God help him.'

———

Rose went down the stairs to the kitchen, where Tyler had laid out their Sunday morning breakfast ritual of croissants. He had already been to Marylebone High Street both to collect the croissants and to fetch a stack of Sunday news-papers, which lay neatly on the coffee table in the sitting room. He was making coffee when she came in. She said, 'That was William on the phone.'

He turned, his hand still on the plunger of the filter jug. 'Oh?'

'He's getting married.'

'Ah.'

Rose settled herself on a stool. 'It seems she wants it. Wants to be Mrs William Woodrowe.'

'Well, if she hasn't been Mrs anything, ever . . .'

'Yes.'

He carried the coffee pot across to the central island where breakfast was laid out. He said, 'Shall I get the papers or would you rather talk?'

She didn't look at him. She said, her hands in her lap, 'I meant to ask you something yesterday.'

'Fire away.'

'Tyler,' Rose said, 'what is this secret plan you have that you know I'll love?'

He grinned sheepishly. 'I didn't want you to know till almost the very day.'

'What very day?'

'Before we fly.'

Rose raised her head. 'Fly?'

He sat on the stool next to her and folded his arms. 'To San Francisco.'

'Oh.'

He leaned forward. He said warmly, 'I wanted you just to have to pack a case and then we'd be off to the airport. I wanted it to be a complete surprise. But everything's planned, everything's in order: meeting Seth and Yuhui, staying with friends, the hotel at the end, all sorted. I can show you all my places, for once, where I lived my life for thirty years.' He stopped and looked at her. Then he unfolded his arms. 'Rose?'

Very slowly and sadly, she shook her head.

'What?' he said. 'What? Don't you want to? Don't you want to meet Seth?'

She said in a whisper, 'It's got nothing to do with meeting Seth.'

'What hasn't? What?'

'Tyler. I'm so sorry. But I don't want to go to San Francisco.'

He looked down at his lap and bit his lip. 'But I've bought the tickets.'

'I'm sorry about that, too. I'm – I'm sorry about all of it.'

He glanced up again at her. 'All of it?'

She nodded. 'All of it.'

It was his turn to whisper. He said, 'What are you saying?'

'I think,' Rose said quietly, 'that you know what I'm saying.'

He put a hand up to his eyes. Then he said in a low voice, 'Don't you love me?'

She leaned forward and put her own hand on his. 'Yes, I love you. But I can't marry you.'

He brushed her hand aside and got off his stool. Then he went across the room and stood with his back to her. After what seemed like an eternity, he said, 'I knew this was coming.'

'Did you?'

'Yes,' he said, 'I knew it.' He turned round. He looked suddenly much smaller, as if something within him had shrunk and pulled his exterior self inwards. 'There's been something in the air, something not quite right, for ages. Weeks. Long before the party. And then . . .' He stopped.

'What?'

'I rang the solicitor. Just after you did. He told me that you'd withdrawn the offer on the cottage.'

'Yes. I was going to tell you.'

'Were you?'

She nodded again. 'Of course I was.'

He said unhappily, 'It wasn't the cottage really, was it? And it wasn't when I told you about Cindy's money. It was before that. Wasn't it?'

'Yes,' she said.

'Is it . . .' he said, and trailed off.

'Is it what?'

'Is it – oh God, I can't even say the word, it's so debasing, so unworthy, unromantic. But – but, is it money?'

Yet again, she nodded. He gave a groan and turned away.

She said steadily, 'It isn't *just* money, Tyler. I mean, money isn't just something sordid and base.'

'Isn't it?'

'No. And certainly not at our age. At our age, it's dignity and choice. It is terrible, at our age, to have the humiliation of no choice or power.'

He said, 'You think so.'

'Yes,' she said. 'In fact, I know so.'

He looked at her. 'But, Rosie, you *have* money.'

'Yes.'

'So what does it matter if I don't?'

'In time,' she said sadly, 'I wouldn't love you enough to overcome the resentment I'd have that you were living off me, that we didn't share the same attitude to money.'

'But you didn't make the money that bought this house.'

'No,' Rose said, 'but I earned it. I earned this house when William ended the marriage and I've earned the possibility of living here.'

'But you're selling it! You're selling it to the Gaffneys!'

'I am.'

'How can you be so calm?' Tyler shouted. 'How can you sit there in the ruin of all our hopes and plans and seem so – Jesus, almost *indifferent*?'

'I'm not indifferent. I'm far from indifferent.' She held her hands out. 'Look how they're shaking.'

He seized them. 'Rosie, sweetheart, please don't do this, *please* think again. We don't need the cottage, we don't need to disappoint the Gaffneys, we can think of some other plan,

I'll bin those tickets to San Francisco, nothing matters, *nothing* except we are together. I can't bear it. I literally cannot *bear* to lose you.'

Very gradually, she withdrew her hands. She said, not looking at him, 'I didn't say I didn't love you.'

'But if you won't marry me! If you don't want to meet Seth . . .'

'I told you. Meeting Seth has nothing to do with it.'

He leaned against the island. He said, 'I can't believe this is happening.'

'But you said you knew.'

'I feared it,' Tyler said. 'I was walking on eggshells. I was telling myself that it would all be fine, sort of to keep my spirits up, but there was a storm brewing. I knew it. I could feel it.' He looked wildly at Rose. 'What the hell am I supposed to do now?'

She looked back at him in silence.

'Tell me, will you?' he demanded. 'Tell me. You bring my world crashing down about my ears, so you can't just walk away. You can't.'

Rose stood up slowly from her stool.

She said, 'I think you use that ticket and go back to San Francisco. And sort yourself out. Sort your pension. See Seth.'

He gazed at her. He was almost gaping. 'And you?'

'I'll miss you.'

'How dare you say that!'

'It's true,' Rose said.

He sighed and shook his head. 'I don't get you.'

'No.'

Clumsily, she pulled the aquamarine ring off her engagement finger and held it out. Her hand was far from steady.

'I think – I suppose – that you had better have this.'

He looked at the ring, then he looked at her face, and then back at the ring. Slowly, he stretched out his right hand, took the ring from her and dropped it in his trouser pocket as if it were no more than a handful of loose change. Then he moved towards the door. Rose watched him. She said hoarsely, 'Where are you going?'

He halted but he didn't look back at her. 'To pack,' he said.

'To – to *pack*?'

He glanced briefly at her. 'Yes,' he said. 'It's what you want, isn't it?'

———

It was something, Emmy considered, that she thought she would never see; Nat and Mallory side by side on the sofa where Mallory slept, sharing a white chocolate and raspberry muffin on the paper bag Nat had brought it in. Nat had arrived bearing the muffin, and three coffees in a recycled cardboard holder, looking so woebegone that Emmy had done what she hadn't done for months, and enfolded him, coffees and paper bag and all, in an awkward but heartfelt embrace and he'd said, 'Don't Em, don't, or I'll just blub again. I've already made an idiot of myself all over Tim.'

Mallory had been up, but not dressed. Her hair, now dark again but with cobalt-blue tips once more, was tangled, and she was wearing flannel pyjama trousers and a faded T-shirt which said 'Look but do not touch' on the front in dark-green letters. Emmy had been getting ready for brunch with Matthew and had texted him, when Nat arrived, to say that she would be late. His message had come back at once.

Let's make it lunch then. Or tea. Or dinner.

As long as I can see you today.

Emmy put her phone in the back pocket of her jeans. It seemed more than tactless to have a happy romantic prospect when, clearly, Nat's own romantic plans had been so cruelly dashed.

Mallory offered him the last piece of muffin. He waved it away.

'You have it.'

She went on holding out the paper bag as if it were a plate. 'No, Nat. *You* have it. You need it.'

'Being dumped,' he said, taking it, 'isn't cured by muffin.'

'Nor by vodka,' Mallory said. 'But it helps.'

Emmy came to sit on the arm of the sofa. 'Did – she just go?'

He sighed. He took a mouthful of coffee then said, 'No. She told me. She was all gussied up to go out somewhere, somewhere not with me, and she just said it was – over. She said – oh, she said all kinds of meant-to-be-nice things, but the bottom line was that she was going. And then she went. Cleared everything while I was at work, and went.'

'Do you know where she's gone?'

'I'm not asking,' Nat said. 'I don't want to know.'

Emmy and Mallory exchanged glances. 'Of course not,' said Emmy.

'She warned me,' Nat said. 'She told me we wouldn't last, that I was just for now, but I didn't think she was planning to go so soon. I never thought she meant kind of *now*.' He sniffed. 'I made an utter fool of myself around Tim.'

'Tim'll forgive you,' Emmy said.

'I wish I could,' Nat said. 'I wish I could forgive myself. I've got a broken heart and bruised pride and I don't know what to do about either.'

Mallory tipped the crumbs off the paper bag into her cupped palm. Then she put her head back and tossed the contents of her hand into her mouth.

'Just wait,' she said indistinctly.

Emmy nodded. 'Exactly. Just wait.' She looked fondly down at him. 'You've got me, after all. And her.'

He sighed again. 'Yes.'

Emmy nudged him with her nearest foot. 'You've missed me, Natty.'

He glanced up at her, briefly. 'I have.'

She bent towards him. 'That's a beginning, then. Tim's staying, so you can afford the flat. That's good.'

Nat stared at the floor. 'There's just this wedding, now.'

Mallory nudged him. 'Cheer up, big boy. We'll be brother and sister.'

He managed a weak smile. Mallory's phone, buried in her discarded duvet, began to ring. She found it, pulled it out and looked at the screen without enthusiasm.

'It's my father.'

'Answer it,' Emmy commanded.

'He can wait.'

'Answer it!' Nat and Emmy said in chorus.

Mallory shook her hair free of her right ear and held her phone against it.

'Dad?'

The others watched her, with a shared air of mild self-congratulation. She was listening and then abruptly, her body stiffened and she stood up. Nat looked up at her and Emmy straightened.

'What?' Mallory was saying. 'What, Dad, what?'

Then she swung round so she was facing the others.

'Oh my God,' Mallory said. 'Oh sweet Jesus. Are you OK?'

CHAPTER TWENTY

Prue looked round Rose's new sitting room with approval.

'It's very nice, Rosie.'

'But there isn't a garden.'

'There's a terrace. A balcony.'

'It's tiny.'

'Now look, Rosie,' Prue said, 'it's not that tiny. You can grow all kinds of things there, if you're clever. And you are very clever with gardens.'

Rose said, childishly, 'Well, thank goodness I am clever at *something*.'

Prue regarded her for a moment. She was holding the gardenia in a pot, trained neatly round a hoop, which she had brought Rose as a house-warming present, pointing out, as she did so, how many promising flower buds it had. She set it down carefully on the coffee table that had come, like all the rest of the furniture, from the mews house. She said, 'Have you heard from him?'

'From – Tyler?'

'Of course Tyler, Rosie. Don't play games with me.'

Rose sat down suddenly in one of the armchairs. 'Yes, I

have. Several times in fact.' She looked up at Prue. 'He's in San Francisco. He thinks I'm mad.'

Prue settled herself in the second armchair and crossed her legs. 'I doubt that. He just can't understand how your mind works. Because it doesn't work like his.'

'No,' Rose said. 'It doesn't.'

Prue waited a few seconds and then she said, 'Do you miss him?'

Rose looked down at her lap. She nodded violently. 'Terribly.'

'I'm not one to beat about the bush,' Prue said, 'so I'll ask you straight out. If he came back and proposed again, would you accept him?'

Rose raised her head. She sighed. 'No,' she said.

'So you miss him but you don't regret rejecting him?'

Rose looked straight at her sister. 'Yes.'

Prue smiled broadly at her. 'Well done, Rosie.'

'It doesn't feel like it. Those emails and texts from him saying how unhappy he is, how bereft, how he misses me, how he absolutely can't understand my priorities . . .'

'Priorities?'

'He's come to the conclusion that I've put money before him. Before happiness. Before the children. He thinks I've gone round the bend, and that all I mind about is money.'

'Have you tried explaining otherwise?'

'Oh!' Rose exclaimed. '*Have* I! I've spent so much effort and energy in trying to explain myself to him, and himself to him, you can't think. It's hopeless, completely hopeless. I don't know if he can't hear me or won't hear me, but the end result is the same every time. He's the lovely romantic who puts emotions first and I'm the heartless materialist who puts money above everything.'

'Face-saving,' Prue said. 'As far as he's concerned.'

Rose struggled to get out of her chair. Then she stood, looking down at Prue. She said, 'Let me make you some coffee.'

'I'd like that. Rosie . . .'

'Yes?'

'If he thinks like that, why do you miss him so much?'

Rose made a clumsy little gesture. 'He's such a nice man. So easy and open. Rooms were sunnier if Tyler was in them.'

'Only at the beginning,' Prue said. 'Everything's always sunny at the beginning.'

Rose took a step back. 'I was in love with him.'

'And he was head over heels in love with you. Is that really what you're missing?'

Rose said good-humouredly, 'I really hate you.'

'I know,' Prue said. She smiled again. 'You said something about coffee?' She let a brief silence fall, and then she said, in her kindest voice, 'It wasn't about money really, was it, Rosie? It was about trust.'

——

Laura had spread lunch out on a table under her cherry tree in the garden. Angus had gone – reluctantly – to a stag weekend in the West Country, and Laura had said to Emmy why didn't she bring Matthew round on Saturday, and they could have a picnic in the garden, if the weather was nice. So she had bought charcuterie and cheeses and interesting bread, and Jack, who was naked except for his gumboots and a grey-plastic Sith mask worn on top of his head, like a saucer-shaped hat held on by elastic, had helped her spread a cloth on the garden table and lay out the food.

Matthew had brought wine, in a cooler bag full of ice. He turned out to be a fan of *Star Wars* too, so was knowledgeable about the Sith mask, which Jack explained wasn't new, but Daddy had found it on eBay. Matthew asked Jack why he was wearing gumboots and Jack said he didn't like the feel of grass on his bare feet, which Matthew said was perfectly reasonable. He then held Adam on his knee for most of lunch, and fed him morsels of cheese and buttered bread, and Adam grew very loving after the food and wanted to stand up unsteadily on Matthew's knee and kiss him ardently.

'Goodness,' Laura said admiringly to Emmy. 'He's a natural.'

Emmy was gazing at Matthew in a way Laura hadn't seen her look at any man before.

Emmy said, almost dreamily, 'He's like that with me, too.'

'What an asset.'

With one hand steadying Adam, Matthew reached out to pick up the wine bottle, which he then gestured with towards the girls.

'Why not?' Laura said, proffering her glass. 'It's Saturday, after all. And the first lunch outside of the year.'

Emmy held her own glass out. She said to Matthew, 'Shall I tell Laura?'

He stretched past Adam with the wine bottle. He said, 'Why not.'

'Tell me what?'

'Well,' Emmy said, glancing at Matthew, 'we're moving in together. I'm going to Matthew's, I'm going to live with Matthew.'

Laura raised her glass. 'Wonderful!'

Jack stopped eating a stick of chorizo.

'Why?' he said to Matthew.

'Because I asked her,' Matthew said, 'and she said yes.'

Jack said seriously, 'She's quite messy.'

'I know,' Matthew said, 'I've been to her flat. But actually I'm fairly messy too.'

'Are you,' Jack said, going back to his chorizo, 'going to marry her?'

Matthew didn't look at Emmy. He said, 'D'you think she'd have me?'

Jack said, 'Grandma Rose isn't going to get married after all, you know.'

'So do you think there ought to be a wedding in the family somehow, then?'

Jack chewed for a moment, then he said, 'Not necessarily.'

Everyone laughed. Laura said to Matthew, 'We call spades spades in this house.'

He was looking at Emmy now. He said comfortably, 'I rather like that.'

She looked back. 'Me too.'

'Enough, lovebirds,' Laura said. She got up and went round the table to lift Adam off Matthew's knee. 'Up you come, you sticky horror. So good to have some happy news. After poor old Mum.'

'Is she old?' Jack asked.

'It was the right decision,' Emmy said. 'It wasn't going to work.'

'What wasn't?' Jack said.

Emmy bent towards him. 'Grandma Rose being married. That wasn't going to work.'

Jack said nothing. He put down his chorizo and slid off his chair.

'Jack,' Laura said warningly. 'You didn't ask if you could get down.'

'I need a wee.'

'Then you ask.'

Matthew got up. 'I do too.' He held a hand out to Jack. 'Show me where?'

Laura watched them cross the shaggy grass together, holding Adam on her hip.

'He's a keeper, isn't he, Em?'

Emmy sighed happily. 'Oh, I think so.'

'I'm so pleased for you.'

'Thank you.'

Laura kissed the side of Adam's head and brushed his hair back with her hand.

'D'you think Mum's OK, really?'

Emmy swept some breadcrumbs on the tablecloth into a neat pyramid. 'I think she will be.'

'It was such a shock. Maybe she even shocked herself. At least she's gone back to work a bit. And we've managed to stop her giving us money.'

'I like her flat,' Emmy said, 'It's a sweet flat. I think she'll like it too when she stops saying how cramped it is.'

Laura went back to her seat, carrying Adam. Once settled on her knee, he began devouring the crusts on her plate.

'Talking of flats, Em, where does Matthew live?'

Emmy immediately looked transported again. 'It's wonderful. A garden flat at the very edge of Ladbroke Grove.'

'And yours? What happens if you move in with Matthew?'

Emmy held out a grape to Adam, who seized it and crammed it into his mouth along with all the crusts.

'Mallory's taking it over.'

'Mallory!'

Emmy nodded. 'She's got a job of some sort, an assistant stage manager or something, and she's going to live in my flat.' She pulled a quick face at Laura. 'Just down the hill from Nat. She's doing a great job consoling him.'

'Do you think . . . ?'

'Who knows,' Emmy said. 'Anything could happen. If I can fall for Matthew, Nat could fall for Mallory.'

'Perhaps stop eating?' Laura said to Adam. She tried to take a cheese rind out of his fist. 'You'd think he had serious deprivation issues. Heavens. Nat and Mallory!'

Emmy held another grape out to Adam. 'It isn't Nat and Mallory that's interesting, though, is it?'

'Isn't it?'

Emmy looked at her sister. 'No, Laura, it isn't. What is really interesting is Mallory – and Mum.'

——

The view from Rose's flat was what had sold it to her. It faced west, and the glass doors of the sitting room folded back so that one could step out onto the – admittedly rather narrow – balcony and watch the sun go down over the miles and miles of London rooftops. There were different birds up here too, swooping, high-flying birds, and wind and cloudscapes, which was some compensation for the loss of trees and shrubs and any earth that Rose hadn't carried up in the lift to her floor in a heat-sealed plastic sack. There were two bedrooms and a narrow kitchen whose end wall was almost all window, and where she could stand at night and watch the tail lights of cars in the street below glimmering like little scarlet sequins.

The translation agency for whom she'd used to work had been taken over and was uninterested in having her back. So she went doggedly, in person, to agency after agency, most of whom seemed only interested in employing people who could speak Chinese or Russian or Korean, until an agency in High Holborn agreed to take her on, at a modest rate per word, and sent her home with a test article in French on juvenile chronic arthritis, which she translated that evening, on her knee, sitting in the armchair that had once been Tyler's favourite in the mews house. It gave her a headache, but also an indefinable satisfaction, intensified by emailing it off the next morning – like a child, she thought, handing a piece of written prep in to a teacher before time, with a flourish. It was in fact, she told Prue almost shyly, on the telephone, like coming home to herself, however heartsore that self was.

Weekends, she had said to Prue, candidly over their coffee, were difficult. Bleaker. Longer. Not eagerly anticipated any more; in fact, there was almost a longing for Monday mornings, for the life of the streets to start up again, for public transport to be crammed with resigned people doing what they had to do in order to earn weekends. She had felt something of this at the end of her marriage to William, but it was more acute now, as if Tyler had not just taken his person to California, but also a sense of the shared joy of time off. There had been walks with Tyler, meals with Tyler, movies and theatres and concerts with Tyler. Above all, there had been talks with Tyler, talks in which his eyes hardly left her face while he asked her what she thought, what she felt, what she imagined.

'I don't think,' she said to Mallory, who had taken to spending most of her Sundays and Mondays, when her theatre was closed, in Rose's flat, 'that I have ever been so valued for my reaction, in all my life.'

Mallory was in her father's chair, holding a glass of wine. She said to the wine, 'I never felt that.'

Rose said quietly, 'I know.'

'He loves us,' Mallory said. 'But he can't empathize. He can't imagine what it's like to be us. Mom couldn't either, but then she didn't want to. Daddy just doesn't have what it takes.' She glanced at Rose. 'With us kids, I mean.'

'I know,' Rose said again.

Mallory put her head back against the armchair. Her eyes were closed.

'Emmy's moving in with Matthew.'

'Yes,' Rose said, 'I'm so pleased. He's so nice. He's helping her find another job because he doesn't think that they should work and live together.'

Mallory didn't open her eyes. 'Is he right?'

'He's right,' Rose said. 'In fact, I think he's right about a lot of things. He's taking Emmy out to Australia for her father's wedding. He said she would kick herself if she didn't go, and it would be hard to go alone.'

Mallory rolled her head sideways and opened her eyes. 'Are the others going?'

Rose shook her head. 'No.'

'Did they talk about it?'

Rose smiled at her. 'None of my business.'

Mallory said abruptly, 'Am I some of your business?'

'You – seem to be.'

Mallory sat up. She said, 'Are you worried about Nat?'

'Not really. He'll get over it. He's never been dumped before.'

Mallory said seriously, 'I'm not getting over it. It's why I came back to London.'

Rose took a sip of wine. 'You're different.'

'How different?'

'Needing healing from family deficiencies is very different to getting over being dumped.'

'Will – Daddy get over you?'

'I think so.'

'He says he won't. Ever. He says you were the one.'

Rose said softly, 'None of us is ever the one. We're just the only ones we meet.'

Mallory took a hank of hair in one hand and inspected the blue ends. 'If Daddy hadn't fallen for you, I'd never have met you.'

'No.'

'You glad about that?'

Rose got out of her chair and went over to the view, darkening to the west above the skeins of street lights. 'Of course I am.'

'You've got Laura,' Mallory said, 'and Nat and Emmy and Matthew. And Angus and Jack and Adam. And Prue.'

Rose didn't turn. Mallory waited.

'There's always room,' Rose said. She moved slightly so that Mallory could see her profile. 'There's always room, for another connection.' She sounded as if she was smiling. 'Family isn't a finite thing.'